THE SCOTSMAN WHO KISSED ME

Iain put his hand under her chin and tilted her face up to his. Studying her face for a moment, he saw no rejection. If anyone asked, he would have to say it was indecision mixed with a hint of curiosity. He did not blame her for the indecision but he would ignore it. He bent his head and kissed her.

Emily placed her hands on his chest to push him away but the moment his mouth covered hers, she clutched at his shirt. She opened to the gentle prod of his tongue. His kiss clouded her mind even as it heated her body. She wrapped her arms around his neck and held on tight, pressing her body up close against his. It was scandalous of her but she enjoyed it.

Desire was not something she had any knowledge of but Emily was sure that was what was flooding her body as he moved his kisses to her neck. She shivered as the feel of the heat of his mouth ran through her body. When he returned to her mouth, taking it a bit roughly, she was as eager as he seemed to be. . . .

The Scotsman Who Saved Me

HANNAH HOWELL

ZEBRA BOOKS
KENSINGTON PUBLISHING CORP.
http://www.kensingtonbooks.com

ZEBRA BOOKS are published by

Kensington Publishing Corp.
119 West 40th Street
New York, NY 10018

All Kensington titles, imprints, and distributed lines are available at special quantity discounts for bulk purchases for sales promotion, premiums, fund-raising, educational, or institutional use.

Special book excerpts or customized printings can also be created to fit specific needs. For details, write or phone the office of the Kensington Sales Manager: Attn.: Sales Department. Kensington Publishing Corp., 119 West 40th Street, New York, NY 10018. Phone: 1-800-221-2647.

Zebra and the Z logo Reg. U.S. Pat. & TM Off.

First Printing: October 2017
ISBN-13: 978-1-4201-4303-4
ISBN-10: 1-4201-4303-4

eISBN-13: 978-1-4201-4304-1
eISBN-10: 1-4201-4304-2

10 9 8 7 6 5 4 3 2 1

Printed in the United States of America

Chapter One

Arkansas Ozarks, 1860

"Is that smoke I smell?"

Iain MacEnroy glanced at his youngest brother, Robbie, who was sniffing the air like a hound tracking a wounded fox. As he opened his mouth to say just that the smell hit him. The breeze did carry the strong, acrid smell of smoke, wood smoke. Since he saw no sign that the trees they rode through were on fire he suspected someone's cabin was burning. It was not an unusual problem but it could mean trouble for them. He halted his mount and struggled to determine where the smoke was coming from.

"We are riding right toward it," he said. "Do we go on?"

"Aye," said Matthew, the brother closest in age to him. "I suspicion it would be wise to ride in as if we approached an enemy."

"Good thinking." Iain shifted his rifle so that it was easier for him to use it if needed and nudged his horse forward in a slow cautious pace. "Stay with the wagon, Duncan. And keep a close watch out, rifle at the ready," he ordered the brother who was barely a year older than Robbie before fixing his full attention on their approach.

The trees began to thin out but Iain and his brothers were careful to stay within the shadows. When the clearing appeared, Iain signaled a halt. He sighed when the source of the smoke proved to be a smoldering cabin just as he had suspected. He could see no bodies but they could easily be inside. To his relief he could also see no sign of the ones who had caused such destruction but then realized they could also still be inside.

"I see no sign of Indians," said Robbie.

Iain dismounted. "Wasnae Indians. Nay sure there are any left in these hills." He glanced at the tracks in the dirt, clear to see in the area around the edge of the clearing but tried to keep an eye on the house for any sign of movement. "Horses were shod. No arrows I can see. Wager we will find boot prints near to the cabin. I keep telling ye that the natives were driven out and we havenae heard or seen them slipping back. This was done by the vermin who slip about these hills doing what they please and none of it nice."

"Should we have a wee look inside?"

"We will walk round the outside first and see what we can see before we step inside." Iain stood and looked at the smoking cabin. "Robbie, ye could try throwing some water on any flames ye see. Just make sure there is no one who is a threat inside. We may need to step inside later and best if it isnae still burning."

It was in the back of the cabin that they found the dead. Iain sighed. The woman's body had been left obscenely sprawled, naked and bloody, at the edge of an expansive garden heavy with ripened fruit and vegetables. The man's body had been pinned to the door and it was clear that he had been tortured. They were both rather young and Iain suspected they had once been a very handsome couple. He could see the remains of the beauty they had had before the ones who killed them had sliced up their faces. Iain had the chilling feeling that part of that torture had been forcing the man to watch as his woman or kinswoman was raped and butchered. Whoever had come here had been the worst of the worst that ran in these hills. They would definitely have to keep a watch out for them.

"Have to wonder what they kenned that the enemy so badly wanted to know," said Matthew as he stepped up next to Iain.

"Aye, I thought the same. I also get the feeling they were nay just brutes who kill because they can. We certainly have enough of that sort in these hills. Nay, ye are right, they wanted something. Ye have to wonder what that something was that would make two people endure this. Sad as it is, it can only be good for us if this was some private fight, some very personal vendetta. Weel, best we get them buried."

"Ye want us to bury them?"

"I will no leave them for the beasts to gnaw on. We have the time and we have the manpower to dig a grave. Get us some shovels." He watched Matthew walk away and then moved to take the man's body down.

As he set the man's body next to the woman's he frowned at the man's hands, something catching his eye, but he was not sure what. Scowling, he used a piece of the man's shirt to wipe the blood off the man's left hand. The gleam of a wide gold ring sparkled in the light of the sun. That told him that the killers had not been driven by the dark need to steal. No thief worth a thought would leave behind such a ring. This was born of some private battle, he thought again. He moved to the woman, straightened her tattered clothing as much as he could and carefully wiped clean her left hand to reveal another gold wedding band. She also wore an ornate gold locket around her neck.

"Got the shovels." Matthew cursed when he saw the locket. "So, it wasnae robbery."

"Nay." Iain stood up and brushed off his clothes.

"Then what reason did anyone have for killing them?"

"I think trying to find the answer to that will take us time we dinnae have."

"But . . ." Matthew sputtered as Iain began to dig the needed grave, careful to toss the dirt away from the garden.

"There is naught we can do except do them the courtesy of burying them. It is not much but I think they have suffered more than enough already." Iain kept digging and only glanced briefly toward his brother who began to dig as well. "Where is Robbie?"

"Getting what we have to collect up this harvest. I told him to. Sorry as we are for these folk, it makes no sense to leave good food to rot."

Robbie arrived a few moments later. Iain could see the horror that filled the eyes of the man who was barely out of boyhood. For most of Robbie's life there had been little bloodletting done around him, and what little he had seen still hit him hard.

"See if there are any blankets or the like in the barn, Rob," he said. "We cannae take the time to build coffins but it would be nice if we could shroud the bodies."

Robbie nodded, his auburn hair falling into his eyes. "Why did they not take anything?"

"They wanted these poor people to tell them something, I am thinking, and I also think they didnae get that information so they left. Go on, laddie. See if there is something we can use for a shroud."

As soon as his young brother was gone, Iain returned to the work of digging a grave with Matthew's help. He did not think these two people would object to sharing a grave. At least he prayed not, for he had more than enough ghosts haunting him already. By the time Robbie returned with two blankets, well-worn and smelling faintly of horses, they had dug the grave. Iain felt uneasy about just tossing the bodies in the hole so he jumped down into the grave. It just seemed so disrespectful to throw them in the hole. He had Matthew hand each one down to him. Matthew handed down the man first and then the woman, who Iain tucked up at the man's side.

Pity filled him as he took a last look then bent to open the locket the woman wore, wanting a brief look at what she kept there. He stared at the small portraits inside. The man stood tall, well-dressed and smiling, on one side and the woman was on the other smiling sweetly down at the babe in her arms. They truly were a handsome couple and much too young to see the end of their lives.

"Jesu," he whispered, and scrambled out of the grave still clutching the locket. "She had a bairn, Matthew." He showed his brother the pictures.

They all looked to the cabin and Matthew sighed. "We dinnae ken how old that picture is. The child may well have died long ago."

Closing the locket, Iain shook his head. "True enough but I have to look. I have to." He glanced down at the bodies. "Take the rings, too, Matthew. They are the kind one would pass on to a child." He turned to Robbie. "Did ye hear or see anything when ye were putting out the fire?"

Robbie shook his head. "Nay, but I was just looking for what needed water thrown on it. Keeping a watch on the fire took all my attention."

"We have to look." He stuck the locket in his shirt and started toward the house.

"They would have taken the bairn when they tried to flee," said Matthew as he followed his brother.

"There was no child with them."

"It isnae a big cabin. We can look close before we finish the burying."

Smoke and ash still tainted the air inside the cabin and all three men covered their noses and mouths with their bandanas. It was clear the fire had been meant to drive the couple out of the back and they had run right into the arms of their killers. There was a sort of viciousness to this attack that he had not seen in a long time. Painful memories he resented were being stirred up.

Lost in ugly recollections he did not watch where he was stepping. Suddenly there was nothing beneath his right foot. He stumbled back but as he put his foot down more of the floor gave way. As he fell, he twisted around in time to grab at the edge of the hole that had opened up beneath him. A heartbeat later Robbie and Matthew each grabbed him by the wrists and pulled him up. Cautiously, he looked down.

"A storm cellar?" Robbie asked.

"Nay." Iain noticed the crude steps heading down and heavy burlap bags set against the dirt wall. "Looks as if it was for cold storage or the like. Just a place to store the harvest, I think. Wonder why the people ran outside instead of down here? They might have been able to survive if they had hidden down here."

Cautiously testing each step before putting his full weight on it, Iain went down. He could hear Robbie coming down behind him, Matthew standing watch above. Once on the ground he discovered it was not a large place. A pile of empty bags waited for more of the harvest to come in.

"No child down here," said Robbie as he looked into the full bags leaning against the walls. "Taters and apples though. Shall we take them?"

"Aye. No sense in leaving it all here to rot."

"Thinking we should take the empty bags, too."

"Good thought. They can be used to collect up anything else useful, like the harvest."

"Iain, why are ye staring at them like this? And thinking. I can hear you thinking."

Laughing softly, Iain shook his head. "I dinnae ken. Just, weel, something about them looks wrong."

"They are not in a tidy pile, that is certain." Robbie stepped over to them and started shifting them. "Hey, there is a wee bit of blood on some of them and"—he yanked a couple away from the wall—"some got stuck in this hole in the wall."

Moving to help Robbie pull all the bags aside, Iain cursed when they uncovered the hole. As they cleared away the last of the bags Iain saw more faint signs of blood. Someone had fled the house. If the men who had burned the place had taken but a little time to look around, they would have found the one who had escaped. If it was the child from the locket picture, Iain could not be sure it was still alive. Men who would torture two people as had been done to that young couple would probably not hesitate to kill a child.

"A tunnel. Whatever went down it was leaking a wee bit," he said.

"We best follow then."

Iain knew Robbie was right. There was a child out there, one hurt, scared, and in danger. He could not allow an old fear to rule him when a child's life might matter. Iain struggled to use that good sense to push back the fear curdling his stomach. He knew it was not an easy fear to push back or even to control for a while.

"Ye go in first, Robbie," he said. "I will follow. And if I falter, ye just come and drag me along. I cannae let my distaste for such places stop me from trying to help a child."

"Then, aye, I will go first," Robbie said even as he started to crawl inside the tunnel. "Need a light."

Iain quickly searched the room and found an old lantern with a thick candle inside. He handed it to Robbie after he lit it and the light it cast eased the growing knot in his stomach. After taking a deep breath he followed Robbie as his younger brother crawled forward. Drops of blood led the way. The acrid smell of smoke still thickened the air they breathed. Iain fought the memories that invoked. If he let them come, fell back into the terrifying horror of crawling through a similar tight spot to save his brother, he knew he would panic. He could not allow that and he forced himself to think only of the child they might save.

Sweat pooled in the small of his back and dripped down his face. He could feel panic gnawing at his insides. He had nightmares about being stuck in small places while fire licked at his heels. It was hard to push such images away each time he found himself in a confined space. He had nearly died the last time he had been in one, had been burned badly and still carried some scars. Iain just kept reminding himself that he had survived and he had saved the life of his brother Geordie.

When they reached the small ladder that led out, Iain clenched his fists to fight his urge to run over Robbie and climb out as fast as possible. Robbie hefted the door at the top open and Iain took in a deep, soothing breath of the fresh air pouring in. When Robbie climbed out then turned to offer a hand, Iain gritted his teeth to fight the urge to race out of the tunnel like a rat escaping a flooded warren. From the way Robbie winced though, he knew he had gripped his brother's hand harder than needed. He climbed out then stood staring at the ground as he fought to calm the turmoil inside of him.

"Are ye well, Iain?"

"Aye." He took one deep breath and let it out slowly. "Aye. I kept my thoughts on saving the child. That is far more important than some fear I cannae shake."

"And that worked for you. It always has. I was worried when I smelled the smoke. Too much like what set the fear in you. We all know the story."

Iain sighed. "'Tis a fear I best conquer. It was years ago. There is no sense in clinging to it. Now, we need to look for the blood trail."

"It looked to be a slow bleed," Robbie said as he began to search the ground.

"Even a slow, steady loss of blood can prove fatal." Iain looked around to see that they were just inside the stand of trees. "Ye cannae help but wonder why the mon and the woman didnae use the tunnel to flee."

"I did wonder. I think the why of all that happened here concerns the child. Here is some blood. Looks like whatever is losing it headed deeper into the trees."

Iain followed the trail Robbie pointed out. He was not sure a child could survive such a steady loss of blood. Slow and steady though it was, it was adding up to a lot. And why had the parents not at least bandaged the wound before sending the child off? He tried to picture the attack and slowly came to the conclusion that the parents had given their lives to protect the child. They had held off the attackers as best they could, for as long as they could, and sent their child off to safety. Had they believed the men were after the child?

"There is something odd about all this," he said as he and his brother stopped to search yet again for the trail to follow.

"What is odd?" Robbie gave a soft cry of triumph as he found another drop of blood. "Found it."

"Changed direction." Iain frowned as he studied the stain and looked into the thickening wood. "Maybe the child was given a particular direction to go in. And it is odd because the child was sent off. Then there is how its parents were tortured. The men had to be after something verra specific and it had something to do with the child. Yet why would anyone be after the child of a couple farming in the hills?"

"Cannae think of any reason. More apt to be after the woman but they just used her and killed her. This way now." He turned a little to the right. "It is strange that the men did not go hunting if they were still after the child. It doesnae appear as if they searched for it at all."

"That would have made sense but the parents may have convinced them that the child was not there or even that it was dead." Robbie paused and stared at the ground. "Weel, we may lose the trail now." When Iain joined him, Robbie crouched down and pointed out the crushed grass and small puddle of blood. "I think the child realized he was leaving a trail and bound up the wound." He stood up and wandered around looking for some hint of what direction the child took next. "So we may be hunting an older child."

Iain stayed crouched down by the spot. It was easy enough to see where someone had sat down. Looking close, he could even see the tiny thread revealing something had been torn to make a bandage. What bothered him were the two footprints he could see. They were small but not, he thought, small enough to be a child's. Neither was the spot where someone had clearly sat for a while. Then he saw the faint print of a child's foot.

"Found another bit of blood, Iain," said Robbie when he returned. "Reckon the bandage wasnae tied on correctly."

Standing up, Iain shook his head. "Or there was more than one wound and the one doing the bandaging didnae consider it worth taking time to tend it."

"Or didnae have enough bandages."

"Possible. Where was the blood?" He looked where Robbie pointed and nodded. "We keep looking. I believe we will soon find the hole they crawled into."

"They?"

"Aye." He crouched down and pointed out the

marks he had found as he said, "One set of footprints here and just there one print of a bairn's foot."

Robbie looked closely and shook his head. "I didnae see them. Good eyes, Iain. So we look for two."

"Could just be one small child and one older one but, aye, two. Somewhere in these woods is a hole they crawled into to hide."

"Then we best be moving again."

It was slow work with only drops of blood to tell them where to go. Whoever was moving through the woods knew how to avoid leaving much of a trail. Iain hoped they found the ones they hunted soon, as the day was rapidly drawing to an end. The last place he wanted to be after the sun set was this far up in the hills near a killing site. He wanted them all tucked up safely behind stockade walls as soon as possible.

Then he saw it through an opening in the trees. One old tree had finally succumbed to age and rot. The top half had snapped off almost cleanly. That broken piece had fallen so that it angled away from the bottom of the trunk, its tangled dying branches providing a good covering for what could possibly be a hollow trunk. He was certain it was the hiding place he searched for.

If he was right, it was actually a well-chosen spot. There was shade enough to make it somewhat hidden from sight. It was not in a straight line from the cabin. Nor was it too close or too obvious. He suspected he spotted it because too much of his life had been spent making sure there was a good place for him and his brothers to hide. If he had found such a spot in his travels he would have marked it as a safe haven.

It was a good place to hide, he thought. The ones running had not run straight to it, either. If he and

Robbie did not have some skill at tracking, they never would have found the trail to follow. The tree was far away from the cabin and, being in a shaded area, one that made it harder to spot.

"O'er here, Robbie," he said as he started toward the tree and stared through the branches, searching for the opening he was certain was there.

"Should we call out first?" asked Robbie as he hurried over to Iain's side.

"Nay, we dinnae want to startle anyone. They are afraid and hurt. They are nay about to step out and say howdy-do. They will either hide by staying silent and dug in or be scared into shooting at us."

"Ah, aye, there is that."

"Let us hope we find our quarry."

Chapter Two

Emily did not think she had ever hurt so badly, or been so afraid. She was exhausted and heartsore. Her arm burned and her leg throbbed in such a way she constantly had to bite back a cry. She knew her sister and David were dead even though she had not seen them fall but she was sure she had heard screams. They had not begun searching for their son, either. There was also no way they could have held off ten men for long, not men who had made it clear they wanted everyone in the house dead. All she wanted to do was curl up on a soft bed and cry but she had Neddy to care for.

She looked down at the boy sleeping curled up at her side, her wide skirts as his blanket. He looked so much like his father that she felt a stab of loss. David had been a good man. His son had the same thick wavy black hair, a sweet little face, and big brown eyes that could convince people to give him anything he wanted. Fortunately, he was not yet old enough to understand the power of those eyes. She prayed he was also not old enough to fully understand what had happened to his parents.

Lightly stroking his hair, she closed her eyes. They were safe at the moment. She needed someone with skill to tend her wounds but, for now, they were safe. Now was not the time to fret. Now was the time to plan. As soon as she felt sure those men who had attacked them were gone, they would run again. She just wished she knew where they could run to.

For a moment the pain in her leg and shoulder was pushed aside by the pain in her heart. Her sister and her husband were certainly dead. Every time she tried to think of them as merely wounded her mind mocked her. The shooting had ended and the taint of wood smoke still hung in the air. The last time she saw them Annabel and David were still desperately trying to hold off their attackers. Her sister had ordered her to take little Neddy and run. She had not wanted to leave them, had desperately wanted to stay and fight, but both David and Annabel had grown equally desperate in their pleas for her to save Neddy. The look in David's eyes had convinced her to go, that look of desperate sadness. It was a plea she had had to obey and she was certain it had cost her. Tears clouded her eyes as the surety that she would never see her sister again swept over her.

She wanted to go back and look, to see if what she feared was true, but then she felt her nephew wriggle closer to her side. Emily could not risk him. If David and Annabel were dead, they had given their lives to save young Neddy, she firmly reminded herself. Done what any loving parent would do. She could not toss away that sacrifice with a foolish action, one driven solely by emotion. The sweet little boy had no skill in protecting himself.

"Mama? Papa?"

Her nephew's query, spoken in a soft tear-choked

voice, acted like an arrow to her heart. She did not know how to explain it all to him. Emily held him closer and began to sort through a number of ways to explain that Mama and Papa were gone. A flicker of hope attempted to spring to life in her chest but good sense ruthlessly smothered it. Then a sound broke through her grief-ridden thoughts.

Emily quickly hid Neddy beneath her wide skirts. The sound she had heard had now clarified itself into male voices. She sat as still as possible and listened carefully as the voices drew nearer. Her fear receded a little because the men spoke differently than the ones who had attacked her family. Those men had not had what sounded very much like a Scots accent.

That made no sense, she thought as she pressed deeper into the hole dug inside a tree hollow. What were Scotsmen doing wandering around the hills of Arkansas? Annabel had often complained about being so completely out of place, so alone despite David always being at her side. The farther west they had traveled the more separated from it all she had felt. Annabel had missed society far more than she ever did or could. She had constantly repeated stories of the places she had gone, the events she had attended, the food and people there, and the fashions she had shopped for. Emily had begun to fear her sister would fall permanently into her world of memories. These men were definitely not ones who had grown up in these hills or come from any sort of high society. She grasped the knife she had placed by her side and waited, tense and wary, as the men drew closer.

Suddenly she fell back into the memory of the attack she had just fled from. The men had ridden up to the cabin so fast David had barely made it inside, barring the door behind him. Emily had stood silenced by shock as her sister had tossed a rifle to her husband then grabbed one of her own and loaded it. Then the shooting had begun. The men outside had demanded her sister hand over her only child. After some colorful threats that had made her blood run cold the shooting had begun and there had been little lag in the assault. Emily had done her best to keep Neddy shielded and safe, sheltered from the bullets filling the air. Soon both Annabel and David were wounded and then someone had tried to set the cabin alight. Annabel had ordered Emily to take Neddy and run, run and hide.

Tears filled her eyes. She had not wanted to leave Annabel and David, had been sure she would never see them again if she did run. The terrified child clinging to her was all that had given her the strength to move, to run and hide as ordered. It was what her sister needed. The knowledge that someone was taking her child to a safe place would give Annabel the strength to keep fighting. It was during the time Emily had been getting Neddy into the root cellar that she had been wounded. Now, with the smell of smoke beginning to fade and the sound of shooting silent for too long, she knew her duty was to keep Neddy alive and safe. She tightened the grip on the knife by her side.

"Let us just hope we find our quarry alive," said a man with a deep voice that was too close to the opening of her hiding place.

Quarry? she thought. That was a word a hunter used. Gritting her teeth over the pain in her leg, she rose carefully to her knees. Determined to protect her nephew, she held the knife at the ready and kept her mind clear. She knew she could not battle all of the men but she would make it cost them dearly to take Neddy from her.

Iain saw the shadow of the opening in the tree and moved closer as he signaled to his brother to help him shift the broken tree limb. As soon as it was moved he saw the opening more clearly. The trunk of the tree was thick enough to make a hollow that could easily hide a child but it was too shadowed to see if it did.

He got on his knees and edged closer. When he stuck his head inside he did so slowly and was glad of it when he felt cold steel touch his throat. He glanced down and calmly met the narrowed gaze of a woman.

"I mean no harm," he said. "I am nay one of the men who burned the cabin." He fought a wince as the blade trembled in what appeared to be a small hand and the point scraped painfully over his skin. "My brothers and I smelled the smoke and came to help." He reminded himself he was speaking to a survivor and kept his voice as soft and pleasant as he could.

"The people who lived there?" There was a hint of dread in her voice as she asked and he suspected she already knew what he would answer.

"Could ye move the blade aside? It makes talking a wee bit uncomfortable."

"Oh. I beg your pardon."

He warily rubbed his hand over his throat when the knife was pulled away and swallowed a laugh over how polite she had sounded. "I fear the people in the cabin are dead." A sound much like a moan choked by a sob reached his ears and he grimaced, knowing he had probably been too blunt, but he had no idea how else he could have answered her question. "We have buried them. Come out and I will show ye where they are." He inched back and held out his hand.

Emily hesitated a moment but then decided she had few choices left. She had already been found and the man had made no threatening move. Toward her or Neddy. Although she had no idea of what she could do now, she knew she could not remain huddled in a shallow hole dug inside the trunk of a dying tree. Trying desperately to keep Neddy hidden by her skirts she allowed the man to pull her out. The shadows helped. They kept Neddy hidden but it added an awkwardness to her movements that she could not hide.

"Are ye hurt?" he asked as she stood up but kept her right hand tight against her skirts.

"A small wound already bandaged. I will be fine." She looked in the direction of the house and fought the urge to collapse, to weep. "Annabel and David are dead."

"Aye." He decided he would never tell her how. "I am Iain MacEnroy and this is my brother Robbie. My other brother, Matthew, is at the cabin collecting all that can be salvaged and I have yet another brother, Duncan, watching over our wagons."

She nodded but her thoughts were centered on how to keep Neddy hidden until she was absolutely certain these men were safe. "I am Emily Stanton. I thank you for burying my sister and her husband."

Iain frowned. There was a distinct English accent to the woman's words, which held that cool politeness her class was so well known for. He told himself not to let that trouble him. He had known some decent English men and women in his time. There were also a lot of them coming to America, as desperately in need of a better life as he was.

"It was nay a bother," he said quietly.

"I must mark the grave," she said as she started to walk back to the cabin, dreading what she would find but determined to do her sister and her husband honor.

He cursed softly. Her voice was slurred, like someone half-asleep. He signaled Robbie and they followed the woman. He noticed that she walked oddly, as if she was dragging her feet. Her left arm hung limply at her side and he could now see the dark stain of blood on the blue sleeve of her gown. The woman was wounded worse than she had claimed. Quickening his pace, he drew up beside her. When he looked at her he noticed that she was very pale and was sweating despite the cool breezes.

Grasping her wrist to halt her, he scowled when she stared at his hand then slowly looked up at him. Her eyes were cloudy and he doubted she was seeing him clearly. Then she began to sway. He grabbed her around the waist as she began to fall to her knees.

"Do not let me fall on him," she said in a rapidly fading voice.

The abrupt increase in the weight he supported told him she had fainted. Just as he shifted to pick her up a small boy scrambled out from beneath her skirts. Robbie caught hold of the child before the boy could grab her.

"Em! Emmy!" The child thrashed in Robbie's hold, reaching blindly for the woman Iain was now cradling in his arms.

"Hush, laddie. Hush!" Iain cautiously stepped closer so the boy could see the woman he held, even touch her slightly. "She has but swooned. She sleeps because she was hurt."

The child calmed although he stuck his thumb in his mouth and shuddered a little with the remnants of his fear. Here was the child they had been searching for. The boy looked physically unharmed but Iain knew there would be scars left from what had happened at his home. It brought up his own memories of trying to explain to young Lachlan that their parents were dead. He quickly shook them aside and started walking toward the burned cabin.

By the time he reached the graveside Emily was stirring. Reluctantly, for he found holding the slender woman pleasurable despite her unconscious state, he set her on her feet, holding her by the waist until she steadied. Even with her disordered appearance and too-pale skin she was a pretty little thing. Her blond hair was in a thick braid tied off by a ribbon that matched the color of her gown.

After she took the child into her arms she turned to look at him. Her eyes were wide, with a lush fringe of surprisingly dark lashes and they were a soft gray with the faintest hint of blue. A small, straight nose cut a line down the middle of her heart-shaped face. Even pinched with pain her mouth looked to be full-lipped. He inwardly shook his head, shoving aside his interest in her looks. She was English. She was also a woman in need of some help who had suffered a hard loss. She was not a woman he should be feeling any sort of amorous inclinations for.

"This is Neddy, my sister's boy," she said, and a lone tear wind down her pale cheek. "Only one grave?"

"We buried them together, holding each other." He glanced at the other marked grave a few feet away and wanted to ask her about it but decided now was not a good time.

"Thank you," she whispered. "They would have liked that. I would like to place a marker if I may."

Iain looked to Matthew who held a crude wooden cross he had obviously prepared for the grave. "We can do that. What do ye want it to say?"

The urge to curl up on the ground and bawl like a child was a tight knot in Emily's chest and throat as she told the man what to burn into the cross. She set Neddy down and held him by the shoulders as she said a prayer while they placed the cross. What she truly wanted to do was curse. Beneath her grief burned rage but she knew she could not give in to it. She now had a child to protect and hide for there was no certainty that the men had seen or believed that second grave held the child they sought. Anger could be dealt with when they were both strong enough to act on it.

By the time they were done, she was feeling weak and light-headed again. Forcing herself to hold fast to her senses, she looked toward the ruined cabin. There was one last thing she needed to do before she could give in to her weakness and pain.

"Was the floor badly burned?" she asked.

"Nay," answered the one called Robbie, his freckled face flushing red as he dragged a hand through his brilliantly red hair. "It seemed steady save for the floor by the opening to the cellar. A wee bit singed and now wet."

Emily nudged Neddy toward the young man. "Will you watch him for me for a few moments? I need to see if I can retrieve something." She started toward the cabin and then frowned at the man who quickly fell into step beside her. "I shall only be a moment."

THE SCOTSMAN WHO SAVED ME   23

"Aye, but ye are still weak and, when ye go down, ye go down fast."

A blush heated her cheeks and she frowned even more, thinking it not quite proper for him to point that out. Then she shrugged and hurried into the cabin. Stepping cautiously, she made her way to the fireplace. The wet sooty mess on the floor made her grimace as she sought out the cleanest spot, tossed down her handkerchief, and knelt on it. The wet made it difficult to lift the hearthstones and suddenly the man crouched beside her.

"Which one do ye need to lift?" the man asked in that voice she found far too attractive.

"These two," she replied as she pointed out the ones she wished to pull up.

Iain lifted the stones and frowned at the square of oilcloth beneath them. He watched as she lifted it out, set it down, and carefully unwrapped a metal box. She pulled a gold chain out from beneath the neck of her gown, unclasped it, and removed a small key. When she unlocked the box she briefly touched the papers inside to test if they were dry. Immediately after that she locked the box again and returned the key to the chain.

"These are important?" he asked as he helped her stand up, noting how she paled and touched her left leg.

"Yes, very important. They matter to Neddy."

He frowned as he followed her out. Her accent had changed again and he wondered just how long she had been in the country. For a moment she had sounded very proper, very high-toned. It was an accent that reminded him all too much of Lady Vera. A chill entered his blood as he suddenly had all too clear a picture of the woman who had driven them from their home. Iain was about to bluntly ask her what place she held within English society when the boy ran over to her.

"My box!" He reached for it and then just patted the top. "Boo? Want Boo."

"What is a Boo?" Iain did not really wish to return to the burned home.

"It is a toy he loves. A little dog his mother made for him. She made it with a very soft material and it is bright blue." She stroked Neddy's hair. "I fear it is lost, my sweet boy. The fire . . ."

"Nay," said Robbie and he grabbed up one of the loaded sacks still waiting to be put in the wagons. "We have been collecting up anything useful and Duncan said this bag held things for the babe we thought we were hunting for."

Her leg throbbing so badly she just wanted to sit down and cry, Emily stepped over to look into the large sack. It was filled with kitchen goods, some books, Neddy's clothes, and a little stuffed dog set on top of a pile of small sweaters. All of it smelled strongly of smoke though nothing appeared badly damaged. She sniffed the small toy and was pleased that it carried only a slight scent of smoke. As soon as she could, she would wash away even that.

"Oh, look, Neddy. These kind men found Boo for you." She took the toy and handed it to Neddy, pleased by how the toy eased some of the worry and fear from his face.

"My Boo." Neddy smiled, then hugged the toy and frowned up at Emily. "Mama?"

"No, sweet boy. Mama is gone and your papa is gone too. I am so sorry." She kissed his cheek. "Emily will care for you, my love." When she straightened up she felt close to swooning but fought the feeling.

"Emmy stay?" Neddy asked in a small broken voice.

"Yes, love. I will stay."

"Stay here?" He looked toward the burned cabin with wide eyes, his small body tense with fear of her answer.

"Nay, lad," Iain said. "Ye are coming with us."

The boy nodded but the woman frowned. Iain thought they had settled the matter but realized they had not actually discussed it. There was nothing here for her. She could not fix the damage done to the house and they had marked the grave. He was about to point that all out to her when he noticed that she had grown far too pale again.

"Mama? Papa?" the boy asked, his bottom lip trembling.

"Ye can come back to visit the place where they rest when ye need to," Iain said, and noticed how Emily's eyes filled with tears. "We have to go now. It will be dark soon and I would like to be closer to the safety of my own lands when the sun sets. Nay sure how far away the men who did this have gone," he added softly, and watched the woman nod.

Iain edged closer to the woman as they moved for he had noticed how heavy her steps were, as if each one required the utmost effort. Her slim figure swayed a little and he knew she was close to collapsing in another swoon. They had just reached the side of the wagon his brothers had cleared for her and the boy when she gave a sigh and started to crumble. He swept her up into his arms, a little annoyed by how good she felt there.

Duncan and Matthew quickly cleared a little more space in the back of the wagon, tossing a few blankets down to better cushion the area. Iain set her down and then helped Neddy to climb in. The boy still clung to his toy and Iain picked up the box Emily had dropped when she had collapsed. He handed it to the boy and then mounted his horse and signaled everyone to start moving.

He studied all they had added to their freight but any joy over the gain of a couple of sturdy plow horses, a pair of cows, chickens, and bags of fruits and vegetables was buried deep beneath the pity for two people so brutally murdered. There were also several bags of clothes and assorted household goods plus a small plowshare. He had learned long ago that if you did not take what the dead left behind someone else would, but still had to wrestle with his conscience when he did. He soothed that troubled part of him by knowing that, when Emily and Neddy had a safe place to go, he would give them what they wanted from these gains and a fair market value for the rest.

By the time it was too dark to continue, Iain was at ease over the matter. He and his brothers set up camp, tended to the horses, and Duncan started to cook them some food. Iain took Emily from the wagon and noticed that the skirts under his hands were damp. He was thinking an extra blanket would be wise when he set her down on the rough pallet Matthew had made for her, but, as he pulled his hands away from her he realized it was not water soaking her skirts. His hand was covered in blood.

"Damnation!" he snapped. "She had another wound and it hasnae ceased to bleed."

Matthew crouched beside him. "Where?"

Iain yanked up one side of her skirts, fighting not to be distracted by her legs. Using his knife, he slowly cut open the leg of her drawers and cursed again when he found the hole made by a bullet just above the top of her stockings. Fighting not to expose any more of her, he turned her onto her side but could find no exit hole for the bullet.

"Do ye ken how to remove a bullet?" he asked Matthew.

"Nay," said Matthew, and a glance at his other two brothers brought sad shakes of their heads.

"Then best we bind this as well as we can and get home as fast as we can."

"Aye, Mrs. O'Neal will ken what needs to be done." Matthew hurried away to get something to bandage her wound.

Iain stared down at the pale, unconscious woman and prayed Matthew was right in his utter faith in the indomitable Mrs. O'Neal. Hate the English as he did, he really did not want to bury this one.

Chapter Three

Another moan came from the back of the wagon as they entered through the gates of the stockade surrounding their home and Iain winced. They had tried to keep the wagon as steady as they could but the trail to his place was a rough one in places. He glanced back at the still unconscious woman and sighed. She was feverish now and he thought that was a bad sign.

Neddy sat beside her looking heart-wrenchingly sad and clutching her hand. Iain had run out of comforting things to say to the boy.

Bringing the wagon to a halt, Iain leapt down from the seat and moved to pick Emily out of the back. He doubted he drove the wagon any better than Matthew or Duncan did but he had insisted and he was still not fully sure why he had. There had been a hard need inside him to be in complete control of her care and he had given in to it. Robbie got the boy out of the wagon and they all headed to the door of their house. Just as he paused to figure out how to get the door open and Robbie stepped up beside him to do it, Mrs. O'Neal flung it open.

A short, sturdy woman, Mrs. O'Neal was inching into her matronly years fighting all the way. There were only a few lines on her face so he suspected she was winning the battle. A widow with three children, she had come to them to cook and clean in exchange for a place for her and her children to stay and be safe. Soon she and her children had moved into the small cabin he and his brothers had built for her. Now, Iain thought, she was as important to their home as the thick stockade walls.

"Who is this and what is wrong with her?" Mrs. O'Neal asked as she stepped back and let them in.

"Emily Stanton and she has a bad wound in her leg," Iain answered. "Bullet is still in there, I am thinking."

"Follow me."

He did not argue but strode right behind her as she headed up the stairs. She turned into the small room that just had a bed and a single small table next to it. It was their sick room. Mrs. O'Neal had long ago designated it so. Even though it was on the second floor she had felt it was necessary for such a full house and, she had insisted, one so full of males who were always getting themselves injured. Iain was proud of how rarely it was used and he set Emily on the bed after Mrs. O'Neal covered it with several old blankets.

"Get me a bucket of hot water, boy," she ordered. "I will be needing it to clean this mess and wash out the wound once I get that cursed bullet out." She felt Emily's forehead. "Fever is building. That poison is already doing its nasty work."

Iain hurried down to the kitchen to do what she asked. As he waited for the water to heat, thankful one of his brothers had already put some on the stove, he watched Robbie walking Neddy around showing him everything and introducing him to everyone. Only Mrs. O'Neal's daughter, Maeve, could be considered a child at just ten years of age. Her sons, Donald and Rory, were already close to Robbie's age and steady workers. His own brothers were all grown. It was going to be hard on the boy. He would have to have a word with his brothers to make certain they understood the need to be patient with the child. Then he watched Donald and Rory take the boy over to meet their dog who had just had puppies and decided he probably did not have to worry. Sadly, all of them understood how it was for a child to lose family and every one of them knew to keep a close watch over the younger ones.

Taking the water upstairs he nearly backed right out of the room again after stepping inside because Mrs. O'Neal was just pulling a sheet over a very naked Emily. He swallowed hard and set the bucket down near the bed. Iain suspected it would not be easy to banish the image of a naked Emily from his mind but he intended to do his best to accomplish that. Even with the glaring ugliness of her wounds, her body was one that would stick in a man's mind. He told himself he had imagined the ivory perfection of her breasts but feared the image of them would definitely linger in his mind.

"Is it bad?" he asked.

"Fear so. I am praying we are in time to clean out the poison those bloody things leave in a body. She is a small lass and that worries me, but then the small ones can fool a body with their strength. I will need you to hold her down and don't you fret about leaving any bruises on her. Better a few bruises than what could happen with the knife I will be digging around her."

"She is unconscious."

"That she is. But even the unconscious ones can still feel pain and I will be trying to dig something out of her." She pulled a sharp, thin knife out of a drawer in the chest where she kept what she liked to call her doctoring tools. "Even the ones you think are out as cold as a body can be and still live will let out a scream or start to thrash. So pin her down hard, son. I need her to be as still as you can hold her. Arms and legs."

Iain stiffened his backbone and studied Emily for a moment to try to decide what would be the best way to do what Mrs. O'Neal wanted him to do. Then he took a deep breath and climbed onto the bed, straddling Emily and securing both her arms and her legs. He nodded and then fixed his gaze on Emily's face as Mrs. O'Neal pulled the sheet out of the way and started to work.

Emily proved to be very strong even though she never opened her eyes. It took all his concentration to keep her from moving. He closed his ears to her cries and moans, fixing all his efforts on keeping her from moving away from the pain Mrs. O'Neal had to inflict. It was not until he heard something dropped into a bowl that he realized he had closed his eyes, unwilling to see the agony on her face. He opened them to see Mrs. O'Neal threading a needle to stitch up the wound.

"Ye got the bullet out."

"I did. All of it. Cleaned the wound, too. So all I need to do now is stitch the hole up." She grabbed a rag from the pile she had placed on the little table and wiped the sweat from his face. "You will have to keep her still just a bit longer."

"She didnae wake up when ye dug the bullet out of

her. Cannae see why the stitching would wake her now. That doesnae hurt nearly as much as the other."

"At times they get close to being awake when you do some work on them so there is no trusting that they will continue to remain quiet."

He resettled himself so that his hold on her was not as tight as it had been. Emily looked nearly gray and he felt the tickle of concern, but let his faith in Mrs. O'Neal help him push it aside. Iain cursed himself for not noticing the second wound sooner, then told himself it would not have mattered. She still would have had to travel to his home so this could be done, and done by someone who knew what they were doing.

"Did ye look at the wound in her arm?" He tightened his hold on Emily when the first stab of the needle Mrs. O'Neal used made Emily flinch.

"I did," answered Mrs. O'Neal. "Nothing needed there. I put in a few stitches just to hold the edges of the wound together. It was more of a scrape than a hit. Deep enough but not as bad as the one on her leg. Thinking the bullet burned her good."

By the time Mrs. O'Neal was done and Iain climbed off the bed, he felt as if he had been through a long, hard battle. He moved to pick up Emily's clothes. Yet again he wondered how he had missed the fact that she had been bleeding. Her skirt and petticoat were soaked with blood. Her stockings and pantaloons were in equally bad shape and he hoped that, in all that stuff they had brought from her sister's cabin, there would be something for her to wear.

"How did she get shot, Iain?" asked Mrs. O'Neal as she tugged a clean nightgown onto Emily's limp form.

"Her sister and brother-in-law were both killed. Some men attacked them. Burned the cabin, too."

"Ah, poor child. So, she is all alone now with no place to go."

Iain ignored the glint in Mrs. O'Neal's eyes, all too aware of the woman's love of matchmaking. "Her nephew survived. She got him to safety. We stripped the place of everything that wasnae burnt and brought it with us. Got two cart horses, a wagon, and a decent but small plowshare. A lot of household goods and food, too."

"Good. No sense in leaving it for others or, worse, to rot. Buried them people, I hope." Mrs. O'Neal started to collect up all the bloody rags scattered at her feet and shove them into a bucket.

"Only one grave, I fear. Put the pair in together and buried them that way. Marked it."

"Good. Might be that the lad will wish to go back and visit. How old is he?"

Iain shrugged. "Three?"

"Oh, sweet Jesus, a babe." She looked down at Emily and patted her arm. "We will watch him close for you, lass. I hope he has a true fondness for this one," she added, and glanced at Iain.

"Aye, I believe he does. Ye can see it clear. I am nay sure he understands his parents are gone though."

"He will, but being so young, and with an auntie to care for him, it might not be so hard on him that his folk are dead. My Maeve wasn't much older when my Tommy was killed and she recovered fine. The lads still carry some anger over it." She picked up the bucket of rags and grabbed the cover she had used to hide Emily's nakedness. "Grab her clothes and I'll get this whole lot in to soak, get the blood out."

"Do ye think ye can get her clothes clean as weel?"

"Maybe. Will take some work. Easier when the blood is fresh."

"Weel, if ye can, it would be good as I am nay sure we have anything for her in what we took from the cottage," he said as he followed her down the stairs.

"Ah, well, I will do my best. Now, I will start on this and ye can bring the mop up and clean up any blood on the floor, if you would. Best if the room and all are as clean as we can get them. I truly believe that can help a body to heal."

By the time Iain finished with that chore Emily was looking less like the dead and more like she was just sleeping. There was still a flush on her cheeks and he felt her face to find she was still a little bit feverish. It was not surprising since she had had a bullet inside her for almost two days. He hoped she had not lost so much blood that she would be unable to fight off the fever.

He went back down the stairs, and then put away the mop and bucket. Mrs. O'Neal was busy scrubbing out the clothes so he went outside to look for little Neddy. He found the boy sitting on a rock by the side of the house, laughing as a puppy tried to grab his toy dog. Iain sat down on the ground next to the boy and noticed that the box he kept such a close watch on was still right by his side.

"Ye dinnae want to let him get to your toy, lad. Those teeth are wee but they are also very sharp."

Neddy looked at the puppy and quickly stuck his toy inside his shirt. "He wants a toy."

"Dogs are easy to please, lad." Iain looked around and grabbed a small stick off the ground.

"A stick?"

"Aye. Dogs like sticks. Ye teach them to chase it when ye throw it and then to bring it back." He held it out and the puppy grabbed it. "Right now, this fellow just wants something to chew on."

After watching the puppy try to pull the stick away, Neddy held out his hand. "May I have that now, please?"

So polite, Iain thought. The boy spoke very well when he wanted to. Neddy had had a look of intense concentration as he had spoken. "Do ye ken how old ye are?"

"Three. I am growing."

"Oh, aye, that ye are."

"Where Emmy?"

"In bed. She was wounded and Mrs. O'Neal tended to her. She is sleeping now. She will heal better if she gets a lot of sleep."

"I see her?"

"If ye want to."

The boy dropped the stick he held, grabbed his box, and stood up. "Now." He blushed and frowned. "Please?"

As they walked to the house, Neddy held the box close. He took the boy by the hand as they walked up the stairs and wondered if he could get the box away from the boy. It held papers that were obviously very important to him and his aunt. Of course none of them knew how to read so he would have to find someone else to look at them and that seemed wrong. He was debating the ethics of that when they entered the room where Emily slept. The papers were private and he had no trouble thinking of how he would feel if someone took something of his that was private and shared it with others. Iain stopped thinking about the box as Neddy pulled his hand free and ran to the bed.

Iain quickly stepped up to him as the child patted Emily's cheek and said, "Emmy?"

"She is sleeping, lad," he said. "I told you, she was a wee bit hurt so she really needs to rest."

"Like Mama?"

The single tear that went down the child's cheek and his fearful expression tore at Iain's heart. "Nay, laddie, your Emmy will be better soon. She but sleeps so that she can heal better."

"Need box open."

"Ye wanted Emily to open it?" The boy nodded. "Why? It is just papers."

"My papers. You open again." When Iain just stared at the box, Neddy yelled, "Now!" Then he looked as startled by his rude demand as Iain felt, blinked several times, and quietly said, "Please?" His bottom lip trembled slightly. "Sorry. I yelleded. Bad boy," Neddy added in a very soft voice.

"Nay, just impatient and ye need to practice how to stop that. I ken that feeling very weel. And ye did say 'please' after." Iain reached out and lightly ruffled the boy's hair. "I will see if I can get the key without waking her."

As gently as he could Iain removed the chain from her neck. She took so little notice of what he did, he found himself checking to be certain she still breathed. When he turned he saw Neddy seating himself at the end of the bed, one hand on Emily's foot as if he feared she might disappear, and the other on the box. The boy watched Iain carefully as he opened the box.

"I dinnae ken why ye want it opened," Iain said as he put the key back on the chain and placed both on the little table by the bed. "Ye cannae read them."

"Emmy teachin' me. I know my name." He took out the papers and carefully unfolded them one at a time. "Edward," he said carefully, moving his finger over each letter in the word on one of the papers. "Emmy says it my birth paper."

Iain sat next to the boy and studied the paper Neddy held. A cold feeling knotted his stomach as he studied the precise handwriting and the official seal on the paper. It was the same feeling he had gotten when Emily had spoken like a high-bred female. Common people did not have such papers. They got a notation in the parish records at most or had it noted down in a family Bible if the family could afford one. They certainly did not have papers signed by half a dozen people or a signet ring to mark the paper as well next to a few of the names. Despite reminding himself that he was dealing with a small child and a wounded woman, Iain felt the heat of anger and distaste flood his veins.

"Lad, are ye gentry then?" he asked.

Neddy stared at him then looked back at the paper and shook his head. Iain sensed he had just been lied to. He wished he could read. It was not hard to recognize the mark of a signet ring as it was so similar to the mark on the papers shoved into his father's face as they had burned their home to the ground. Cursing softly in Gaelic, he knew the boy would tell him nothing, had probably been well trained to keep his silence, but there was no denying the mark.

"I think we should put these back, Neddy," Iain said. "Then we can clean ye up and have ourselves something to eat."

"I am hungry," Neddy said, and began to fold the papers back up.

As soon as the child allowed him to help return the papers to the box, Neddy then settled his Boo on top of the papers. Iain knew there would be no locking the box this time. He helped the boy get off the bed then turned to look at Emily. Before he could reconsider his action, he reached out a hand to brush it over her cheeks and forehead.

"Emmy sick."

"Just a little." He took the boy by the hand. "We will just wander down into the kitchens and see if Mrs. O'Neal has anything for us, aye?"

The boy smiled and nodded. "Aye."

Mrs. O'Neal was just tucking the last of the buckets with the blood-stained clothes and rags in between the sink and the back wall when Iain led the boy into the kitchen. The woman had ears like a prize hunting dog. She must have heard their approach and put out of sight anything that could upset the child or bring awkward questions. Mrs. O'Neal wiped her hands on her apron and hurried over to greet Neddy.

"Are you hungry, lad?" She smiled when the boy nodded. "Come in and have a seat. The evening meal will be set out soon." She took his hand from Iain's and tugged him over to the table.

It was not until Iain was helping her get the plates to set the table that Mrs. O'Neal quietly asked, "How fares the lass? Resting easy?"

"Aye," he replied. "Still has a fever though it doesnae feel too high. She sleeps like the dead though."

"Some folk do. My boy Rory sleeps like that. I will go have a look in a few." She glanced toward the boy. "Can you get that box away from him?"

"Aye, but I dinnae think he will let it go far. It holds a lot of papers and I think he was taught, verra thoroughly, to keep it safe. I think they might be gentry. The papers have a seal I am sure was made by a signet ring. No one uses them in this land. Or, very rarely."

"Irish, Scottish, or English?"

"English. They both have that accent."

"What the devil would English gentry be doing in these hills?"

"Hiding? Running? I do not think the attack was just random so it means someone is looking for them." Iain shrugged. "The boy has no answers or doesnae wish to give any to me."

"Then we best get the woman fixed up right quick so she can tell us."

Iain had every intention of doing so. He did not like the thought of English gentry being anywhere near him. They had finally found a place, actually owned it. It was what their parents had wanted but had not lived to see. All the death and misery they had endured had been caused by the English gentry. He needed to know if he was right about what he suspected. If he was he would see that the Stantons left. He would make certain that they were safe but they would be safe far, far away from him and his family.

A sound from the back porch drew his gaze and he grinned. Through the window he could see his six brothers and Mrs. O'Neal's three children cleaning up for supper. They started splashing one another and, as always, Robbie stepped in front of the girl to save her from getting wet. The concerns he had had when he had allowed the O'Neals to move in seemed foolish now. Their two families had blended perfectly.

Moving quickly to help Mrs. O'Neal put the meal on the table, Iain wondered what could be done about getting some sustenance into Emily. She was too small and slender to go without food for long. He hoped Mrs. O'Neal had some solution.

He was pulled out of his thoughts by young Neddy. The boy was up on his knees so that he was at a height to reach the food. Iain went into the food pantry and

got the large block of wood they had used when the
youngest O'Neal was small. He picked up the boy,
who was still clinging to that box, set the block on the
chair, and sat the boy back down.

Taking the seat beside the boy, Iain asked, "Why
dinnae we put that box under your chair?"

Neddy frowned. "I will forget."

"Nay." Iain took the box and put it under his chair.
"I will remind you."

"Promise?"

"Aye, I swear to it."

The boy nodded and then all conversation paused
as the food was passed around. As soon as everyone
filled their plates, talk of what work had been done
and what was still needing to be done began. The
only bad news was that they had lost a lamb to wolves
but the rest were thriving. Iain decided it was probably time to do some hunting.

By the time the meal was over, Iain had a list of
chores in his mind and was eager to plan out the next
day. He took time to see to Neddy though, cleaning
the child's face and hands off and returning the box
to him. Then he took the boy up the stairs to get him
ready for bed.

A small cot had been set up in the room where
Emily still slept. Mrs. O'Neal had put out a little
nightshirt for the boy and Iain got him into it and
then tucked him into the bed. Neddy never let go of
the box. Iain's need to know what those papers said
grew even stronger.

"Story," the boy said as he got his Boo out of the
box and held it in his arms.

"Ye need a story?"

"Aye." Neddy briefly grinned. "Story."

Iain sat on the floor next to the cot and searched his mind for one of the stories he used to tell his young brothers. Settling on the one about dragons that his brothers had so often asked for, he started. He got halfway through it when he realized Neddy had fallen asleep.

Standing up, Iain tucked the covers around the boy and then studied him for a moment. He suspected Neddy was one of those young children women cooed over. There was little doubt he was a well-behaved boy. What tightly gripped Iain's heart was that he was now an orphan, just as he and his brothers were although they had been a bit older than Neddy, had had a chance to enjoy some life with their parents. They had not had an aunt to look after them, however. He lightly smoothed his hand over the boy's curls and then left. The boy was going to be a problem in deciding what needed to be done about the aunt.

Chapter Four

Emily carefully opened her eyes. She knew she had been asleep for quite a while but had little sense of how long that while was. Brushing her fingers over her eyes she found no crustiness that often formed after a long sleep. She wondered if someone had bathed her face for she was certain her sleep had been a long one. The various aches and stiffness in her body told her she had been lying in the same position for quite a long time.

Pushing herself up so that she was propped up against the headboard, Emily hissed as pain tore through her arm. Once it began to ease, she began to remember what had happened to her. Her sister was dead, as was her husband. Their cottage had been badly burned. Tears flooded her eyes and Emily brushed them aside as she looked around the room.

Fear crept in slowly as she realized she recognized nothing. Looking down at herself she found she was wearing her shift but little else. Who had undressed her? The walls were white, there were two windows framed with light yellow curtains she had never seen. On the floor were rag rugs she did not recognize.

The bed was a bit high, wide enough to hold two people, and made of thick, sturdy wood.

She was breathing too quickly. Emily knew her fear was rapidly increasing and she fought to calm herself as she looked for signs of danger. Panic would cloud her thoughts and she needed them clear now. There was no one guarding her and Emily decided to take that as a good sign. If the enemy had taken her, she doubted they would have had her wounds tended to so well and they certainly would not have left her on her own. She stared at the painting on the wall opposite the foot of the bed and felt calm begin to smother her agitation. It was a picture of home, or someplace similar. Just looking at the small stone cottage with its high thatched roof put her more at ease.

Sitting up a little straighter she realized it was a painting of a place somewhere in Scotland. She had traveled there once with her mother and father and recognized what the Scots called a glen. Memory returned in a rush and she could almost hear that deep Scottish brogue telling her they would be safe. There was a man who had helped her but there was no sign of him. Listening closely, she could not even hear that voice.

And where was Neddy, she thought with a surge of sharp panic she could not hold back. "Neddy? Neddy!" she yelled as she struggled to get out of bed. "Neddy, where are you? Neddy!"

A few moments later she heard someone coming quickly up the stairs and braced herself. Although she prayed it was Neddy, she knew it could be whoever had brought her here and she would need to keep her wits about her. The pound of footsteps was far too loud and heavy to be those of a small child. Neddy's life depended on her being careful about who she trusted with the truth. Saving her life and treating her well could simply be a more subtle way of getting her to tell them what they wanted to know or leave Neddy unguarded.

Iain watched Neddy carefully as they worked to weed the kitchen garden. He had planned to fix fences but the boy would not leave his side. Deciding Neddy was too young to be wandering the fields with him, he chose to do the simpler chore of weeding the garden. He had pointed out what needed to be pulled in the pathways between the plants and away from the crops and the boy dutifully stuck to them. Iain kept a close watch though.

Suddenly Neddy leapt to his feet and looked at the house. "Em!"

The boy was already running toward the house before Iain heard what the boy had. Emily was awake and calling for the child. He grabbed the box the child always kept close and caught up with Neddy, hooked his arm around the child's waist, and helped him up the stairs. He had not considered how fearful she would be to wake and not see the child. They entered Emily's room and Neddy wiggled free to run over to the bed. Before Iain could catch him again, Neddy climbed on the bed and into Emily's arms. Iain stood by the side of the bed and saw her quickly hidden grimace of pain. He could not be certain which wound the boy had jarred, however.

"My box!" The boy suddenly cried and looked around. "I lost it."

"Nay." Iain held the box he had scooped up as they had rushed away from the garden. "I brought it."

Neddy grabbed it and held it close. "Mine!"

"Rude, Neddy," Emily said, and tried not to grimace over how dry her throat was. "Say thank you kindly."

"Thank you kindly, Iain," he repeated carefully, then opened the box and took out Boo. "Do you want Boo, Em?"

Emily stared at the box. It should not be unlocked. She reached up to touch her neck and realized the chain holding the key was gone. When she looked at Iain, he pointed to the table beside her and she saw the chain and key lying on the table. Trying not to wince she reached out to pick it up. Then she looked at Iain but he just smiled. Next she looked at Neddy, who avoided her gaze, patting his Boo.

"Neddy? Why is the box open?" she asked softly. "The papers need to be locked up."

"Why?" Neddy frowned at her then held Boo up in front of him and stared at her.

"Because they are yours and very important. Those who are not family should not be looking at them. They are private papers."

Neddy smiled. "I know. He cannot read. So, you teach him, too."

Emily noticed the faint hint of color in the man's cheeks and realized he was embarrassed. She was not sure why he should be as she was well aware of the fact that many of those not born to privilege could not read and not every parent felt it worth the loss of an extra pair of hands to work to send their child to the schools that were now set up. At best those people learned what words they felt were important like *poison* or *danger* and felt that would do well enough. Nor could such people afford the books to read so the skill was of little practical use in their eyes. She had taught the tenants' children back home on the estate and knew that few of their parents had felt it was really necessary.

"If he wishes it, I can do so." She glanced at Iain. "Might I have some water, please? My mouth is horribly dry." She lightly rubbed her throat. "How long was I asleep?"

"Three days," Iain replied as he made use of the glass and pitcher on the bedside table and poured her some water. "We got some food into ye a few times. Mrs. O'Neal tended to your wounds and said they were healing nicely." He handed her the glass of water.

Taking a sip, Emily nearly moaned in pleasure as the water washed away the dryness in her mouth and throat. It was not cold but it was not too warm, either. She drank it down as slowly as her raging thirst would allow. Once done she attempted to turn enough to place the glass back on the table only to have her wounded arm loudly protest and she gasped.

Iain took the glass from her and set it down. He watched her as she took slow, deep breaths to banish the worst of the pain and the color returned to her face. She sagged back against the pillows he had quickly plumped up at her back. Then a worried Neddy gave her his Boo.

Although she was startled at how weary and weak she felt, Emily tried to look sternly at Neddy. "You should lock the box, love. The papers are then safe from dirt or water."

"And prying eyes?" Iain asked as he picked up the key and locked the box before holding the chain out to her so that she could slip it back on.

Emily took the chain and quickly realized she

would not be able to put it back on. Her left arm simply could not be moved in a way that would allow it. She sighed and looked at Iain.

Tired and sore though she was, it annoyed her that she could not ignore how good the man looked. His hair was in need of a cut but suited him, the mahogany waves with touches of red brushing his broad shoulders. His deep green eyes were rimmed with surprisingly lush lashes. There was a faint bump in his long straight nose that hinted that it might have been broken once. When she looked at his mouth she was shocked by a tiny tug of strong attraction for it was not something she had ever felt before. He had a slightly wide mouth with a full lower lip. Emily decided he was a man she had best avoid as much as possible while she healed.

"I fear I cannot put this back on," she said. "It requires the full use of two arms."

He stood up, made certain the key was secured on the chain and, as carefully as he was able, put it on over her head. To his relief it fell perfectly. The last thing he wanted to have to do was adjust it. That could cause him to have to get very close to her and, perhaps, even touch her skin. Just seeing her bare shoulders and arms was already straining his control. Iain decided he needed to get down to the Trading Post soon for he had been far too long without a woman.

"What is so important about those papers?" he asked as he tugged a small chair over to the bed and sat down.

Emily wished her head did not ache as she rubbed her forehead and tried to decide just how much she should tell him. "There is proof of his birth and papers to prove he has a claim to some property back in England as well as proof that the cabin and land here also now belong to him. Then there is a will which names me his legal guardian."

Iain believed she was telling the truth but also omitting a lot of things from the explanation. The fact that the boy needed a fancy proof of birth and papers to prove a claim to property told him more than she realized. They were gentry. He just did not know how high they sat at the table. The thought stirred old angers and he decided he needed to get away from her before he lashed out at her with an anger she did not deserve.

"I will tell Mrs. O'Neal that ye are awake," he said as he stood up. "She will want to look at your wounds," he added as he walked to the door, "and I suspicion there are things ye may wish her help with."

A blush stung Emily's cheeks as she watched him leave. Then she noticed how Neddy watched the man. It was clear the boy had a budding attachment for the man. It might be kind to try to gently put an end to that but she could not do it. David had loved his son but protecting his small family and the fight to keep them fed and housed had used up most of his time and often consumed all of his thoughts. He had had little to give his son aside from the occasional pat on the head as he hurried from one chore to another.

"Do you want to go with him, love?" she asked the boy as she lightly stroked his hair.

"We were working. I pulleded weeds."

The boy looked so proud of himself she could not help but smile. "Well, go on then. See if he still needs your help." She looked at the sturdy woman who had just appeared in the doorway. "I believe I will be busy with other things for a time."

Neddy moved to kiss her cheek and put his hand on her wounded leg. Emily bit the inside of her cheek to stop from voicing a moan of pain, which she suspected could quickly turn into a scream. Mrs. O'Neal grabbed the child around the waist and lifted him off. She then patted the boy on the back, set him on his feet, and gently nudged him on his way. The moment Neddy was gone, Emily sank back against the pillows and fought the urge to cry.

"Ah, poor lass. Is it passing?" Mrs. O'Neal asked as she got a cool wet rag and bathed Emily's face. "Take deep breaths. Good," she said when Emily did so. "Passing now? Pain easing?"

"Yes. It just throbs a bit."

She opened her eyes and studied the woman standing by the bed. Mrs. O'Neal had a pleasant face and a white cap that vainly struggled to contain thick curly brown hair. As the woman set down a bowl she had brought up, Emily noticed she had hands well worn by hard work but they were strong. Emily also saw that Mrs. O'Neal's arms, which had looked as sturdy as the rest of her, actually rippled subtly with muscle that moved beneath the skin and the plain brown gown the woman wore. Mrs. O'Neal was a woman who worked hard.

"You are probably a bit hungry," the woman said. "Twice you roused enough for me to get some soup into you though I am thinking you don't recall it."

"No, I cannot, but I thank you for it."

"I mean to have a quick look at your wounds now. The one on your arm was not as serious as the one in your leg. They showed no signs of festering but it may be best to keep a close watch for a while yet."

Emily nodded but could not stop herself from tensing as the woman undid the bandage on her arm.

She looked at it along with Mrs. O'Neal, although she could not see it as well. Just as she began to feel a little queasy over the sight of the stitches on her skin, Mrs. O'Neal lightly touched the wound area and Emily closed her eyes as she winced.

"Still painful?"

"Just a little. I think it was mostly seeing you touch it that made me wince."

"It is looking very good. I think we will leave off the bandage tomorrow," she decided as she put the bandage back on. "You do not move much when you sleep so it should be fine."

"I sleep like the dead."

"You know?"

"My mother and sister complained about it as they always felt compelled to see if I was still breathing. At least I do not snore, I think. I am sure they would have told me if I did."

"Never heard any from you and believe me, I have heard every type and tune of snoring in this house." Mrs. O'Neal began to take off the bandage on her leg. "My eldest boy is the same. Spent many an hour setting by his bed trying to see if he was still breathing." She sent Emily a smile as she got a cloth to gently bathe the wound. "Once I got accustomed, I thought it was sweet. He was, in that way, like a babe or a kitten, a puppy. Awake one moment then sleeping like the dead in the next. This looks like it is healing well, too."

"Will we leave the bandage off it tomorrow as well?"

"I think not. It looks good, only a little redness from the boy bumping it. But that bullet tore a hole through your leg and it's best to give it more time under the cover of a good bandage. It was a much deeper wound. Takes longer to close up firm and all.

Needs to heal deep down inside. You will have a scar, I fear."

Emily tried to shrug but a pain in her left arm curbed that gesture. "It does not matter."

"Well, I have something I can try on the one on your arm that might lessen the mark left. Don't think anything can stop the leg wound from leaving a scar but we can try. Might make it fainter," she said as she bandaged the wound again.

"It would be nice if the one on my arm is not too stark but it truly does not matter. I am alive and so is Neddy. My sister"—Emily fought the urge to cry—"and poor David are not."

Mrs. O'Neal sighed and shook her head. "I am sorry. This land is beautiful round here but it is also dangerous. It took my Tommy, too. Lazy scum who didn't want to work for money decided he should hand over what he had just gotten for our apple harvest. Stubborn man wouldn't give it over so they killed him."

"A hard loss. My deepest sympathy for your loss and pain. So, you came here then?"

"We ran here fast as we could because now I was a single woman, a widow with three children and easy prey, and he let us in. So we settled on what we could do for him, on pay, and then the lads built us a small cabin. That was a gift we didn't expect. I was happy enough to be behind these walls. Saw them as we fled into the hills and thought it a good place to be. There is a chance of safety here, I thought. Been here six years this winter."

Emily nodded and watched Mrs. O'Neal uncover a tray of food. "I do not think I have ever seen a house with a stockade fence round it. Not in all my travel to get here." She pressed her hand to her stomach, afraid it was about to loudly announce how empty it was.

"Iain was insistent. The lad had suffered and wanted his brothers to be safe. It took a lot of work." Mrs. O'Neal put the tray of food on Emily's lap, careful to avoid the bandaged area around her leg. "Something more solid and filling for you this time. Want me to cut that meat?"

Since Emily had already discovered that movement hurt her arm, she nodded. "If you would, please, I would be most grateful. It all looks so good."

"Hope it tastes the same. Been a long time since I prepared something for a lady."

Quickly looking at the woman as she tried to hide the alarm she felt, Emily decided Mrs. O'Neal did not know anything. She had used the word *lady* as no more than a simple form of address. So Emily pushed aside her concerns and enjoyed her meal. She also learned a lot about the running of the place she had been brought to as Mrs. O'Neal entertained her with tales of the brothers.

"How many MacEnroy brothers are there?" she finally asked, wiping her face and hands with the damp cloth Mrs. O'Neal gave her.

"Seven." Mrs. O'Neal shook her head as she collected the tray and set it on the table by the bed. "Every one of them a handsome strapping lad. Their parents must have been so proud."

"Do you know how their parents died?"

"Their father and mother were bringing them all west. There was really nothing for them back east. Then their small wagon train was attacked. Both died in the battle." Mrs. O'Neal shook her head. "That fool boy Iain still blames himself for not helping, thinks he might have saved them if he had joined the fight but his folk had told him to watch his brothers and watch over their money."

"That was a very important job. Can he not see that?"

"He is a man, child. All he sees is that he ran from the battle." She picked up the tray now loaded with the plates as well as the bowl of water and rags she had brought up. "I will wander back in an hour or so to see if you are in need of any help."

Emily mumbled a thank-you but her thoughts were already on the MacEnroys and the place they had brought her to. The MacEnroy brothers must have been very young when they had found this place yet they had built themselves a home. They had been given skills for, rough as it was, the house they had built looked strong and was sealed tightly from what little she was able to see. And they had to be blessed with sharp wits to avoid being cheated on the price of things they had needed to begin. David and she had taken care to learn the prices of things so that he and Annabel did not lose all their money.

Settling into the pillows, Emily sighed. She had to confess, if only to herself, that she had found Iain MacEnroy a true pleasure to look at. He had apparently not found her so as he had been stiff and cold. No, she thought and frowned. He had grown cold right after she had said what the papers they protected were. That made no sense to her for surely everyone had some sort of paper to prove ownership of land if nothing else.

The man had certainly not leapt at Neddy's offer to have her teach him to read despite his obvious curiosity about the papers. It could be simple manly pride. He might not have wished her to know that he lacked that skill. She had faced that problem with some of the tenants at home. When she was back to her full strength she would see to that.

Closing her eyes, she tried taking slow, deep breaths to ease the last of the pain tending her wounds had caused. She was still heartsick over the deaths of her sister and David, the long sleep she had taken not easing it much at all. They had not deserved it, were only trying to keep their child safe. The moment the men had demanded they hand over the child, they all knew it was not some random attack.

What Emily did not understand was how their enemy had discovered where they were and how he had then gotten men to come hunting them. She had to wonder if Annabel had been writing to someone back home, giving them just enough information to point to a trail for their enemy to follow. David could have also written to someone in his family, she supposed, but he had claimed, loudly, that he was done with all of them.

It was a puzzle she was determined to solve, if only because the answer could serve to keep her and Neddy safe. The need to sleep meant she would have to do her thinking later. Fear for her nephew tried to push aside the sleep creeping over her, but she told herself the MacEnroys were watching out for the boy. That knowledge proved enough to allow the need to sleep to win over her fear.

A hand shook her by the shoulder and Emily scowled. Then she opened her eyes and stared into the deep green ones of Iain MacEnroy. That was enough to push aside the last dregs of sleep. Before she could speak he nudged Neddy forward. Iain stepped away and she felt a pang of disappointment before fixing all of her attention on Neddy.

"Hello, love. What have you been doing?" she asked as he pulled off his shoes and climbed up on the bed to sit on her right, uninjured side.

"Working. Pulleded more weeds." He gently took his Boo from her arms and held it close. "Iain showed me."

"Ah, so now you know what weeds look like."

"Some. I pulleded the things between rows. Hard work."

"I suspect it is. Where are you sleeping now, Neddy?"

"Here." He looked around. "My bed is gone."

"It is over there in the corner, laddie," said Iain.

Even as she wondered why he was standing across the room now and staring out the window, she glanced in the direction he pointed. There was what looked to be a folded cot, blankets, and a pillow tucked neatly in the corner. Neddy was sharing her room. The knowledge eased her mind. Emily turned to say something like that to Iain and found him staring out the window again.

Deciding he was intent on ignoring her, she talked with Neddy. It took her only a moment to realize Neddy was at ease, that she knew she did not need to fret about his care. The way the boy talked of Iain told her the man was skilled with small boys and she had to wonder again just how old he and his brothers had been when they had lost their parents.

A few moments later she found herself hoping Mrs. O'Neal would soon come. The last thing she wanted to have to do was ask the silent man by the window if he could fetch the woman and, worse, have to explain why she needed her. As if she had heard that thought, Mrs. O'Neal appeared and shooed Iain and Neddy out of the room. Iain left without a word or even a glance. Emily had only a moment to wonder why the man who had been so kind and helpful now seemed cold, before all of her thoughts were taken up by the humiliating business of having to be helped in the use of the chamber pot.

Chapter Five

A sharp curse escaped Emily as she tugged on her stockings. She was healed enough to move around now, and eager to do so after more than a week in bed, but her leg wound did not appreciate the feel of the stockings and garters. After trying again to pull them up, she removed them. She would just have to go without and hope no one noticed her bare legs. At least her drawers caused no pain.

Tying back her hair and pleased that her arm only gave her a small twinge, Emily stood up and brushed down her skirts. She had seen little of Iain MacEnroy but told herself that suited her just fine. The few times he had entered the room he had exhibited all the life and warmth of a marble statue. If he spoke to her it was in short, biting sentences and at times she was sure she saw a cold fury in his eyes. That made no sense for she had never done anything to the man.

Deciding she had fretted enough over Iain MacEnroy, she took a few steps to test her strength in walking. There was still a faint throb in the wound on her leg but she shifted to keep as much weight on her uninjured leg as possible when she walked. Going down the stairs proved tricky but she was not in too much pain when she finally reached the bottom.

There was no one around so she decided to have a quick look at more of the house before she went on to the kitchens Mrs. O'Neal had given her directions to. Emily peeked into the room on the right. It was the parlor, she decided. It held a heavy, overstuffed settee in a brown upholstery that almost matched the wood. Two sturdy chairs faced it and there was a plain low table set between them. Scattered around the room were other mismatched chairs with small tables, plain and fancy, set beside each one. She suspected the rugs in the room were handmade. What caught her eye was a painting over the fireplace. It was of a little valley, surrounded by hills both rocky and green, with cottages scattered through it. Some other glen in Scotland, she guessed, and turned to go into the room across the way.

It was the same yet much fancier. The furniture looked more expensive, there were fewer chairs scattered around the room, and they all matched. This had to be where they greeted guests, she thought. Here the rugs were almost certainly purchased. She wondered what the MacEnroys did for money. Again there was a large painting over the fireplace and she suspected she was looking at yet another picture of Scotland. Emily could not help but wonder how they had managed to bring the paintings so far without damage. Then she saw the sword on the mantel and fought against the urge to go over and have a closer look at it. It was a very large sword and had been polished to a pure shine, the scabbard hanging beneath it.

Shaking her head at her odd fancies, for she had never had the slightest interest in weaponry, she headed toward the kitchen, pausing only to peek into what was obviously a dining room and wonder what was behind the closed door on the other side of the hall. The MacEnroys had built themselves a big house but she supposed it was needed when there were seven of them.

Mrs. O'Neal sat at a large wooden table peeling potatoes. Emily carefully sat down on the bench opposite her and idly smoothed her hand over the table. Someone had a true skill in working with wood, she mused. Whoever it was truly knew how to bring out the beauty of the wood.

"Matthew made this," Mrs. O'Neal said. "The lad has a true gift."

"The benches as well?"

"Yup. Took a while as he had to work but then winter came and he had the time to finish it all. They did most of the inside work on this house during the bitter months. Built the outside walls and all then did the inside bit by bit."

"A good skill to have when you are starting a home. If you have another paring knife I could help with the potatoes."

"Thank you, dearie." Mrs. O'Neal quickly got a knife and pushed some potatoes in front of Emily. "We give the peels to the pigs. Just make a tidy pile and I will add them to the food bucket."

"They raise pigs?" Emily asked as she began to peel the potatoes.

"I and my children tend the pigs. The lads raise sheep. Between the meat of both and the wool of the sheep we don't do too badly."

"Is there not some trouble from the other people here about them raising sheep? I heard the beasts are loathed out here. In fact, Annabel and David discussed it a lot as they had considered having a few sheep. They decided to stick to just crops."

"They aren't near any grazing lands so we don't get bothered much. And they never go into town alone so few are brave enough to trouble them there. And, they give some folk work in the readying of the wool for market. As long as we stay up here it seems they find it tolerable enough. Our biggest problem is wolves. The boys are out hunting some now as we recently lost a lamb to the beasts." Mrs. O'Neal shook her head. "I tell them they should just kill the things but, mostly, they harry them until the pack moves away."

Emily sighed. "Fair, I suppose. The wolves have to feed themselves too. It is just that the very idea of wolves in the area gives me a chill."

Mrs. O'Neal nodded. "Feel the same way but you are right. Animals are just trying to stay alive. Do you knit?"

"A bit. Small things. You have yarn? Some from the MacEnroy sheep?"

"If there is a plentiful amount, yes, I get some. I do the scouring and scrubbing and we have some women in the town who do the carding and spinning. It works out well for all of us."

"It certainly seems to."

"Especially since we do not grow enough crop to make much money. We grow for us and some for market but we could not live on that. I often think there is nothing these lads can't do."

"You sound like a proud mama," Emily said, and grinned when Mrs. O'Neal laughed.

"Can't help but marvel at all they do." She tossed the potato peelings into the bucket. "I think they knew how to build things since they were small but everything else they just learn. They decide which one of them will find someone skilled at it, then he goes and learns the skill and comes back and teaches the rest."

"It is the best way." Emily added her peelings to the bucket. "I did it before we came to this country. I felt one of us should know some basic skills like cooking so I hunted down ones who were willing to teach me. I was rather surprised how difficult that proved to be. It turned out to be very fortuitous as I think my sister could burn water." She smiled sadly when Mrs. O'Neal laughed.

Mrs. O'Neal put the bucket by the back door, washed her hands, and then began to prepare the meat for roasting. "Why did you come here?" she asked. "I can tell you are educated and all." She noticed Emily's look of unease. "'Fortuitous'?"

"It is a common word," Emily said, not wanting the woman to keep asking questions for she knew she could not lie to her.

"About as common as that dress."

"Oh. I thank you for cleaning it. You did an excellent job."

"I got it soaking before the blood dried. Now, don't try to distract me. Why did you leave England?"

Emily sighed. "My sister was beginning to show that she carried a child. David was only the local blacksmith's son and it would be a match everyone frowned on." A partial truth that she hoped would satisfy the woman.

"A bad match." Mrs. O'Neal shook her head. "I was considered the same for my Tommy. He was an educated fellow and I was only the daughter of a seamstress. He was also Catholic and Irish and I was not. My Tommy realized his family was going to make our life hell and so we came out here. His sister was saddened about it, and Tommy was their only son, but he was adamant. We had ten lovely years and I am still trying to forgive them for driving us away."

"Because he died here," Emily said softly.

"Which is silly of me. Some fool in Boston could have killed him. Killing an Irishman wasn't all that unusual there." She put the meat in to cook then turned to study Emily for a moment. "I think you feel something like that."

"Yes. Something like that." Emily suspected what she felt was far stronger and more bitter than what Mrs. O'Neal felt. "Is there anything else I can do?" She wanted something that would dim the sad memories stirred up by their talk.

Mrs. O'Neal set a huge bowl of pea pods on the table. "Shell the peas. Done that before?"

"Yes. That is a lot of peas."

"We have twelve, no, thirteen people to feed and many of them male. Several of them still growing boys. They are like locusts in a field after a full day of work." She set down a bowl to put the peas in. "Then we do some carrots and, after that, apples, as I mean to make a couple of pies."

"A couple of pies?"

"They all have a sweet tooth."

Emily laughed and concentrated on the peas. It was pleasant to sit in the kitchen talking recipes and helping Mrs. O'Neal prepare the meal. She thought of her friends back home and knew many would be an even mixture of horrified and fascinated. A smile twitched at her lips as she thought of her friend Penelope Whitman, who had been her friend since they were very small. That woman would fall down laughing if she could see her now. Emily missed the long talks and laughter they had often shared over tea.

By the time Mrs. O'Neal had all the apples she needed for her pies, Emily was exhausted. It embarrassed her that helping with such simple chores had worn her out. When she stood up she had to grab the edge of the table to support herself. She glanced toward the door leading out of the kitchens and was not sure she would be able to reach it without sprawling gracelessly on the floor.

"You are looking very pale," said Mrs. O'Neal as she stepped close to Emily. "Done in now, are you?"

"It is ridiculous," Emily muttered. "I have done nothing but lie abed for days and all I have done now is sit here and ready vegetables for cooking. That should not weary me so."

"You may have been lying abed but your body was working hard." Mrs. O'Neal put her arm around Emily's waist to help hold her up. "When folk stay in a sickbed for a while they always find the first few days of being back on their feet hard work. Let's get you back up to bed. There are a few hours for you to rest before the meal is set out."

They were slowly starting up the stairs when a voice behind them demanded, "What are ye doing?"

Both women screeched and Emily grabbed hold of Mrs. O'Neal. When they turned to see it was Iain behind them their fright turned to annoyance. Emily scowled at him.

"You should not sneak up on people like that," she said.

"You scared us half to death, son." Mrs. O'Neal patted her chest as she fought to calm herself. "I am helping her back to bed so she can rest before tonight's meal. She was helping me. Too much too soon, I am thinking. What are you doing?"

Iain tugged Emily free of Mrs. O'Neal's grip and swung her up into his arms. "I will do it. Ye can go back to your work now."

Mrs. O'Neal just raised her brows, nodded, and hurried away. Emily silently cursed and tried to ignore the broad chest she was being held against. She stared at her hands to keep from looking at his face. Then he faltered in his step and she quickly wrapped her arms around his neck. His pace up the stairs immediately smoothed out and she frowned as she glanced up at him.

"Better," he said. "Before it was akin to toting logs up to the fire."

"I am unaccustomed to being carried about."

"What? No servants to carry ye about back home?"

"I suppose you think yourself amusing. You may have noticed that Annabel and David had no servants." Except for her, she added silently, but quickly buried that bitter thought. "And I left England almost four years ago."

"Where in England?" he asked as he set her on the bed.

"Hertfordshire. My sister chose the wrong man to love and was carrying his child."

"And that made her need to run here?"

Realizing she was close to telling him too much, Emily shrugged and looked at him. "Why did you and your family leave Scotland? I have seen the paintings you have. You loved that place. One can see it in each painting."

"We were not given a choice." He looked down at her feet as he fought down an old anger. "Where are your shoes?"

Emily blushed. She had hoped he would not notice that. Once she had realized she could not put on her stockings she had seen no point in struggling with shoes.

"I left them off because I was unable to don stockings. I am not ready to bend down and put them on, either." She tried to pull her feet up under her skirts but the slight bending of her upper leg caused her wound to protest enough to make her hiss with pain.

"Dinnae be a fool," Iain said, and tugged her feet down. "I have seen unshod feet before."

"Not mine," she muttered.

"Why did your sister feel the need to leave just because she carried her husband's child?" He sat on the edge of the bed near her hip.

"I told you, she chose the wrong man to wed, one our parents did not approve of." She sat up against the pillows and gave him her best polite smile. "She could not raise her child where he would always be looked upon as less, as a terrible mistake. Where she and her husband would not be accepted in the places she always went to so freely."

"Aye, that would be hard on a lad and a woman but harder yet to leave all your kin as weel."

Not liking how intently he was studying her, his expression pleasant enough but his dark green eyes narrowed, Emily settled herself more comfortably against the pillows. "I came up to get a little rest before supper so I suppose I best get to it."

He knew she was hiding some piece of the real truth, quite possibly the piece that would explain why her sister was dead. She held his stare for a moment and then closed her eyes, tensing when he moved up the bed until he was face-to-face with her. He thought of that box the boy kept such a close watch over, of the mark on that birth certificate, and her talk of papers proving that the boy owned land in England and the land his parents were buried on. He also re-called the rings and the locket, all worth more money than a blacksmith's son and shamed daughter could gather. Emily was gentry but for some reason was determined to keep that a secret. He had to wonder what kind of trouble he had brought into his home.

Emily opened her eyes and frowned at him. "I do not need to be watched until I go to sleep."

"I think there is something ye are hiding from me."

"Why would you think that? What reason would I have to do so?"

Iain tried to think of a good reply, one that would help to pull the secrets out of her, but all that filled his head were thoughts of her mouth and if it would feel as warm and soft as it looked. It was a foolish thought but he could not shake free of it. She was trouble. Every instinct he had honed over the years told him so. Yet, even as those thoughts went through his mind, he realized he was lowering his mouth to hers.

Her mouth was sweet and warm. She offered no re-sistance when he slid his tongue between her lips, needing only a light push to get her to open to him, although he had felt her give a start of surprise. He pulled her close and she wrapped her arms around his neck. It was the tiny sound she made as she raised her wounded arm that snapped him out of the haze of pleasure he had fallen into. He pulled away, ignor-ing the wide dazed look in her eyes as he leapt to his feet. There was also a lingering warmth in her gaze that called to him and he needed to get out of there before he answered.

"Best you get some sleep now," he said, then turned

and hurried out of the room. *Running like a damned coward,* a small voice whispered in his mind but he sternly ignored it.

Emily stared at the door wondering what had just happened. He had kissed her as if he was starved for the taste of her yet he had then backed away as if she had suddenly become venomous. She had little experience with kisses but felt certain that was not a common reaction. His parting words had been pleasant but his voice had been cold enough to chill her blood. It had certainly robbed her of any lingering warmth offered by the kiss.

She mulled over what he had said before he had so abruptly kissed her. Relaxing back against the pillows she touched her lips and sighed. She could not answer his questions yet felt that she should. The man had saved her life and Neddy's, too. Emily closed her eyes and tried to calm herself, to reach for the sleep she needed. She had spent too many years keeping secrets, fearing that she would slip and give something away, something that would cost her sister her child. Now she had lost her parents, her sister, poor sweet David, and she was all that was left to protect little Neddy.

Well, Iain MacEnroy could continue to believe she kept secrets. She did and no matter how sweet his kisses, no matter how much his coldness upset her, she would not give them up. Neddy was the only family she had left. Then there were the ones determined to wipe out the Stantons, most especially the young heir. Secrecy was necessary to keep the child alive. She could not, would not, gamble with trusting her feelings about who could be told those secrets.

As she slid into sleep her fears and worries followed her, darkening her dreams.

Iain dismounted and then plucked Neddy from the saddle and set him on the ground. The boy laughed and Iain smiled. Neddy had a great laugh, one that drew a person in to share his joy. Iain could only assume the boy had not seen any of what had happened to his parents. He had been saved that trauma. His mind and spirit carried few shadows of the violence he had survived.

As he watched Neddy play with the puppies that ran out of the barn to greet them, Iain wondered if Emily Stanton was more than just an aunt to him. It was not unusual for a female to use some indigent relative to raise her child. It better explained the child's lack of scars than anything else he could think of. In Neddy's heart and mind, Emily was more his parent than the two people murdered had been. It was sad but he did not blame the boy's parents for that. Starting a new life in a new country took up a lot of one's time and strength. They had not had the time or energy to build a bond with their child before they died.

Knowing he was postponing seeing Emily, he finished stabling his horse and then took Neddy by the hand. It was cowardly to use the boy to shield himself but Iain knew he would do it. It was time for him to face whatever consequences there were for his actions. Iain had no idea of how she might greet him but there was no forgetting how he had kissed her then walked away. He had the distinct feeling that was not something a woman shrugged off easily.

It had been a mistake to kiss her. He was still not

sure what had possessed him. One moment he had been admiring the lines of her face, thinking her mouth would be sweet, and the next he had been tasting that mouth. He had definitely discovered just how sweet that mouth was. Then he had run off like a rabbit scenting a hungry fox. He could not really understand what had sent him running but he certainly knew a lot of reasons why he should not be kissing her.

There was no denying that there were many good, solid reasons not to go kissing the woman. Emily was a woman in danger, one he had taken in. She was, in fact, under his protection as was the child with her. It was something he continually reminded himself of. He should not then turn into one of those dangers, even if his desire was not one to kill her. It might kill him though, he thought, and chuckled softly as he led Neddy up the stairs.

Just before stepping into the room, he sent up a quick prayer that she would be asleep. Neddy pulled free of his hold and ran to the bed. Emily's eyes opened and she smiled at the child. Iain decided he might need to live a more righteous life if he expected his prayers to be answered.

"And what did you do this afternoon, love?" she asked as the boy climbed up on the bed.

"I rode a horse."

Emily had been trying hard to ignore the man standing behind Neddy but Neddy's announcement had her looking at him in alarm. "Surely he is too small to ride a horse."

"Which is why he rode with me, nay alone."

"Ah." She kissed Neddy's cheek. "Did you have fun then?"

"Aye. I saw sheeps. Lots of them."

Iain watched as she talked with the boy about all he had seen and done. There was such a close affection between the two he would think her his mother if he did not know she was only his aunt. Suddenly he was certain of one of the reasons why she had been dragged to this country with her sister. Her sister had wanted someone to help her care for a child. He might be unfair but he doubted it. Emily had been given the care of the baby probably from the time he was born. That was why Neddy was not suffering from the loss of his parents because as far as the boy was concerned the most important person in his life was by his side.

Knowing it was almost time for the evening meal Emily nudged Neddy off the bed and carefully stood up. Iain stepped forward to slide his arm around her waist to keep her steady and support her. Despite the things he thought about her, about her kind, he could not help but appreciate the way she felt in his arms. He wanted Neddy to be gone so he could pull her firmly into his grasp. It was a strange fever he had no explanation for and was having a hard time curing himself of.

"I do not need so much support to walk down to the evening meal," Emily said quietly as Neddy led the way.

"Nay? Legs arenae wobbly?"

"Not at all. I am actually quite steady and need no help."

"Oh, I think it would be best if you have a little. Wouldnae want ye to tumble down the stairs. Ye might hit Neddy on the way."

She looked up at him and caught the hint of a smile. "I will be very careful. I think I could make certain to fall to the right if I weaken and then he is safe. I do so hate to inconvenience you."

"No bother at all." He pretended not to hear her soft sigh of exasperation.

Once they reached the kitchen, he helped her to a seat and then took one right next to her. As the food was passed around, she concentrated on helping Neddy and listening to all the talk. She covertly watched each brother as they ate. Mrs. O'Neal had been right. The MacEnroys were a handsome lot. Even Robbie, although he was a little bright with his vividly red hair, freckles, and blue eyes. She suspected that would tone down as he got older. Iain was not only the oldest but clearly the leader. It occurred to her that she had never seen so many shades of red and wondered if both their parents had had red hair.

Emily carefully worked to figure out where each one stood in the family line. Matthew held the place of the second in command. Nigel, who looked a great deal like Iain but had a softer shade of green eyes, was next, she decided. Then Geordie, she thought, as she studied the shortest one of the brothers. When it came to the other three brothers she only knew that Robbie was the youngest. Lachlan, strangely enough, had very dark hair and what looked to be brown eyes. It was as if he had been the cuckoo in the nest yet no one treated him as anything other than a brother. Duncan was quiet. His dark auburn hair was thick and prone to curls and she knew he was only a year older than Robbie. He was the studious one, she decided.

If this had been a family from her part of the world and society the doors would have to be barred against the women seeking husbands. She thought it odd that none of them appeared to be calling on anyone and they never spoke of any woman either. She sighed and felt sad for the parents they had lost. It would have been good if they could have seen what their sons had built.

By the time she finished dessert Emily was ready to retire. Despite wanting to join everyone in the parlor, she excused herself and made her way to her bedroom. Once she was settled in bed, she sighed. She was going to have to tell Iain more about what she and her sister had been fleeing. It was wrong to leave such a family ignorant of what might come kicking down their gates. They had worked hard for all they had and accomplished a lot. It would be horrible if they lost any of it because she made them stand between her and her enemy.

Chapter Six

Singing softly to herself Emily brushed flat the cover on her bed. She straightened and looked over the room. Everything was clean now. It had taken almost all day, which she found annoying since it was one of the smallest rooms in the house. Even after two weeks she still tired easily and had needed to sit down too often and rest. She told herself to be patient. What had been done to her required a long period of healing and she needed to accept that with grace.

She looked at the freshly washed curtains, the completely cleaned and fluffed bed, the clean rugs spread on a swept, washed, and polished floor and decided how long it had taken her did not matter. Although Mrs. O'Neal had polished the floor, Emily had managed the rest. Feeling proud and increasingly confident about her recovery, she started down the stairs.

Voices filled the dining room and she paused to look in. All seven MacEnroy brothers were gathered around the table, which had what looked to be maps spread over it. They were an amazing array of handsome men. She was still astonished the place was not besieged with women trying to catch their eyes, even young Robbie's, but she had quickly become aware of the shortage of available women as they had traveled west. Women were not inclined to make such a journey without a man at their side, which left the single men with few choices.

Mrs. O'Neal was pouring them all glasses of cider. Each one took the time to thank her kindly. What fascinated her, though, was the two somewhat disreputable men who were hunkered on the floor intently inspecting one of Donald's puppies. It was an adorable black-and-white mix and obviously a breed that was far from pure but young Donald was doing a fine job of espousing all of the dog's fine points.

"Hello, dearie," said Mrs. O'Neal as she started toward the door where Emily stood. "All done with the room?"

"Yes, finally. What is going on?"

"The lads are arguing over where the wolves might be and whether they should fence in the sheep. They have that argument every year," she added softly. "Always ends up with them agreeing the sheep don't do well all penned in. One spends too much time moving them from pasture to pasture. The Powell brothers are here looking at my boy's puppy. They think he may be able to be trained to help with the sheep. Their dog is getting old, though not too old he can't breed puppies with my bitch, and they want another up and trained before the old girl dies. Might need to breed her again."

"In England they have very simple fences or hedgerows."

"They don't have wolves."

"True. What do the Powell brothers do here?"

"Sheep herders or shepherds if you prefer."

"But there are seven brothers."

Mrs. O'Neal nodded. "And guess who they learned about sheep from. The Powell boys are out in the fields during the night now. They really had no other place to go," she said softly. "I best get started on the food. All this planning and arguing seems to give them a hearty appetite."

"They always have a hearty appetite."

"True enough. Hey, Owen?" Both Powell men stood up and looked at Mrs. O'Neal. "You and David are staying for a meal." Even though it was more a command than a request both men nodded.

"I will give you a hand," Emily said as she followed Mrs. O'Neal out of the room. "Oh my, something smells very good," she said as they entered the kitchen.

"Mutton stew. Got two pots of it cooking. We just need some biscuits and something for a sweet after."

"Never had mutton stew."

"Fairly common amongst farmer families." She gave Emily a sideways glance.

Ignoring the woman's look that begged for some answers, and with only a little instruction, Emily fell into the work of making biscuits. She was finding work in the kitchen soothing. A little smile touched her mouth as she suddenly recalled the reaction of the head cook at Stanton Manor when she had tried to help in the kitchen. Flush with new knowledge she had wanted to hone her skills. Instead she had nearly caused their head cook, Mrs. Paxton, to swoon. Then had come the lecture.

Not the place for a lady was an often-repeated phrase. It had infuriated her so she had finally stomped out of the kitchens and never gone back. The one good thing that had come out of that confrontation was that one of the kitchen maids had quietly offered to teach her a few things. Between that girl's help and the lessons with Mrs. Cobb, the tenant's wife, she felt competent in the kitchens. Making up the meals, with no help when living with her sister, had given her more confidence in her ability. Emily was contemplating asking Mrs. O'Neal if she could cook a meal sometime with the woman helping as much as was needed. In her mind she planned the whole meal out as she helped Mrs. O'Neal with the biscuits and her need to do so grew stronger.

When everyone started to arrive for the meal, Emily was surprised at how well the Powell brothers cleaned up. They had cast off their somewhat ragged coats and washed up, revealing that they were probably not much older than Iain. They had even taken the time to scrape the scruff off their faces revealing fine features. Both had thick black hair and dark blue eyes. They might have been twins, perfectly matching, except that Owen had a few age lines that David did not as well as a ragged scar that ran from the side of his right eye right down to his neck. Someone had once tried to kill the man, she thought, and then fought back her curiosity about the man's life.

She ate her meal surrounded by the accents of Scotland, Wales, and America. Glancing at Neddy she saw only happiness on his face as he ate his meal and listened to the men talk. It hurt her to realize he was not still grieving for his parents, had only done so mildly before settling in with the MacEnroys, even as she accepted that it was probably for the best. What hurt was the knowledge that her sister would not be dearly remembered by many. Emily promised herself that she would tell Neddy about his parents. While it was sadly true that they had not dealt much with their child, they had given him life and died to make sure he stayed alive. For those things alone they should be remembered.

By the time the meal was done, highly praised by the men, and she and Mrs. O'Neal had cleared up the kitchen Emily was tired yet not ready to go to sleep. Her mind was too full of worries about what she and Neddy would do once she was fully healed. That time was swiftly approaching for even her leg wound was only mildly aching if she worked on her feet too much or it got bumped. It would not be long before her strength fully returned either. Soon there would be no reason for her to stay with the MacEnroys.

"Is it safe enough to step outside for a while?" she asked Mrs. O'Neal.

"If you stay within the walls. There is a porch front and back. The back porch has a swing." Mrs. O'Neal removed her apron and slipped on her coat. "Just stay inside the walls," she warned again, and hurried out to go to her cabin.

Emily went upstairs to tuck Neddy into bed and make sure he was asleep. She got her wrap, one of the many things retrieved from the cabin, and then headed back down. Thinking that sitting on a porch swing was a wonderful idea, she stepped out onto the back porch, the cool night air a pleasure after working in the kitchen. She had only taken a few steps when she saw Iain standing at the end of the porch, leaning on the railing and studying his domain.

"Ye dinnae need to scurry back inside," he said, and turned to face her.

"I never scurry," she said, and watched his lips twitch as if he suppressed a smile.

"Come to sit on the swing? Matthew made it. We chided him for his fancy but it gets a lot of use."

Although a small voice in her head told her it was not a good idea, Emily walked to the swing and sat down. "He does wonderful work," she said as she ran her hands over the seat.

"He has a gift."

"Has he thought to make anything to sell?"

"Now and then for, when he has the wood, he wants to make something but we dinnae always need it. His skill is helpful in bargaining for what we need, too."

Iain sat down next to her, draping his arm over the back of the seat. Emily immediately tensed but she realized it was not a tension caused by wariness or fear. It was born of anticipation, that she wanted him to put his arm around her. She inwardly cursed herself for being an idiot. She complained about the man not knowing his own mind but it appeared she did not know hers, either.

"He is good enough to make a business of it," she said.

"Perhaps, if we lived in a city, or near one. We live out here and there just isnae the market he needs. There isnae the money here to give him a good living."

"Ah, probably not. A bit of a shame."

"Aye. He did much of the finishing off of the house. I recognize his skill and it would bring good money elsewhere but he has no wish to move."

"I cannot blame him for that. It is quite lovely here, at least, from what little I have seen of it and the problem of wolves eating lambs aside. And he has no great needs as you seem to do well enough here."

"It serves." He moved his hand so that he could stroke her hair. "Did your sister and her man do well where they were?"

"We were not there long enough to find out." She

sighed. "They had such hopes." The main one being that they had found peace and safety, she thought.

"Aye, it is sad that they were killed before they could attain them. This is a fine land but it can also be cruel. There are a lot of desperate men and not enough law."

"That is because it is so new, is it not? They have not had hundreds of years, thousands even, to set in their rules and laws. Although a judge we stayed with for a few days in Boston said it is those laws and legal customs they follow somewhat."

Iain just grunted. After what had happened to his family he did not feel anything good about English systems and laws. He had not yet decided this country did it any better. For most of the time he had been in this country he had either lived outside towns or been traveling to someplace. The threat of violence was always with them as well.

Shaking aside that thought, he looked at the woman sitting beside him as he moved his arm so that it lightly encircled her shoulders. She sat looking out at the yard which, he thought, was not the best view. She had relaxed even though he had changed his hold on her and he took that as a positive sign.

"It is very nice out here but I think a chill is rolling in."

"Could be. Getting that time of the year." He turned her so she was facing him.

"I am not sure this is a good idea and it is certainly not what I came out here for." Emily was pleased with her calm tone for her insides were leaping with what she could only call anticipation.

"I just came out for a smoke."

"A bad habit."

Iain decided he had lost all interest in a smoke.

Emily looked lovely in the soft light of the moon. He thought of her sprawled out on the swing beneath him and his whole body hardened. A dangerous thought, he mused, but one that now crowded his dreams. He just had to catch a glimpse of her in the distance and he grew hard. It was becoming embarrassing. Reminding himself that she was gentry, even if she would not say so, no longer cooled the heat of wanting and that troubled him more than the almost consistent want did.

He put his hand under her chin and tilted her face up to his. Studying her face for a moment, he saw no rejection. If anyone asked, he would have to say it was indecision mixed with a hint of curiosity. He did not blame her for the indecision but he would ignore it. He bent his head and kissed her.

Emily placed her hands on his chest to push him away but the moment his mouth covered hers, she clutched at his shirt. She opened to the gentle prod of his tongue. His kiss clouded her mind even as it heated her body. She wrapped her arms around his neck and held on tight, pressing her body up close against his. It was scandalous of her but she enjoyed it.

Desire was not something she had any knowledge of but Emily was sure that was what was flooding her body as he moved his kisses to her neck. She shivered as the feel of the heat of his mouth ran through her body. When he returned to her mouth, taking it a bit roughly, she was as eager as he seemed to be. Then he slid his hand over her breast and the surprise of the touch brought a hint of sanity. Slowly she pulled her arms from around his neck and pressed her hands against his chest, this time giving a very gentle push.

Iain lifted his head and stared at the hand he had put on her breast. Reluctantly he moved it but could still feel the hard tip of her breast nudging his palm. That he could feel it even through the material of her clothes told him that she was as stirred by their kisses as he was. Sighing softly, he met her gaze and the look in her eyes told him he had gone too far too fast. Emily Stanton was not some woman who worked at the Trading Post.

"I will see ye in the morning." He turned and walked away, knowing that distance was what he needed now.

Emily stared after him and shook her head. She hurried back inside and slipped into her room then began to change into her nightdress. The man was confusing. He had not even apologized for touching her so, just walked away.

As she climbed into bed she decided the look on her face must have told him that he had gone too far. Kisses could be allowed but anything else was forbidden. Or it should be since she was an unwed lady and she knew that rule held in this country as it did in England. Emily was not sure she had the strength to refuse if he put his mind to having her, however.

The very thought of being touched by him, made love to by him, made her tremble and she was not even completely sure how that was done. She was in trouble. There was definitely a part of her that welcomed the idea of him showing her how that was done. Shaking her head, she closed her eyes and told herself to go to sleep. It might be time to start planning what she and Neddy should do once she was completely healed. There was no doubt in her mind that, if she stayed here too long, she would give in to the man and since he offered no hint of having feelings for her that would be a tragic mistake.

She suddenly thought of her parents, which surprised her because she rarely thought of them any longer. Yet now she could see her mother, a woman who was never terribly happy. *Resigned* would be the word to best describe her mother. Her marriage to Emily's father had been arranged. Emily had always sworn she would not enter an arranged marriage but had never had much hope of being able to stick to that vow.

From listening to conversations she had not been supposed to hear she had learned that her mother had been with child when her parents married. That had stunned her when she had reached an age to fully understand all the ramifications of such a thing. It was truly the kind of scandalous behavior her mother had never revealed any inclination for and had often lectured her daughters thoroughly on any behavior she seemed to think was worthy of scandal. Now Emily understood that, in so many ways, the freedom of choice had been taken away from her mother by her own lack of restraint.

It was sad but a part of her was angry that her mother had not made a better effort to make herself happy. Her father had not been a bad man compared to many another husband and at some point her mother had obviously found him attractive enough. Now she rather understood what could have happened. Iain had shown her the heady power of need and passion. She promised herself she would be careful. There was no need of a forced or arranged marriage here but there was always a chance of finding herself carrying the child of a man who could not love her but would feel compelled to marry her. She needed to guard against that chance. Perhaps, she thought as sleep started to nudge at her, it was past time she turned cold to him.

Iain lay in his bed staring at the ceiling. It was going to be a while before his body relaxed enough for him to find sleep. This time telling himself he needed to go visit one of the girls at the Trading Post brought nothing but a feeling of distaste. That did not please him and he knew that was a sign of trouble. The girls at the Trading Post could ease the sharp bite of need but he realized it would never help him to stop wanting Emily Stanton.

He then realized he had not once thought of Emily as a lady tonight, as one of Lady Vera's ilk. That cold fury at gentry had not rushed in to cool his interest or make him angry about feeling it. In the days she had been at the house he had somehow separated her from that class of woman. He knew it had been unreasonable to ever think of her that way but the fact that he no longer did seemed another sign of trouble to him.

"Oh, hell," he muttered.

Emily opened her eyes and stretched. The sight of Neddy's empty cot pushed aside the lazy pleasure she was enjoying and she sat up. Her door was ajar and she could hear voices in the kitchen. She had slept past breakfast call. Blushing, she got up and gathered her clothes, slipping behind the privacy screen that had been brought in so she could dress.

Quickly running a brush through her hair, she tied it
back with a ribbon and rushed down the stairs, ignoring the occasional twinges in her leg.

"Oh, I am sorry, Mrs. O'Neal," she said as she
stepped into the kitchen and saw everyone seated
and eating. "I should have been up to help you."

"Nonsense. You clearly needed your sleep. I have
been making the food for this lot for a long time.
Have your breakfast." She set a plate of eggs and ham
in front of where Emily usually sat. "I saved you some
in case you came even later."

"Thank you, Mrs. O'Neal."

Emily did her best to ignore Iain as she ate. She
knew if she looked at him even once her blushes
would tell everyone at the table far more than she
wanted them to know. It was difficult to keep anything secret from such a large group of people.
Somehow she was going to have to train herself to not
think of kisses or touches when she looked at him.

Finished with her meal, she looked up and found
everyone gone until she turned to the side. Iain
straddled the bench at her side, studying her carefully. As she frowned at him she felt the burn of a
blush on her cheeks and inwardly cursed.

"You do not have any work today?" she asked.

"Always have work but today is my day off."

"You get one?"

"Aye, I get one though I dinnae often take one. I
am about to head out to clean out the stables. They
need it and it will save me having to see it done tomorrow. What do ye plan to do?"

"Clean. I think today I will attempt to clean the
dining room."

"Why? It looks clean to me."

"Well, you are a man."

He laughed abruptly. "You have been around Mrs. O'Neal too much. Truly, why do you want to clean the dining room?"

"A good hard clean and not just a sweep and a dust. I have decided to do a room a day and by winter this place will be pristine."

"Still dinnae see why it needs it." He shook his head as he stood up then leaned toward her and gave her a quick kiss. "Dinnae exhaust yourself and set your healing back. We are happy with just clean and dinnae need *pristine*."

Before she could get over her shock at that surprise kiss and tell him she was healed enough to work as hard as anyone else, he was gone. She shook her head then wondered where Mrs. O'Neal had gone as she took her dishes to the sink. Seeing that no one had washed up yet, she rolled up her sleeves and got busy.

She frowned as she thought about Iain. He had actually been pleasant to her, chatting as if they were old friends. The kiss had been a light brush of affection. The man had too many moods. Just as she got adjusted to his passion followed by cold anger, he found yet another mood to confuse her with. Emily supposed she would have to find a way to treat each change with calm.

She was wiping dry the last pan when Mrs. O'Neal came bustling back into the kitchen. "Oh, child, you did not have to do that."

"They were there and needed cleaning."

"Well, thank you kindly. Had a small emergency with Rory. The child has a deep and abiding fear of wasps and one was flying around too near to him. So had to go to his rescue."

Emily laughed softly. "I can fully understand the fear of wasps."

"Nasty devils. So what do you have planned for today?"

"I plan to clean the dining room. Top to bottom just like I did my room."

"Are you sure you are strong enough?"

"I may need to sit down and rest a minute more than I like but, yes, I am strong enough. It will probably take me all day though."

"I will polish the floor for you."

"Thank you." Emily grinned. "I was hoping you would offer." She laughed when Mrs. O'Neal gave her a light slap on the arm. "The floor in my room looks wonderful and I have no idea how you got it to look that way."

"Just let me know when you are ready for it. Best we shift some of the furniture first."

Emily wiped her hands and followed Mrs. O'Neal into the dining room. One look was enough to tell her they would need to call the men in to move a few things but the two of them took everything else to the parlor. With much complaining about why they had to do this, the men came in and moved the two largest pieces and set them in the hall.

"The room is far larger than I thought," Emily murmured as she looked over the empty room.

"I can help whenever you need it. Just need to make a lunch and prepare the supper."

"Then I had best get started."

She bent down to roll up the carpets and Mrs. O'Neal helped. Then they carried them out to the porch, flipped them over the rail, and Mrs. O'Neal got her rug beater and started to work. Emily went back into the kitchen, got a mop and a bucket of light soapy water, and went to wash down the walls. She hoped she had more strength than she had had the last time she cleaned because this room would not allow her many rests if she was to be done by the end of the day.

She looked around after she had finished washing the walls. "This is going to look magnificent."

"Huh. I would never have guessed the walls had gotten so dirty. We shall have to have a meal in here when it is not a holiday."

Emily looked at Mrs. O'Neal. "You only use it on holidays?"

The woman shrugged. "We don't have dinner parties. So, carpets clean, walls clean, and I have some time before starting the midday meal. What next?"

"The windows."

Both women looked at the windows and groaned.

By the time the men had arrived for supper, they were ready for them to put the furniture back. Emily noticed some frowns as they looked over the room while bringing in the furniture. She found she was nervous about their opinion. Mrs. O'Neal's frown deepened as they did their work and said not a word.

It was not until they were all seated for the evening meal in the kitchen that Iain said, "So we arenae allowed to eat in the room now?"

Emily laughed when Mrs. O'Neal cursed and tossed a napkin at him. "We are eating here because the room needs airing or one ends up tasting the smells of window cleaner, polish, and the like. Everything in there, even the walls, was cleaned and that can make a smell hard to breathe in."

"It looks nearly as new as when we built it," said Robbie.

"That it does," agreed Lachlan. "Even the carpets."

"Nice as it is, the question is—why?" asked Iain.

"It is what we used to do at home before winter," said Emily. "It makes everything all fresh so when you close up the house it is nicer." She placed the potatoes on the table and then took her seat next to Neddy. "Then one sometimes does some of the same things in the spring. Clean off the smell of fires going for days." Emily looked up to find even Mrs. O'Neal staring at her and just shrugged.

"Ye had servants to clean for you," said Iain.

Emily heard no real anger in his voice so she just shrugged again. "I do not think that room has been scrubbed down since you built it. It won't need such a hard clean for a long time."

Iain looked at Matthew and then each of his other brothers and nodded. "Just how many rooms do ye intend to do that with?"

"All of them. One a day."

"Weel, ye will tell us when ye plan to do it to any of our rooms."

"If I must."

"Aye, ye must."

Emily bit back a smile as she turned her attention back to her meal. As ever, the men talked of work done and work they thought needed doing. When they all got up to leave she turned in her chair and watched them walk down the hall. Each one of them paused to look over the dining room. Satisfied, she turned her attention to clearing up after the meal.

Chapter Seven

Determined to see what the town had to offer, Emily went to the stables thinking she would ride into town. All she would need was some directions. Looking around the dimly lit stables she only found a pair of plow horses and no saddle she could use. Frustration was a hard knot in her belly for she needed to get away from Iain and his home for a while but it appeared she was stuck.

As she stood outside the stables considering how she could get away from Iain and his ever-changing moods for a while, Robbie strolled up. He was eating an apple and walking as if he had nowhere pressing to be. Emily wondered if she should try to use one brother to hide from another for a little while. It seemed wrong in some inexplicable way but she had no choice.

"How can I get to your town?" she asked. "There is neither horse nor saddle for me to use."

"Weel, we never had need for one of those silly woman's saddles," Robbie answered, and tossed his apple core into the pig pen that was right beside the stable. "I can take you in the buggy."

"I would not wish to take you away from your work."

"No work today. My day off."

"You have a day off too?" she asked as she followed him back into the stables.

"We all do. Iain decided that since we cannae all stop working on any day we choose that each one of us will have a day to do as we please. There are still times when we are all needed but it works out well." He started to hitch one of the plow horses to the front of a small buggy. "Slept late. Did some weaving and was just thinking of having a ride, an ambling kind of ride, one with no purpose."

"You do weaving?" she asked, startled, and then smiled at his blush.

"Aye. Some."

She smiled as he helped her up into the buggy seat and realized he was not going to tell her much about his skill. "Are you sure you want to do this?"

"More interesting than riding aimlessly." He hopped into the seat and carefully steered them out of the stable. "Need a few things myself so this will suit me." He reined in right in front of the house. "I will just tell Mrs. O'Neal so everyone knows where we are."

"Oh, of course. Please ask her if she will watch over Neddy if it is needed."

As she waited Emily realized Robbie had a lot less accent than Iain, actually spoke more like an American. She suspected the occasional slips came from growing up surrounded by people who spoke like Iain did. When he returned and got in the seat, he handed her a scrap of paper upon which was a list of what looked to be badly spelled words.

"Mrs. O'Neal wants a few things. She told me but thought it might be best to make a list. Took her a while. Said she didnae know the spelling. Can you read it?"

"Tell me some of the things she said so I can puzzle it out. There is usually some logic to the way people who really do not understand how to spell will write their words."

"Huh. First thing is flour. Second thing is sugar."

"Ah, that will do. I can see it now. You cannot read?"

"Nay. First, the tenants were usually doing work if it was ever offered. No time. Then we were always moving on. Even here. Then you just reach an age where you simply give up on the idea. You have found no need for it so why bother. Other things that need doing."

"I could teach you if you want."

"Really? There was a teacher on the wagon train and our mither had us go to her but it was only for a few days before the attack. Teacher died as did our folks."

"I am sorry. When was that?"

"Near to fifteen years ago. Me, Donald, and Lachlan were born here. Tale is that Lachlan barely waited for our mither to get off the boat."

"Oh, my, your poor mother. She left Scotland when she knew she was carrying a child?"

"Had no choice. Laird decided that stock was cheaper than tenants. We were tossed out of our cottage. They came in the night. Dragged my parents out, shoved a paper in front of my father's face but he could not read it, could he. Slapped him around a bit before they understood that."

"Surely you had some right to live there."

"Only the laird's word. Even though the same thing was happening all over Scotland and had happened over and over before our turn came, Da never thought our laird would do it."

"Greed can be a powerful persuader."

Robbie nodded. "One soldier was a good fellow and let my mither and Iain get a few things before they set the place on fire. To keep us from sneaking back in, they said. She grabbed a few of my da's paintings, his painting supplies, his sword from when he was in the army, and a few other small things. Nearly lost Geordie because he had run back in to get something. Iain went in after him. Got him out but it was close. See, Da had a tunnel under the house. He said that with reivers and soldiers always wandering through, it would be useful. Iain got singed but he brought Geordie out. We also saved our money, which proved useful. Passage was costly. Did ye hear nothing of the clearing of the lands in Scotland?"

"Not much, I fear. Females are not to be troubled by such things. Too weighty for our tiny female brains," she drawled, and Robbie laughed. "Perhaps the men think we will riot or some such nonsense. I did hear a bit but nothing to tell me it was so harsh. Tenants usually have some agreement with the man who owns the land. The paper they sign gives them a little protection from just being tossed out or so I was told."

"If Da had a paper he did not ken what it said. And Lady Vera, the laird's new wife, got angry over how long my mother was taking to get her things and ordered it stopped. They set the place on fire before Iain and Geordie could get out. When they did get out we picked up what little we had saved and headed to a city where we might find some work. We did but Da had also heard about this land and wanted to come here." He frowned. "So, yes, I would like to learn how to read. I have seen how it can cause one trouble if you cannot read."

"Well, we will see what others wish to do, and then settle on a time to do it. It takes time, you know."

"Most learning does from what little I have seen of it. I would like to get good at it. I want to read a book."

A simple wish, Emily thought, and she was determined to fulfill it. She then thought on what they had suffered, what had driven them from the land they were born in. It was sad and so very wrong. Now she also had a clue as to why Iain would go from being warm to acting cold around her. As the eldest his memories would be the clearest about what the gentry had done to them. He was convinced she was gentry even though she had yet to confess to it. It was wrong for him to blame an entire class of people for what had happened but she could understand it. Sad to say a lot of her ilk would be just as cruel to their tenants if it brought them money.

She winced. It made her even more reluctant to tell him the truth but she knew she had to. Emily had almost convinced herself that her actions since coming into his home would show him she was nothing like the ones who had hurt him and his family when Robbie stopped the wagon.

Emily started and looked around. There was one large store that was called the Trading Post. The sign hanging on the wall of the building indicated it was also a tavern. Robbie's glances at it and faint blush told her it was probably a place that offered some other services men sought. Her opinion of that was confirmed when they stepped inside. As Robbie hustled over to a door at the side she glanced up at the upper floor and saw a man stepping out of a room as he adjusted his clothing. A scantily clad woman stood behind him. Her expression was one of utter boredom.

Then she was inside what looked to be a perfectly normal store. She glanced to the front of the building and noticed it too had an entrance. Then she looked at Robbie but he was blushing so brightly she did not have the heart to tease him. A big woman came out from behind the counter, walked over, and rapped Robbie on the head.

"Mabel!"

"Idiot! You don't go bringing some proper woman in through that tavern." She pointed at the door. "We have a door. Next time you bring her here, use it. Now, can I do anything to help you?" She turned and smiled at Emily.

"Yes, please." Emily proceeded to ask for what Mrs. O'Neal wanted and followed the woman as she marched around the store collecting up everything asked for.

Emily took the time to look over the goods offered and was surprisingly impressed. As the woman piled the goods she asked for on the counter, she checked over a few dresses, some shirts, and even looked at the skirts. Her things saved from the cabin were not meant for riding around outside and she decided she could use a simple cotton outfit. Checking what she had for money she picked up a pretty little dress and walked back to the counter only to find Robbie getting candy.

"How nice of you to pick up some sweets for the children." She nearly laughed aloud when he gave her a narrow-eyed look.

"That is a good idea. I think I will pick some other

candies up for them." He finished filling the bag he held and grabbed another.

Feeling a little sorry for him as she had no idea of how much money he had, she slipped him a couple coins. "Include some from me as well. Neddy loves lemon drops."

As Mabel added up what they had bought, Emily looked around for a lady's saddle. The woman hurried over to her and asked, "Do you want one?"

"Actually I was looking for a lady's saddle."

"Huh. Never have understood how some ladies sit on those things let alone ride about."

"It does take a lot of training. Do you have one?"

"All I have is some used ones. After living here for a while a lot of ladies give them up for a normal saddle."

"Fear I am not ready to do that. Is there a way I can look some of them over?"

"Sure can. Come with me. We keep them in the back room with some other things people got tired of. Maybe you will see something else you have a liking for."

Emily shook her head when the woman turned and started to walk away. She had to marvel at the woman's skill at selling things. Her remarks about the type of saddle she was looking for did sting though. Emily was not sure she could ever change to ride as the men did.

The cost of the saddles quickly put her off. They were priced well for being secondhand goods but it was still more than she could afford. She was stroking the fine embossed leather of one when Robbie walked in.

"That is one of those funny saddles ladies ride." He

stroked the leather. "Thinking the woman didnae use it much. Nice work on the leather though."

"It is but it is also too rich for me. That little table is cute though. I wonder why someone would get rid of it."

"I bet Matthew could make you a little one if you want it."

"I suspect he can too, but"—she leaned closer to him and whispered—"the woman hoped to sell a saddle and I cannot oblige her, but I can afford to buy that little table."

Robbie nodded. "You sure?" Emily nodded and he lifted the table. "Got good weight. We'll take this, Mabel. Emily, do you want me to put it in the buggy?"

Emily went back to the counter with Mabel and paid the bill. She discovered that Robbie had already paid for the things Mrs. O'Neal wanted plus the candy. When she stepped outside and adjusted the bonnet she had just bought several men stepped out of the tavern. From beneath the rim of her bonnet Emily looked at one of them and nearly stumbled. Then he spoke and laughed with the other men and her blood froze. She tried to hide her upset and went to the buggy. A glance back showed the man staring at her and she grew afraid.

"Robbie, we must go. Now."

Hearing the fear in her voice Robbie looked around and then started the buggy on its way. "Those men?"

"The one who was looking our way is one of the men who attacked our cabin. I recognized his voice and his laugh. Then he looked at me and I truly fear he recognized me as one of the ones in the cabin."

Robbie cursed softly and urged the horse to a faster speed. It was just a plow horse and although it tried, the men were gaining. Emily was terrified that

Robbie would be hurt when she noticed several horsemen headed their way. It took them drawing closer for her to realize it was Matthew, Iain, and Geordie.

"Why are ye pushing this poor old horse to a speed it probably never ran before?" Iain asked as he rode up on Robbie's side of the buggy.

"Those men behind us? They are the ones that attacked the cabin where Emily was. They are the ones that made poor Neddy an orphan."

All three men turned to look behind them and the men after them slowed down and drew their guns. Robbie pushed Emily down and tried to prod the plow horse back into a harder trot. He was pulling away from the confrontation when the shooting began. Emily struggled against a rising hysteria. The sound of guns, the looming threat to her and these men who had taken in her and Neddy was almost more than she could bear.

Emily listened to the guns for a moment and then tried to look over the seat, needing to see how everyone was faring. Robbie used his foot to push her back down again and she cursed. "I just want to be sure no one gets hurt," she said, hanging on to the seat to steady herself.

"Ye'll just get yourself shot."

"We are too far away."

At that moment a bullet ripped into the top of the buggy seat. Emily screeched and ducked down all the while keeping her eyes on Robbie, who appeared to be unhurt. Then a horse without a rider galloped past them and she took a chance at a fast look back, raising herself up just enough to see a body in the road. Iain, Matthew, and Geordie were chasing the other men into the hills.

"Can I get up now?"

Robbie looked around and nodded as he eased up on the reins so the plow horse could return to its long steady stride. "Just keep a close eye out for them trying to circle back this way."

"But one of them is dead."

"That willnae make any difference to men like that. If they think about it at all, it'll be to consider how they will split his share of whatever they are getting for this crime."

Holding on to the side of the buggy, Emily kept a close watch out for the men. They were almost to the house when she saw three riders coming back down the hill. Everyone looked hale and she breathed a sigh of relief. She came to a decision. She and Neddy had to leave before they got one of the MacEnroys killed. It was wrong to bring this trouble to their door.

When Robbie pulled to halt in front of the house, Emily got down and pulled out her purchases. Just as she was about to get her table, the brothers rode up. Matthew looked at the small table Robbie pulled out of the buggy for her and frowned.

"Ye bought furniture?"

"She felt bad for Mabel, who had hoped to sell her a saddle so she bought this instead." Robbie frowned when Matthew dismounted and took the table. He stood there testing every joint and studying the legs. "Not bad. Women like these little things?"

Emily nodded. "I will see if Mrs. O'Neal wants it for Neddy and I cannot carry that about when we leave."

"Leave? Where do you think you are going?" asked Iain, surprised at how shocked he was by the idea of her leaving. Shocked and, he realized with dismay, hurt.

"I have no idea but it is clear we need to leave here.

Those men will tell someone where I am and there will be more." She needed to get to her room for she feared she was going to break down and cry if she stayed there talking on the need to leave.

"Actually dinnae believe those men will be saying much to anyone."

She stared up at him. "Of course they will."

Iain shook his head. "Hard to tell anyone a thing when ye are dead."

A part of Emily was relieved by the news and she felt ashamed of it. "I cannot have killing following me wherever I go. There has to be some way to stop this. But even if there is not, I can stop it touching you and your family by leaving. It will follow me and Neddy."

"Is there anyone you can trust to speak to about it? Anyone here that you trust aside from us?"

"No." She still desperately wanted to have a good cry but she held back her tears. "There is no one." She walked into the house and straight up to her room.

Seeing the box sitting on the bed, she walked over and picked it up. She sat on the edge of the bed and opened the box. All the papers rested neatly inside just as they had for nearly four years. Emily doubted she would find anything in them to help her but she carefully unfolded and read each one. When she picked up one it felt a little odd and she thought Neddy may have refolded it wrong. She opened it and out fell several letters. She stared at them as if they were poisonous snakes for a moment before she picked them up. Arranging them by dates received, she began to read and soon tears filled her eyes. Despite her best efforts to stop them, the tears slid down and she had to hold the letters out of the way.

Every single one was from their cousin. Annabel

had written to the woman about her marriage, her child, and even where they had settled. In a sad way Annabel had signed the death warrants for the last of her family. David had to have known what she was doing yet never said a word.

"What is wrong?"

Emily looked up to find Iain standing over her. "My sister wrote to our cousin. Our cousin is also Albert's cousin. My own sister, who had sworn she understood the danger we were in and how we had to hide, sent letters to our cousin. I do not have copies of her letters but the answering letters give me a good idea of what was said. Constance spoke of how wonderful it must be to have a son. Then about how beautiful it sounds at the cabin. She would have told enough about it to give them a good place to start looking. I can barely read this they so infuriate and sadden me. I told her! I told her there had to be no contact, nothing said to anyone."

Tears choked her and she tried to hold them back but she could feel them continuing to slip free and roll down her cheeks. It was hard to accept that her older sister could be so careless. Even if she had not fully believed everything Emily had told her she should have at least felt some sense of caution. Their parents had been killed and someone had tried to kill them at least once. That should have been warning enough for anyone.

The bed dipped and a strong arm went around her shoulders. Emily leaned against Iain and tried to soak up some of his strength. She was both furious and heartbroken. Her sister was dead and Emily did not want to be angry at her but she was.

"So your sister wrote to someone and that is how the men found you. It seems a long way to come. Why not just leave you here out of his way but with no blood on his hands?"

"I begin to think Albert likes to get blood on his hands. He killed our parents and we are pretty certain it was him behind two attacks on us. So we fled. I thought she had listened to me. She swore she understood that we were in danger, and that David and Neddy were, too. She swore to me that she would write to no one or talk to anyone. But she did and she obviously did so for a long time."

"I am sorry her foolishness has hurt ye so." He kissed her lightly and held her close. "Ye need to sleep, Emily. Ye have had a harrowing day and now discovered what has to be verra bad news." He took the papers from her hands and carefully put them back into the box. "I think ye are also upset that ye are angry with a dead woman, your sister. Get some rest. It may help ye see things more clearly."

She sighed. "Yes, it may help." She got the key from the chain and relocked the box. "Thank you. It was just such a shock." She took a handkerchief from her pocket and wiped her eyes. "Oh, I should help Mrs. O'Neal with the meal."

"She has been making the meals here by herself for a few years. She will be fine. Rest. I will have her put together something for ye for if ye wake up hungry. It will be right there on your new table."

Emily looked over and saw the table she had bought and had a hard struggle not to start crying again. "Thank you. I did not insult Matthew by buying it, did I?"

"Nay. He understood what ye did. Saved a little face for Mabel. Not a bad thing and he was impressed at the way it is built."

She smiled and surprised herself with her ability

to calmly lie down. She really needed to tell him the whole truth, she decided. There was no question he deserved to be told. At least then he would know what he was up against. Although she thought it wrong to sleep, her eyes closed in minutes. Emily fought to try to sort through her thoughts as she waited for sleep to take her but it came over her quickly and she sank into it with a sigh.

Iain stared down at her. He could not even imagine how her sister could have ignored so many warnings that they were all in danger and written to anyone at all over in England, especially to a woman Emily considered too closely connected to the man she was sure was hunting them. Shaking his head over the idiocy, he walked away to deal with his own work before supper and try to think of a way to stop his anger over the past from coming to life and aiming for her. Even he was getting tired of it.

Chapter Eight

Iain frowned at the paper he held and could make out only a few words. The lessons he had been forced into by Mrs. O'Neal and his brothers were actually working, but slowly. It had only been a week of regular lessons but he felt he should have been able to read more than a few words. If he was to get the small loan he needed, however, he needed to understand every word before he signed it. That meant he had to go to Emily and he sighed. He had done a good job of angering her with his wavering emotions and he doubted she would want to be helpful. Then he told himself not to be a fool. Emily would help because she was one who could not do anything else.

Standing up, he headed out of his room, deciding it was best just to steel his spine and get it over with. It was late so he hoped the meeting would be over quickly. He rapped on the door to her room and she opened it, her look of surprise changing quickly to one of wariness. To his astonishment she stepped out into the hall and shut the door behind her.

"Neddy is asleep," she said quietly.

"Ah. Weel, I need ye to read a paper for me."

"What sort of paper?"

"I need a loan from the bank and they said they wanted me to sign this." He held out the paper. "Your teachings helped me guess at only a few words. I dinnae want to sign anything until I ken exactly what it says though."

"That is wise. A rule my papa lived by. Is there a place where we can sit for a moment?"

"We can go down to the dining room. No one there this hour of the night."

She allowed him to lead her down the stairs. He was not in one of his cold moods and she was pleased he had turned to her for help but she remained cautious. The way he could go from warm and seductive to coldly formal in the blink of an eye was unsettling and, to her disgust, hurt her feelings. She was not going to be made to suffer for wrongs done by the others of her class.

By the time they reached the dining room, Emily was calm but determined. She would not allow him to play his confusing games of kissing her one moment and treating her like a complete, and somewhat disliked, stranger the next. Since she intended to tell him the truth, that might well end his games anyway. With his rancorous feelings about the English gentry, the truth would certainly end the strange bouts of warmth he showed her. Sitting down, she frowned when he pulled a chair closer and sat right next to her then handed her a couple of papers.

"Dinnae ken why they need more than one page," he muttered.

"Probably written by their lawyers or one of them has learned the craft. I have never known a lawyer to use one word when he could use six. They are always trying to make certain they do not lose or forget a thing. Do you wish this to be read aloud?"

"No need unless you find something you think is important. My agreement was to put up my flock in exchange for a loan."

Emily nodded and began to read. She was pleased she had read several such legally binding papers before now so she knew how to dig her way through the massive collection of unneeded words. Then she hit the section that spoke of what Iain was to put up as collateral and frowned. Her frown deepened as she slowly read it again then finished reading the whole document.

"Did they know you cannot read?" she asked.

"I didnae say. I told them I needed the night to think on this. But, then, not many folk around here can read and I suspicion they guessed."

"Quite probably, because if you looked at the whole document . . ."

"I did."

"Then you would have immediately objected if you had been able to read it. You offered them your flock as collateral. Right?"

"Aye. I saw that word."

"Oh, it is there. It says if you do not repay this loan in the time agreed upon they have the right to take your flock as payment, and your land, and your house and all belongings which they will be permitted to sell at auction to recoup the money owed."

Iain sat stunned. "Jesu. I never mentioned our lands. We could recover if we lost the flock but would never recover if we lost the house, land, and all else. What were they thinking?"

"That you cannot read, would sign this, and thus give them the chance to make a gain. It very nicely says for repayment of loan, all interest accrued, and other expenses including a penalty for being so rude as to not repay as agreed. Even if they left it as you asked those last two should not be there as they are left vague as to how much and such things can be fiddled to their liking."

"Ye mean raised to whatever they want."

"Yes. A fee added for nonpayment or even late payment would be acceptable if stated clearly but not this. It was always stated clearly, the cost and how it could rise. Is there a lawyer in town? A man you trust?"

"There is a lawyer but I dinnae ken the mon weel. Cannae say if he is trustworthy or nay. Then again, I thought I could trust the bank."

"I suppose I could meet him with you and give you another opinion to work with."

He sighed and took back the paper. "Or I can try to get what I need without the loan."

"No. These things tell me they have made some bad loans. This is being done to help recoup their losses off the back of an honest man. Sad to say, banks are not above such chicanery. Has there been a change of ownership at the bank since the last time you dealt with them?"

"Weel, the son took over from the father last year."

"Ah, and obviously the son has the morals of a snake."

"I dinnae ken how anyone can ken the morals or lack of 'em in a snake."

"Hush." Emily cupped her chin in her hand and stared at the wall as she thought, trying to recall her father's various dealings with banks. "I think you need to judge the trustworthiness of this lawyer. It would be best if you returned to the bank with someone on your side, someone who has the power to cause trouble."

"I trusted the bank," he muttered. "How good are ye at kenning who ye can trust?"

"Good enough, I think, but I also understand lawyers and can tell you if he just talks a lot of idiocy."

"Then we shall go to see him on the morrow. He doesnae have much to do so I've suspicion he will be glad to see us," he said as he stood up and helped her out of her chair.

As they walked up the stairs, Iain sighed. "Thank ye. I would have signed this, I think. Now I find myself wondering if they already had plans to ensure that I couldnae pay them back."

"It is possible. It is also possible it would have occurred to them at some time before you could pay them back. Hard to know. They were obviously underhanded enough to try to trick you with this paper so they may well have done more. Let us hope this lawyer is an honest man," she said as she stopped by her door. "Do you wish to go in the morning?"

"Morning," he replied as he placed his hand on the doorframe and gently pinned her against the door. "I have the feeling ye have dealt far more with lawyers than I have."

"Possibly. Cities are much fonder of the use of them than the outlying towns."

He kissed her forehead. "Gentry are fond of legal papers."

"Which is wise of them considering they usually have more to protect or pass on and often are cursed with family that cannot always be trusted." She hoped she sounded just like someone stating a simple fact rather than someone trying to deter him from the conversation as she was.

He kissed her forehead. "*And* gentry are fond of legal papers."

"Most people with things they value are."

The heat of him was seeping through her body and Emily knew it would be a good idea for her to put an end to this. Then his mouth was on hers and she decided the good-nights could wait a few moments. Feeling his arms wrapped around her, her body pressed close to his, was enough to clear her mind of all thought. All she became concerned about was what he made her feel.

Then all her warm feelings fled as he did as he usually did. He let her go, stared down at her, and she could almost see the cold that entered his veins. A moment later he wished her a good sleep and walked away. Emily sighed before entering her room. She hoped she could put all the questions she had out of her head so she could actually get some sleep.

Morning was as busy as always with hungry men and children to feed. Then everyone went off to tend to their work and she walked out to meet with Iain, who was fetching the buggy. Emily hoped the lawyer was there because spending a lot of time sitting close to a man who could not decide if he wanted to kiss her or ignore her was asking too much of any woman. As they engaged in idle, empty talk, she had to clench her hands into fists to keep from beating on his arm.

The lawyer had his cabin on the edge of town. Emily wondered why the man had not set up an office in town where everyone would know about him faster. As Iain helped her down from the buggy she told herself not to prejudge the man. If he had only just set up his practice it might be a simple matter of using what he could best afford.

Iain rapped on the door and Emily heard some yelling from inside followed by a thud. She glanced at Iain but he seemed unconcerned. A young voice joined the deeper one of a man and then the door opened. The man who stood there brushing his clothes off and smiling did not make her confident. He was handsome with his somewhat too long brown hair and hazel eyes but he was so young she could not believe he had finished all his schooling.

"Do come in. How can I help you?" he asked, waving them inside.

"Mr. Bannister?" she asked, and he nodded. "We wished to see if you can help us with a problem," she said, and was not sure the way he looked so delighted was encouraging.

"Of course." He led them to a large room furnished with a desk and two chairs facing it then waved toward those chairs. "Please sit down." As soon as she and Iain were seated, he sat and clasped his hands together on the top of the desk. "What is your trouble?"

Emily looked at Iain but he just waved her on, so she explained how they had come across a problem in the papers needed to get a loan. "It seems to me they have, well, erred."

"May I see the papers?"

Iain handed it over without hesitation. Emily sat a little tensely as the man read it over. She was certain there was something underhanded in what the bank had done but she had no idea of what the laws were about such things in this country. The frown forming on the man's face could be encouraging or it could mean he simply could not see what her problem was with the agreement.

"What did you offer up as collateral?" he asked Iain.

"My flock. I gave them the number of sheep I had and the value of the flock and it is well above what the loan was for," Iain answered.

"You said nothing about your land or house or belongings?"

"Nay. Then again, most people ken where I live and what I have. Probably even ken where my lands stretch to."

"Then they should not be listed." He looked closely at Iain. "May I ask you a personal question?"

Iain shrugged. "Aye."

"Have you done business with this bank before?"

"Only one in town so the answer is aye. Took a loan from them when we were setting up, as buying the land and all took more of our money than we anticipated. Put our money in there as weel. Been a customer of theirs for years. The father's, not the son's."

"Ah."

Iain grinned at Emily. "That is what ye said."

"And can you read?" Mr. Bannister asked.

Iain could not fully suppress a blush but he shook his head. "Thinking it might be time to learn."

Mr. Bannister smiled. "It can be helpful. This is very close to fraud," he said, and patted the paper. "They were obviously trying to trick you into offering more than you wished and, I suspect, had every intention of trying to make sure you could not meet payments so they could make a land grab. I would suspect there is one of their customers who would like your lands and they thought to win his favor. Maybe get hold of it all and make a profitable deal with that man. It is fortunate you did not sign this."

"Had a bad feeling so took it home, said I needed a night to think on it, and had Emily read it to me."

"Good, good. Best to never sign anything you can't read or cannot understand. What do you wish to do about this?"

"I still need a loan but I need the paper to be right. Need it to say what is right and fair."

"I can help you with dealing with the paper and the bank if that is what you wish."

Iain looked at Emily and she nodded, her brief qualms about the man having faded. In the large mirror on the wall behind him she had been watching the door slowly open and a curly-headed child peeping in. The child dropped to his knees and had just started to crawl toward the desk when adult arms reached in and grabbed him. Then he was gone. Emily suspected that child was behind the thump and yell they had heard.

"When would you like to deal with this?"

"Soon as we can. I am supposed to get back to them sometime today."

"Then we shall go. I can go along to the bank with you, now. We will let them see that you have legal representation. But, perhaps I should first tell you what my fees are." He blushed and glanced at Emily.

Realizing he was one to fret over speaking business before a woman she smiled and stood up. "I will just step outside."

"Nay too far and keep a close eye out," said Iain.

Emily nodded and stepped out of the office. She turned to go out the door and found herself facing a plump brunette holding a very young boy. "Hello. I am Emily Stanton."

"Sorry that William was disturbing you. I am Charlotte Bannister." She moved to a settee. "Come and sit down. I suspect they are talking money. George still finds it hard to discuss such things in front of a woman."

"Yes, a strange habit some men have. Probably think it will give us a brain fever." She grinned when Charlotte laughed.

"I am trying to break him of it. So you and the man are hiring him?"

"Iain is. He needs a bank loan and the paper they wanted him to sign is not, well, right. Mr. Bannister said he can help."

"That is his strength. The paperwork." She frowned. "Our bank tried to cheat him?"

"I suppose you could say that. They did not write down what he verbally agreed to."

"Oh, dear. We were thinking of going to them to try and set up a proper law office in the town. Now I do not know what George will do."

"I doubt they would try a trick with him as he can read and understands all that wordage."

Charlotte relaxed and then smiled. "I have not seen you in town. Are you new to the place?"

"No. I am staying out at the MacEnroys." Emily could see by the slight frown Charlotte could not hide what the woman was thinking and she smiled faintly. "I fear I was living with my sister and her husband and their cabin was attacked. They did not survive. The MacEnroys saved me and my nephew."

"Oh, I am so sorry. How terrible for you. There are so many dangers out here. My family was not happy when George said we were headed here so that he could set up an office. He did not wish to just become another man in some other lawyer's office, a simple worker who did most of the paperwork but got none of the thanks. It is all he has ever wished to do."

The little boy wriggled out of her arms and hopped off her lap. "You do not go into Daddy's office, William. He has a client."

William had a look on his face that told Emily he intended to go anyway as soon as he could when Iain and Mr. Bannister walked out. She stood up as the boy ran to his father. The way that man took the time to hug his child before handing the boy back to his wife made Emily feel even more sure of him.

Mr. Bannister got his horse and rode beside them as they went to town. He and Iain carried on a varied conversation with complete amenity. When the man spoke of some incident he had in the university and the name Harvard came out, Emily relaxed even more. Even she had heard of that place. It also explained why he wanted to be head of his own office. The way Mr. Bannister appeared to soak up the conversation as if he was starved for some began to make her understand the way the wife talked so freely. This young couple was still new, and had probably not yet made friends. She had to think hard on how she might ease that. The boy was close to Neddy's age, she mused, and smiled to herself.

When they got to the bank, Emily was not sure what she was to do. Iain had someone to stand for him so she was no longer needed. By the time they got admitted to the office she found out she would not have been allowed to aid him even if she had wanted to. Mr. Colton allowed no women in his offices while business was discussed. It infuriated Emily but she held back her anger and silently nudged at Iain when it looked as if he was about to protest. Instead she sat in a chair outside the office as the men discussed things. She hoped Mr. Bannister had the spine to put the fear of God into Mr. Colton. A young woman stepped up to her holding out a cup of tea.

"Mr. Colton says we should offer some to any of the ladies waiting for their menfolk to do business," the young woman said, her voice shaking with nerves.

Accepting the cup, Emily smiled and said, "Thank you kindly. Have to offer a lot of these, do you?"

"Enough. He made the rule the moment he stepped into the office so one cannot claim it was some bad experience that caused it." She shrugged. "We had not expected him," she added softly.

"No? Who did you expect to be the new boss?"

"Oh, I should not say."

"Oh, please do. I do not live in town anyway and I am no gossip."

"We expected the younger son as he really liked working in the bank and helping folk and all." She sighed. "If we were not the only bank in town I think we would be losing our customers by now." She blushed and clapped a hand over her mouth. "Was that Mr. Bannister?" she asked after calming herself down.

"Yes. He has come along to help Iain MacEnroy sort out the terms of a loan."

"MacEnroy? One of those brothers up in the hills?"

Emily nodded and spent the time waiting for Iain answering the woman's many questions about all those bachelors in the hills. When Iain and Mr. Bannister stepped out she handed her empty cup back to the young woman who was staring at Iain in a way that made Emily itch to loudly claim he was not up for bid. Iain took her by the arm and led her out, then paused when they reached the buggy and turned to grin at Mr. Bannister.

"One thing good about having a lawyer is it makes

it hard for the man you're dealing with to spit out his anger."

Mr. Bannister laughed. "He was angry. Makes me really wonder who he was trying to grab your lands for."

"That is something I would like to know as well." He reached out and shook Mr. Bannister's hand. "I will send you the payment within a day or two. And, be sure of it, I will tell anyone I can how good you are at your job."

Mr. Bannister blushed and thanked Iain profusely. He then mounted his horse and rode off. Iain helped Emily into the buggy and headed toward the hills.

"I ken I didnae really let ye give your opinion," he started.

"There was no need. I think we were both of the same mind. Not sure if Mr. Bannister even knows how to be sly."

"Nay. He is an open book."

"So is his wife. Seems they were thinking of getting a loan from that same fool so that George could set up an office in town. I suspect his son is part of the reason he needs one."

Iain laughed. "Cute lad and I suspicion he was the cause of the thud we heard."

"Well, I was trying to think of a way to aid his wife in getting out more. Her William is of an age, or close to, with Neddy. But there is that problem of not being able to let Neddy be as free as other children."

Iain just nodded. He would be meeting with George tomorrow to send out a few letters. He intended to do his best to find the one behind the attempts to kill Emily and Neddy and put an end to it. With the help of a woman in town who was willing to read and write for him for a fee, he had kept in touch with a few people and he meant to reach out to them now to try to find something to prove this Albert's guilt and get him locked up for it. It might not get him anything but he saw no wrong in trying.

They had to put a stop to the man's attempts to kill all the Stantons. What he needed was to get Emily to tell him exactly what she thought, who might be involved, and what exactly the man thought was worth so much death. He might well pick up another name or two of people to contact. If nothing else, he wanted to know why some idiot in England was trying so hard to wipe out the Stantons.

Chapter Nine

The day was glorious, Emily thought as she stepped out onto the front porch. The sun shone bright, the sky was as blue as a robin's egg, and fluffy white clouds skimmed across it. The air was clean and the light breeze held a hint of the summer's end.

She decided she would make use of the saddle Iain had gone back into town to buy for her after they had met with the lawyer, the one she had so admired when she had gone to town with Robbie. He had promised there would be a horse she could ride in the stable by the week's end. All she had had to do was prove to him that she could saddle her own mount and knew how to ride and ride well. Emily buttoned up her coat and hurried to the stables. A lovely chestnut mare stood placidly in her stall and Emily wondered where the horse had come from, then she decided she simply did not care.

A short time later she rode out of the stable feeling wonderfully free. She had told Mrs. O'Neal she was going for a ride, even though she had not firmly decided on it yet, so she knew Neddy would be watched. Neddy and Mrs. O'Neal had become very close but

Emily was not surprised. Mrs. O'Neal was very motherly and Neddy responded to that.

She followed the trail Iain had shown her, enjoying the scenery, which was an intriguing mixture of rough wildness and the gentle green of the hills back east, even back in England. She thought she could probably find scenery in this huge country that would remind her of every country in the world. Emily knew it could also be dangerous but she refused to allow that to steal away her appreciation of its beauty.

For a moment she paused at the top of one rise on the trail and looked over the flat lands below. There was a small pond down there along with a lot of sheep. She looked over the area spread out below her and caught sight of the MacEnroy brothers. They were working on the fence and she suddenly knew that was what Iain had taken out the loan for. She hoped it would help to keep his flock protected from predators. It would, at least, make it more difficult for the predators to reach the sheep. The Powell brothers were there, too, keeping the sheep away from the men working.

The trail started downward and a little farther on she passed a small cabin. The Powell brothers, she decided. Looking out from their front yard she realized they had an excellent view of the fields the flock wandered over. It certainly made the night watch of the flock easier. What they needed, she thought as she turned around to make her slow way home, was a few goats. There could be milk, which could be made into cheese. They only had three cows and, with so many people to feed, there was little left for butter and cheese. It was something to consider, she thought, and then frowned. Such thoughts were only useful if she was going to be staying here and there was no indication that she would be. A sadness washed over her and she had the lowering feeling it was because Iain had never indicated that he wanted her to stay. That showed her that she was not keeping her feelings as well guarded as she had thought.

A sound pulled her out of her musings and Emily frowned. She realized she had stopped yet she was sure she heard the sound of hoofbeats. Looking around, she finally glanced up the hill gently rising on her left. Six men were cautiously making their way toward her. A chill gripped her heart when she recognized one of the men who had sent her fleeing town. Iain must have missed one or the man had stayed behind while his friends had ridden out and died.

Emily kicked her mount into a hard trot and heard the men curse. Not sure how long it would take them to get down the rest of the hill to the trail, she nudged her mount into a gallop as soon as she believed the trail safe enough for such speed. She knew the men would do the same and prayed that her mare was faster. There was a shot and Emily urged her mare to go even faster.

Once inside the gates, she leapt out of the saddle and ran back to the gates to try to shut them. Mrs. O'Neal was at her side a heartbeat later. The two of them got the gates shut and barred then sagged against them. The men outside fired at the gates and the two women hastily stepped away, not trusting the thick wood to stop the bullets.

"The boys won't be able to get in," said Mrs. O'Neal.

"I know, but what else can we do?"

"Think these men will give up soon?"

"We can only hope or they will run when the men

return." She saw Neddy standing in the doorway of the house and her heart sank as she hurried over to him. "Neddy, you must stay inside for now." She picked him up intending to carry him inside but the boy clung to her with his arms and legs while shaking his head.

"No! No! The fire will get me!"

Mrs. O'Neal hurried over and rubbed the child's back. "There is no fire, lad. It is safe inside the house."

"Where Iain?"

"I am sure he will be back soon." Emily looked at Mrs. O'Neal. "How far does the sound of a shot carry?"

"A long way in this valley but it all depends on the wind, where the men are, and how much noise they are making."

Emily sat down on the steps and held Neddy close. She knew it would be impossible to get the boy to stay inside without them. Neddy might not be suffering much from grief but he evidently still suffered from fears bred by the attack that had killed his parents. There was a sudden burst of shooting and she prayed the gates held firm.

Iain stretched and rubbed at his lower back. He was not sure how well the fence would work or if it would prove no more than a mild blockade quickly overcome. Taking off his hat he ran his hand through his hair and hoped he had not taken a loan for nothing. Although Daniel had seen to it the loan papers were written up fairly and just how Iain wanted them, he had lost all trust in that bank. Unfortunately, it was the only one around.

The faint sound of a gunshot caught his attention

and he looked at Matthew, who stood beside him. "Did ye just hear a shot?"

Matthew frowned. "I am hearing a lot of shooting. I think it is coming from over there."

Looking in the direction Matthew was pointing, Iain realized it was their home. "Damn it, it is coming from the house." He slapped his hat back on and ran for his horse, Matthew right behind him and calling for all their brothers to come.

Iain did not wait for his brothers but mounted his horse and rode hard for the house. He could think of no one who would attack them so he had to wonder if this was some of the men who had attacked Emily's family. If the women had gotten the gates closed there would be time to reach them.

He reined in at the top of a small rise and stared down at the five men trying to break through his gates. It surprised him a little that the two women had managed to shut them and even to secure the huge gates but he was grateful that they had found the strength. Undoubtedly, they had found it because their children were inside those gates.

Matthew drew up beside him and pulled his rifle from the saddle holster. "Ye think they are after Emily and the boy?"

"Aye, but how the hell did they trail them here?"

"Something to do with the men in town that chased her and Robbie? Must have been one man who peeled off from the others or never even left with them, so we were not able to make sure he never talked. It would be easy to find out who she came to town with, and then find us."

"We need to get inside those walls without exposing the women," Iain said quietly. For a short while

they sat silently, noticing that none of the men trying
to break through the gates bothered to look behind
him. Whoever Emily's enemy was, he wasted no time
trying to find skilled men. "We need to get to the
back way in without alerting these idiots."

They finally decided to go two at a time; the last
ones to go would be the last three. Iain waited tensely
as Lachlan and Robbie rode off, getting into the trees
to the east of the house so that they could circle
around to the back of the wall unseen. Iain wished
that at some time in the future, not long, they could
have a house safe enough to leave the gates open. He
was growing tired of always fortifying the places they
lived in.

Shaking his head for he considered it a poor time
to spend even a moment on wishing, he looked down
at the pocket watch he had gotten from his father.
When five minutes had passed, he signaled Duncan
and Geordie to go. After the last five minutes had
passed he, Matthew, and Nigel made their way around
through the trees. They left their horses secured beside
their brothers' and crept toward the house. Robbie
opened the back door for them and they hurried in.
The women and the children were all huddled in the
kitchen away from the windows and doors. Iain
nodded and led his brothers all to the front.

"I will go up on the walls and see what is there and
how many of them there are now," Iain said.

"No need. They just broke the bar and are coming
in the gates," said Matthew. "Knew it should have
been a bit longer and thicker."

Iain swore and hurried to one of the windows in
the parlor. The six men were in the yard studying the
house. They obviously did not know the women were

no longer alone. Iain took careful aim and shot one. Even as the body hit the ground the gunfire started from both the men in the yard, desperately trying to find some cover and the men in the house.

The attackers fell fast but one ran. Despite their best efforts the man got back out the gates and mounted his horse. He was just racing for the hills when a shot came and he nearly flew out of his saddle. Iain could see just enough to realize the Powell brothers had come and grinned. There would be no news taken back to the one who had hired them. He was beginning to think that lack of news would not buy them much time though.

"Now we need some new windows," said Lachlan as he walked in.

"Only three and not the whole window either. I haven't looked upstairs yet, though," added Matthew as he strolled in with his rifle over his shoulder.

"Not too high a price then." Iain stood up from where he had been crouched by the window. "But ye are right, Matthew. Gates need a longer thicker bar. We shall also have to think of some way of making it so it can be barred without requiring the strength of two men. But, for now, we have a mess to clean up."

The brothers all gathered in the hall and Iain looked toward the kitchen doors to find Emily peering out at them. "It is done. Are all of you all right?"

"We are. Just going to clean up." He noticed that she paled a little but she said nothing, just nodded.

Emily watched the brothers leave and turned back into the kitchen. It was over, she thought, as Mrs. O'Neal shooed her children and Neddy out of the kitchen. No one had been hurt except the ones who had tried to hurt them. Emily knew she should feel relieved, perhaps even happy that they had prevailed, but she just felt cold.

The odd mood clung to her all through the preparation of the meal. She barely spoke during the meal although she carefully studied each of the brothers to reassure herself they were all hale. Iain kept giving her looks filled with concern but she ignored them. Emily knew she needed to be alone to shake off this strange mood. For now, she did only what she had to and spoke only when spoken to directly.

"What troubles you, dearie?" asked Mrs. O'Neal after the others left the table and she had begun to help with the cleanup.

"I brought killers to your home, to Iain's home," she answered.

"Nonsense. They brought themselves. Whoever wants you and that boy dead will chase you wherever you go, you know. Better to be in a place with high walls and a lot of strong men then out on the trail as you run to some place or even in a boardinghouse," Mrs. O'Neal said as she washed the dishes and Emily wiped them.

"This is not Iain's battle."

"Ha! It is the battle of any man with a backbone and some sense of what is right. This cousin of yours wants to kill a woman and a child. A child with no ability to defend himself. And all for gain. It should turn any decent man's stomach. It is just sad that there are so many men willing to take money to do his dirty work."

"The MacEnroys saved our lives, mine, and Neddy's. It is a poor repayment for that kindness to drag them into this mess."

Mrs. O'Neal shook her head. "When you start thinking like that, I want you to do one thing for me."

"What?" Emily asked suspiciously.

"Think of that boy. Of those big brown eyes going cloudy with death. That is what your lofty principles will gain you."

Chastised, Emily finished the dishes. She poured herself a glass of cider and went to sit on the porch swing. It was time to stop being vague and let Iain know exactly why Albert wanted her and Neddy dead. She had hoped the tale of a greedy cousin and vague references to property or land that would be given to him instead of Neddy would be enough.

It was going to increase those moments of being cold to her. She understood what did it but was resentful of how he included her in that condemnation. She would never throw tenants from their home. Her father had been insistent about their responsibilities to their tenants. Emily sighed, knowing she now faced a difficult few moments with Iain. She just hoped he listened and did not throw his anger, righteous though it was, at her.

Iain poured himself some cider and looked at Mrs. O'Neal, who was taking off her apron and getting ready to go to her cabin. "Where is Neddy?"

"With my lads. They were going to play with the pups for a while," the woman replied.

"And Emily?" he asked casually, and could tell by the sharp look Mrs. O'Neal gave him that his casual inquiry did not fool her at all.

"Out on the porch swing. See you in the morning," she said, and went out the door.

Iain gave the woman enough time to get to her cottage and went to join Emily. It took only one look at the woman to know she was still in that strange mood that had hung on her all through dinner. He cautiously sat down beside her. Iain wondered if she was shocked and upset over the deaths of the men who had planned to kill her and said as much.

"I do understand that," she said a little sharply, and then sighed. "You need to know everything, to understand why this will not stop. It will not stop until Albert is dead or Neddy and I are."

"Just what have ye done that makes the mon hate ye so much?"

"We were born. We stand in his way. We have what he wants and will hold it as long as we live and our children, if we live long enough to have any, will then hold it."

"Property?"

"Yes. Quite a lot actually. I have the deeds to five fine English properties and papers affirming Neddy's right to all the money that comes with such lands. A little cottage by the sea is mine but the rest belong to Neddy. Two manor houses and two fine London town homes. There are more but his grandfather holds the deeds to them until he dies."

Iain was shocked. This was far more than he had expected and he suspected she was about to add more. Five properties, manor houses no less, meant she was far higher born than he had thought.

"And if he succeeds in killing both you and Neddy what titles does the man then claim?"

"Well, he really only has to kill Neddy. Neddy is the one standing in his way but he will kill me for being witness to it all and for the possibility that I will wed and have a son thus taking some of the property and money he covets. I believe he is fully aware that it was I who uncovered his murder of my parents."

"What title?"

"Well, Neddy is now the Baron of Dunning and"— she took a deep breath—"the Marquis of Collins Wood. When his grandfather passes on he will be the duke."

"*Jesu.* That is practically royalty."

"Not really. It is not that kind. It was a gift during Elizabeth's reign. My ancestor did a very large favor for her and had the wit to then remain in the background, confronting no one and outlasting Henry and others. He also got the right to pass his title on to the sons of his daughters. Not an easy feat. None of it." She stopped talking, realizing she was babbling to fill the silence.

"And that box Neddy watches so closely has the paperwork to prove his right?"

"It does. The man after us is my father's first cousin, the only other male born in that generation, and he knows he is the heir after Neddy but has no wish to wait who knows how long for the boy to die. Or bother himself with any sons Neddy might breed. My father's will is quite clear on who is his heir. He had a deep distaste for Albert and needed to do all he could to insure the man could not steal Neddy's inheritance. I doubt he ever expected the man to turn to murder to get what he wants."

"How did your parents die?"

"Killed in the town house. The authorities decided it was thieves for a few things were missing."

"How did ye find out that was nay true?"

"It was rather odd that the things stolen were ones that Albert had always openly coveted. I could get no help from the authorities because I was just a woman and what could I possibly find out that they had not."

If he had not still been in such a state of shock, Iain knew he would have smiled at the note of irritation in her voice. "There was no one to protect you in England?"

"There were a few people we thought of but we kept running into the same problem. No one believed us when we said Albert killed my parents and wanted us dead as well. We were just grieving women who wanted to blame someone, see someone hang, for the deaths of our parents and had picked on Albert because it was well known in the family that we had never liked the man. If I had had more time, I think I could have convinced my grandfather but Albert had no intention of granting us that time."

"And you thought coming here would be enough to keep you safe?"

"It is a huge country. Not many in England understand just how huge, I think. I thought we could lose ourselves in this country until we could, perhaps, get word to one of the family who might believe us. Unfortunately, even as we left the country we discovered three of those people had recently met a tragic fate and that was when we knew. We had to run, and hide, until we had the skill and strength to stop Albert. As I said, I believed this country big enough to hide in. And it probably would have been except that, as we now know, my sister wrote to a cousin and somehow Albert found out what was said in those letters."

"Do you think he killed your cousin?" He could tell by the horror slowly dawning on her face that she had never considered the possibility.

"He may well have. Then again, Constance is a lovely woman but not especially bright so he may well have gotten ahold of one of the letters and she just did not notice. She may have even left it out without thinking and he peeked when she stepped out of the room. Who knows, but I am now certain he knows where we are and I should take Neddy and leave."

"Nay. Ye would just give him an easier target. Think. Ye and a boy traveling alone would be seen, remembered. He just needs to poke around a bit and he can run right after you. Ye are safest here."

He finished off his cider and stood up. "Nay. Ye will stay here. I admit I may nay have much love for the gentry but I would never toss a boy and a woman to the wolves because of it. My brothers and I can handle this."

"You could all be hurt and it is not your fight."

"Let me decide what to fight for." He bent down, cupped her chin in his hand, and kissed her. "You stay."

By the time he reached his room Iain was torn between anger and shock. He had known she was gentry but he had never guessed she was so high up. What he had told her was the truth, though. He would never throw her and Neddy out to face all this alone. What he needed to do was figure out if there was any way to get in touch with ones who might help. The killer already knew where she and Neddy were so writing to relatives who might help would make no difference, he decided as he undressed for bed.

He thought of little Neddy and his fury rose. It was unfathomable that anyone could consider killing the boy just to lay claim to some lands, titles, and money. That was one of the things he had always held against the gentry. They thought such things were worth far more than any life. Lady Vera had had the cottage set on fire even knowing that he and Geordie were still inside because she could not abide people she thought of as peasants blocking her plans.

He knew in his heart that Emily was not of that ilk but still wondered if he should stay as far away from her as he could. Then he thought of the kisses they had shared and decided he would never do so. He had to force his stubborn mind to adjust its thinking. She probably had as blue a bloodline as anyone he had ever met but he knew, deep down, she was not like Lady Vera and never could be.

Climbing into bed, he crossed his hands behind his head and wondered how long it would take to get Emily in his bed. Then he thought of how she had been cooking and serving his supper for days now and grinned. Emily had been forced to do things most gentry women never had to do and he had to marvel at how well she had managed. She had insisted on scrubbing their home as it had never been scrubbed before and she spent a lot of hours trying to drum the skill of reading into his head and those of his brothers. She was unlike any gentry lady he had ever seen.

Now he needed to get a few names and such from Emily so he could round up some allies. It would not be easy because he would not be able to meet with them face-to-face and judge their trustworthiness himself but it still needed to be done. There had to be someone in her family that would understand what was happening and come to her aid. He decided the duke she spoke of was probably the one to get in touch with. It was his title and lands Albert sought to grab. Once he got rid of Emily and Neddy what was to stop the man from killing the duke? It would not be easy but that had not stopped him from killing off the man's son and his wife.

It was a sad mess, he decided, and he was glad they had none of these problems in his family. The MacEnroys had no land, no fortune, no power and never had. It had often angered him but he could find some reason to be grateful for it now. Everything he had he had built with his brothers, their safety always at the fore of his mind. They owned all they held and could only lose it through their own mistake, not just because someone decided cattle deserved grazing more than people deserved a place to live.

Emily had tried to do the same with her sister. She had struggled to get her sister to safety and keep her safe. He blinked as that thought wound through his mind and knew that it had settled deep in his heart when he was not looking. He knew he no longer had that surge of anger when he thought of her heritage. It was gone for good.

Now he needed to decide what he really wanted from Lady Emily Stanton. Iain grinned. He knew what he wanted to do. With his confused feelings finally sorted out he decided he could work on that. Whatever happened with all the lands, titles, and money, he planned to bed Miss Emily Stanton.

Chapter Ten

"Shut the gates behind us," said Matthew.

"Aye, Mother," Iain drawled as he lifted Neddy and placed him in the buggy next to Maeve.

Matthew just grunted. Mrs. O'Neal was headed to visit with her family who were staying at the boarding-house in town. It had come as a total surprise to the woman and she had been a bundle of nerves since she got the news. The whole family was headed to California and she wanted to see them. Neddy was going because he wanted to and Mrs. O'Neal had happily included him. Once they were all settled, his brothers were going to patrol the area to see if any men were looking for Emily and Neddy.

After they had ridden off, Iain shut and barred the gates. Emily had wanted to keep Neddy with her. Still shaken by the men coming to the house where she had thought the two of them well hidden, she had been wary of letting the boy out of her sight ever since. A week later and it had still taken a lot of per-suasion from him and Mrs. O'Neal to convince her the boy would be safe, would appear to be no more than yet another child in a large family.

Iain walked back into the house and paused to savor the quiet for a moment. He loved his brothers, even loved Mrs. O'Neal and her children, but there were times when the house felt entirely too crowded. To get some time to just think, he often had to go to his room or find the needed solitude outside. Now he had a few hours of an empty house and he had no intention of using the time alone to do anything but be with Emily.

He walked into the kitchen to find Emily kneading bread. The look of concentration on her face was intense. Obviously, he and Mrs. O'Neal had not fully calmed her nerves concerning Neddy leaving the safety of the house. Iain still found it hard to accept that anyone would hire men to kill off an entire family right down to a boy of three, but there was no denying the sad truth of the battle he had been drawn into.

"I think ye can overdo that if ye are nay careful," he said quietly as he stepped up to the table.

Emily stopped and stared at the dough under her hands for a moment before putting it on a board and draping a cloth over it. She then carried it over to the counter and set it down next to the other three she had done. Her arms ached, she realized, and she sighed as she began to clean up the mess she had made, then cleaned off herself. All the time she did she was fully aware of the man silently watching her.

"He will be fine," Iain said when she poured herself a glass of cool cider. "I would like one of those, too, please."

She poured one for him and brought them both over to the table. They sat opposite each other and Emily tried very hard not to look at him. At some point during the cleanup she had shifted from being terribly afraid for Neddy to being far too aware that they were alone together. They did not have to worry that someone might walk in on them kissing.

Then her eyes met his and inwardly cursed. There was definitely a look on his face that told her he was also intensely aware of how alone they were and he had plans. Emily was not sure she would be able to refuse his plans. She was not sure she would want to.

"I know he will be fine," she said. "You are right. He will be well hidden in a crowd of people. I do not think any of these men who hunt us actually know what he looks like, just that they should kill any small child they find with us."

"All this blood just to get a title," he murmured, and shook his head.

"It happens more than you think. Enough so that many people attending a funeral wonder if the man's collapse was truly because of a bad heart or a nudge from his heir. And it is not just a title, is it. It is the land, the money, and the power that comes with it. With all the Stantons dead, there is no one to dispute him."

"Weel, the men I had Daniel write to for me will find something."

"If there is anything to find. The attacks are coming here now. Too many will decide it is just an unavoidable danger that comes with this new country. The English do see you all as uncivilized here, almost like a place that is here to take the poor in when they flee from England."

"How kind of them. There are rich English here."

"Oh, yes, but they probably became rich through business. Very unacceptable."

He grinned at her tone, one of pure sarcasm. "I do miss Scotland though."

"And I miss England. The hedgerows to the cathedrals." She shrugged. "But there is beauty here. One just has to become accustomed to the differences. Like that spot on the trail you showed me where the hills turned rocky and if you look over the edge there is water. On the other side of the water there is a lovely treed spot which is clearly and beautifully reflected in the water."

Iain smiled. "I know the place. Have a few drawings of it and am thinking of painting it."

He had spoken almost absently and it took her a moment to understand what he was saying. "You paint?"

Nodding reluctantly for he had not meant to let that secret out, he said, "Nay as well as my father, but good enough. My father did all the paintings of Scotland we have."

"They are very beautiful, very peaceful to look at. He was admirably skilled. Did he sell paintings?"

"Aye, when he could. Sold a lot when we stayed in Glasgow until we could afford the voyage over here. There was a lot of work in the city but the pay was poor so we all worked. It was my father's paintings which got us the most money. We were on our way out faster than any before us. He painted while we were sailing here and sold them when we got to New York and that helped pay for our journey here." He smiled with an odd mixture of sadness and amusement. "I was the only one interested and he showed me all he could in the time he had."

"He passed on his skills," she said softly. "That would have pleased him a great deal."

"Aye, I think it did." He finished his drink and stood up. "I need to do a final check on all the animals. Will ye feel all right here alone? If not, ye can come along."

"No, I shall be fine. I will start supper soon."

Iain just nodded and strode away. He decided the work that needed doing came at a good time. Sitting there talking with her, knowing they were alone, had his thoughts going to all he wanted to do with her. Later, he promised himself. He was going to ignore the voice scolding him for his plans for a woman who was undoubtedly a virgin and that voice that warned he was sinking more deeply into the trap all women were for a man. If Emily Stanton was a trap, he would step into it willingly and not spend any time worrying about the consequences.

Emily decided to make a stew. The bread was baking and would go well with a stew. It would also be easily warmed up when the others returned home. She had to decide on what to have for dessert. Mrs. O'Neal had made it abundantly clear that the men of this house had a sweet tooth that needed some feeding as badly as their stomachs did. She had no intention of displacing Mrs. O'Neal but had to admit it was nice to have the kitchen to herself for just a while.

For a short while she could pretend it was her house, her kitchen. It was a foolish fancy, if only because she would never put Mrs. O'Neal out of a job, but Emily enjoyed it and soon the kitchen was full of the good smell of stew and bread. She fussed over a dessert and realized she was trying hard to impress Iain with her culinary skills. Shaking her head at her own foolishness she set the table and was just filling the glasses with milk when he walked in.

"Something smells good," he said as he sat down opposite her place at the table.

"That is a relief. It is the first time I have prepared a meal all by myself. Well, except for the ones I cooked for my sister." Emily filled their bowls, put the bread and butter on the table, and took her seat.

After tasting the stew, Iain smiled. "She must have been pleased."

"I suspect so. David was and often said so. I fear each of his compliments made Annabel less, well, appreciative of my efforts."

"Jealousy. A poison, my mither always called it."

"It is in a way, isn't it. Annabel also sorely missed the food she was accustomed to. I tried to make some things that were similar to ease her homesickness but they did not match her memories."

"I doubt anything ye did would have worked."

"Why do you say that?"

"She did not want to leave, did she? She liked being a lady of the manor. She liked all that went with that position. Aye, she wed the wrong man but I suspect she never thought it would drastically change her life. And ye were only here for a few years so she hadnae yet accustomed herself to the change in her circumstances."

"You and your brothers accepted."

"Not immediately and it was a while before we saw the good in what we now had. We concentrated on survival. By the time we kenned we had succeeded the worst of the yearning had passed. Oh, we still have memories but I am nay longer sure they are true ones or just the lingering fancies of the children we were then. We both lost what really mattered, didnae we."

"Our parents," she whispered, and sighed when he nodded.

They ate the meal and Iain praised her apple-berry cobbler. Then they moved into the parlor to her surprise, for the family rarely gathered there, and he served her a glass of wine. He sat next to her on the settee, and she had to turn away, hoping he did not see her blush. She concentrated on her wine and suddenly he was there, achingly close to her.

Iain took her glass of wine and set it on the table next to his before pulling her into his arms for a kiss. She knew he was going to kiss her and dreaded it all going sour as it so often had in the past. Yet, when his mouth touched hers, she wrapped her arms around his neck and held on tightly, letting him pull her close to himself. A little voice told her she should say no, push him away. Emily ignored it. Iain was big, strong, and the warmth of him seeped deep inside her as he held her in his arms. She had no inclination to push that away. His kiss made everything inside her go wild and hungry and she was a little uncertain of such strong feelings, ones she had never experienced before.

Talking over dinner was torturous enough, Iain thought, when his mind had kept taunting him with soft images of what he wanted to do with her. He ran his hands up her rib cage and slowly over her breasts. The way the tips grew hard and burned against his palms made him anxious to strip them bare, to kiss them. Something he could not do in the parlor, he suddenly thought.

Standing up, he grabbed her by the hand and led her up the stairs. She was still lightly flushed with desire when he led her into his room and shut the door. He pulled her back into his arms as he gently walked her back to the bed. He kissed her, her lips warm and giving beneath his, her body moving against him in clear eagerness.

Emily trembled when he pushed her down onto his bed, pressing himself against her. She could feel his hardness nestle between her thighs and found herself lifting her hips up slightly to rub against him. The feel of him made her insides cramp with hunger and she shivered. The way her body was reacting to his kisses shocked her yet she did not push away the feeling. She found it all too wonderful to force him to stop.

Then his long fingers were undoing the bodice of her gown as he kissed her throat and each new bit of bare skin exposed to him. Emily put her hands on his chest thinking to push him back only to find her hands touching warm, taut skin. Beneath one of her palms she could feel the hard beat of his heart. She opened her eyes to see her palms on his chest and the passion she was struggling to understand soared. Smoothing her hands over his chest, she reveled in the heat of his skin and the light brush of hair she found there. She had the strong urge to kiss him there but fear of acting too boldly held her back.

Her thoughts were abruptly interrupted when Iain pulled the front of the gown down, gently easing her arms out of the sleeves. That slipped into the haze of desire she had been under, cooling the heat of it, and Emily crossed her hands over her chest when he also tugged down her shift. He was raised above her staring down at her breasts and Emily was suddenly all too aware of her near nakedness. No man had ever seen her unclothed, even partly.

"Iain," she began, and he kissed her before she could continue.

Emily sank beneath the force of her own desire. She could feel Iain's desire; it was hot and greedy. That greed fed her own needs and she began to move her hands over his back, sliding down until she cupped his backside. He groaned into her mouth and moved against her. He gently stroked her stomach, telling her all the while how beautiful and soft she was, then slid his hands inside her pantaloons. She was just beginning to tense up, afraid of such an unknown intimacy when he touched her there, stroked her, and she gasped as she lost all inclination to pull away. Part of her was afraid of everything going so fast while another part reveled in the greed she could not seem to control.

Iain felt the damp heat of welcome beneath his fingers and nearly groaned. He kissed her hungrily as he undid his pants. The way she moved her hand over his chest, his back, even his backside, told him her passions were riding her as hard as his were him. Despite that as he settled himself between her restless legs, ready to make her his, he still asked, needing to hear her accept him.

"Emily," he said, "do ye want me?"

"I am here, am I not? Do you need a yes?"

"Aye."

"Then, yes, Iain. Are you ready now then?"

He laughed softly and gently joined his body with hers. When her heat surrounded him he gritted his teeth, determined not to find his release with the embarrassing speed of an untried lad. Then she wrapped her arms and legs around him and he began to move. Every move she made, the soft sounds that escaped her revealing her pleasure, all worked to fire his need until he feared he would be done before she got the satisfaction she needed.

Then he felt her tighten around him and Iain nearly yelled out in relief. He kissed her, smothering her cry of release as his tore through him. He collapsed upon her but kept his wits about him just enough to fall a little to the side. As he gently stroked her back and her hair, he kissed her cheeks. Finally, he met her gaze, braced for shock or repudiation but she smiled at him shyly.

"What are ye thinking, lass?" he asked.

"That breaking every rule should not be such fun or so pleasurable." She frowned as he chuckled, a bit hurt that he whispered no words of love to her but told herself they would come when he was ready.

Iain gently kissed her breasts and then got out of bed. He came back in a moment with a warm damp cloth and bathed her off. Emily tried not to blush but knew she failed. He chuckled softly as he settled down next to her, pulling her into his arms.

"We shouldnae linger here as someone might be home soon," he said as he slowly ran his hands over her body as if trying to mark every rise and hollow.

"Oh." That was a cold slap of reality for Emily and she tugged the blankets up over her breasts. "You are right." She looked around. "Where are my clothes?"

Iain gave her her clothes and grabbed his own, ashamed to see that he had not bothered to take much off. As he dressed he kept a close eye on her. She was beginning to act shy and, he feared, ashamed of herself. Once she did up her gown he leaned over her and brushed a kiss over her mouth.

"Leaving this bed is the last thing I want to do but it is best if we do. I cannae judge when the rest will begin to return."

"I know."

For the first time he caught a hint of shame in her eyes. "Shall we go for a ride?"

"A ride?" she said as she got out of the bed and adjusted her clothes then began to put on her shoes. "Is it not dark?"

"Not very. Still but dusk out. There are other things we can do."

Emily let him take her by the arm and lead her out of the room. It felt odd. They had just made love and now acted as if all was normal. Nothing felt normal for her. It had been something she suspected she would think of for a very long time and probably too often. But then, she thought, with a quick sideways glance at Iain, perhaps for a man it was not such a meaningful experience.

And it had been so quick, she thought. For something that could change so much between a man and a woman she would have thought it would last longer. He had not even gotten completely undressed. For some strange reason she found that the most upsetting of all. She tried to comfort herself with the reminder that they could not have any idea of how long they would be alone.

Iain decided it was too close to dusk to ride anywhere. Going out would be fine but coming back could get dangerous. So he just walked her around the compound and pointed out all the things he thought he would do. Since he seemed to be looking at her for some response, she agreed with each idea and added a few opinions.

They were behind the stables looking over the area he thought might be good for some kind of chicken coop when he backed her up against the outside wall of the barn. Emily looked at him in question but he just kissed her. She held on to him as the kiss grew hungry and stirred her need for him again. When he pulled away he rested his forehead against her as he caught his breath and then grinned at her.

"Maybe we could sneak back upstairs," he said.

"You no longer fear someone is due home?"

At that moment they both heard the approach of the buggy. Iain swore and Emily felt a little calmer about what they had done. A few of the older women had said that once a man got what he wanted out of a woman he did not return. It was obvious Iain wanted to return so perhaps the things she fretted about were all in her imagination.

Mrs. O'Neal already had the buggy in the stable when they came around the corner and Iain hurried in to lend her a hand. She was concerned that she was too late to make any supper and Emily was pleased to tell her about the stew. As Neddy ran up to Emily to tell her everything he had done and seen, Mrs. O'Neal rushed off to the kitchen to prepare anything that might be needed to feed the other brothers when they arrived.

It was late when Emily finally made her way up to her bed. She was surprised to find Iain waiting outside her door. "Is something wrong with Neddy?"

"Nay." He pulled her into his arms and kissed her then held her close and rested his chin on the top of her head. "I just wished to see ye before I had to crawl off to bed. Alone."

Emily blushed, her doubts and fears receding a bit more. "Oh. Well, I must do the same."

"And strangely enough, that gives me great comfort." He kissed her again and walked to his room.

Emily shook her head and went into her room. She undressed behind the screen, checked on Neddy, and then crawled into bed. It felt oddly empty to her, which she decided was silly. It was not as if she had spent many nights with Iain, had barely passed part of a long afternoon, yet some part of her felt he should be there with her.

Stupid, she told herself, and closed her eyes. She had given the man her virginity and that had not prompted him to hold her in his bed. Nor had it brought her any sweet words or vows of love. He was good with flattery but not anything more serious.

Emily feared she had been a complete fool. She had given herself too quickly, too easily. Although she did wonder how a woman could resist a man when his kisses made her body burn. Yet she could hear all the warnings whispered by the older women, warnings of how a man expected innocence in his wife and the ever-present chance of conceiving a child from a man her family would never accept. It would not be just her family that would scorn any child she bore, but all of society.

And none of those lecturing people had ever envisioned a situation like the one she found herself in. She had spent more time with Iain than many of her class spent with the man they were to marry and all of it unchaperoned. Even if she and Iain had not made love everyone would believe they had. In fact, she began to understand the insistence upon chaperons. If there was any true feeling between two people, the temptation to get as close as possible could be overwhelming. Her own mother was a perfect example of such a situation.

The question she needed to answer, for her own peace of mind, was if she loved Iain. Love might not be reason enough to please those who gossiped and condemned but it would ease her sense of guilt tinged with a hint of shame. Emily closed her eyes and decided to stop fretting over it all. She had wanted him and the why of that would come to her eventually.

She was sure she had not let herself be seduced because he had saved her and Neddy. Nor because he was such a handsome, strong man. She had seen such men before and had had no inclination to bed them. There was so much more to what she felt for Iain, a more that made her burn and ache with need. She wanted to slip over to his room and crawl into his bed, wanted to sleep with his arms around her.

"Oh, damn," Emily muttered as she opened her eyes and stared at the wall. She was in love with him.

Chapter Eleven

Iain stretched and breathed deep. It had been a week since he had been able to make love to Emily and he began to think it could be months before he got another chance. The next chance he got to make love to her he wanted to take his time, to show her all the pleasure they could share. He blamed his long spell without a woman for his speed the last time. The fact that she had been ready and found her own pleasure had been more luck than skill and that embarrassed him.

Taking another deep breath, he could now smell fall's approach in the air. There were apples to pick and he tried to sort through his plans to find the best time for that harvest. It could be a good idea to set the women and children on that detail, he decided as he started to open the gates. Iain saw few openings for time spent alone with Emily and he sighed with regret. He suddenly paused in trying to work in some time alone with her and stared out at his lands, not sure of what he was seeing.

Then the fog of a lingering sleep cleared and he cursed. A lot of men were riding hard straight for his home. It was a small army, he thought angrily. He had the feeling that bastard after Emily and Neddy had decided more force was needed. Iain hastily closed the gate and barred it then rang the alarm bell.

In minutes his brothers were racing to his side, a couple of them still buttoning up their shirts. Iain ordered them up to posts on the walls, hearing their curses as they saw what they faced. Iain hurried up to the top of the stockade and stood next to Matthew.

"The fool has hired himself a damned army. He is wasting a lot of men," Matthew said.

"He doesnae care. He thinks the woman and child stand between him and all he covets. Greed is what drives the bastard. E'en if he thinks they mean to live here, he just cannae take the chance. They change their mind and run back to England and he loses it all."

Matthew calmly shot a man out of his saddle. "Where is he getting them?"

Iain shrugged as he took aim at another. "Any saloon, I would guess. He just makes it known he needs some men to rid him of a woman and a child and names the fee offered for the job. Probably went to a couple saloons to get this many. It would sound like easy money to men like these. Doubt they learned the facts of the place they had to attack until they rode up and saw it." Iain shot the man he aimed at. "Saw a few at the back who hesitated and then turned round and left."

"Not enough. We have to keep them from reaching the gates, Iain. We can't shoot them easy when they get too close to the walls of the stockade, at least not without one of us exposing ourselves to a bullet, and that gives them a chance to find a way in."

Nodding, Iain shot another man. "Then we had best shoot faster."

"I dinnae ken why these fools think they can get in here," Iain muttered, reloading his rifle even as the men retreated back, out of firing range.

"Aye," agreed Matthew as he relaxed against the wall of the stockade, "I would have thought they would see it as a fort as so many others have." He joined Iain in glaring at Robbie when he laughed.

"Sorry. I just thought on the folk that thought it was a fort at the beginning and sought a night's shelter. They always looked so surprised to find out it was just us." Robbie fired at a man trying to get close to the gates and watched as the man ran back toward the others. "They have now taken to staying out of range. Well, my range, as I am a poor aim the farther away a thing is."

There was a shout from the back and several shots sounded from behind them. Iain ran to where he had placed Duncan and Nigel. He had placed them there because he had thought it would be safer than in the front. Neither Nigel nor Duncan had the stomach needed for battle. They could do what was needed but they suffered for it. Nigel was sitting down, his face pale and his mouth twisted in a grimace of pain, and Duncan was tying a bandage around his arm. Iain crouched down beside them.

"Is the bullet still in there?" he asked his brother, who was already looking less pale.

"Nay," answered Nigel. "It just took a bit of meat off my arm. Ruined my aim. Think my bullet went into the house. I am not worried. It is much like the wound Emily got and if she can recover easily then I should be able to."

Iain peered over the top of the stockade. There was a group of men tucked into the rocks and shadows that marked his land in so many places. It would be difficult to hit them but he suspected they could do it. Iain just did not think it a good idea to waste their ammunition in trying.

"Do ye think ye can still shoot?" he asked Nigel.

"Not well but, aye, I can hold the rifle and pull the trigger. Why?"

"Because I think they are going to make a charge at us soon. They may well have spotted our weak point."

"We had to have a back way in, and out, Iain," said Duncan. "Most times I forget it is there. The door blends well with the rest of the stockade fence."

"But nay perfectly. It is barred but I am nay sure it can hold firm against a hard attack. So those men have to be kept from getting close. I need to ken that ye two lads can do that."

Duncan and Nigel exchanged looks and then nodded firmly. Instead of hurrying around to the front, Iain went down the wall. He jogged to the house and slipped into the parlor. He cursed himself for giving in to superstition as he grabbed the scabbard and sword that had belonged to his father. It had saved him on the day his parents had died and held off danger time after time as they finished the long journey alone. It might not actually be good luck to go into battle with it, but right now he needed the strength the belief he had in it gave him.

Once back on the wall with Matthew, and assuring him that everyone was fine, Iain studied the men who had sought cover by the small hills and gullies facing their stockade. Iain had never envisioned the wall proving its worth this way but felt a certain pride in how well it was holding up. It was the land's dark reputation of being plagued by outlaws and his fear of losing any more of his family that had made him decide they would put their home behind a stockade. The labor they had put into it while building it had been far more than he had anticipated, but they had not suffered from any sudden attack by the thieves or outlaws who called these hills home.

He looked to the side just as an arrow went sailing toward his house, the flame it carried making it easy to see. He could only hope it did not catch anything alight as he and his brothers could not leave the walls. It infuriated him that they were trying to set his house alight but then he wondered why they had not shot their arrows toward the fence. Because the women and children were in the house, he realized, and swore viciously. They wanted the fear for the others to make him and his brothers err. He tapped Matthew and pointed out the man in the tree on the side of their property. Matthew had a good eye for hitting the more hidden targets. In minutes the man was no longer a threat.

The men at the front began to move forward and Iain readied his aim. Just as he was about to shoot, the man he was aiming at screamed and fell from his horse. Iain looked beyond the now panicked group of men and grinned. The Powell brothers had come to join the fight. He patted the sword hanging on his hip. Even as he told himself it might be ridiculous superstition, he could not fully banish the sense that the sword had brought him the luck he needed yet again. Now if he could just finish this job up quickly he could check on where that arrow landed and what damage there was.

Emily let Mrs. O'Neal in the back door, her children close behind her. "I think there are a lot more men attacking than there was last time."

"There is an army out there," said Rory.

Mrs. O'Neal scowled at her son then looked at Emily, who had moved to lock the door. "This fool went up on the walls. Thank heavens Robbie sent him right back down." She lightly slapped the boy on the back of the head. "I told you to never do that." Then she looked at Emily. "That man after you and Neddy put down some hard money to get this group. If Rory calls it an army it must be a fair-sized force of men. Boy's not one given to exaggeration."

Emily silently cursed her sister and, at that moment, felt not the slightest pinch of guilt for doing so. "I cannot believe how foolish Annabel was. She knew Albert was out to get rid of our whole family. How could she have been so silly as to write to our mutual cousin and tell her about her son?" She shook her head. "No, I will not let all this make me speak ill of the dead. I must cease gnawing on that bone."

Mrs. O'Neal patted her shoulder. "It is all that greedy Albert's fault."

Glad she had told Mrs. O'Neal the full truth as she had found keeping so many secrets hard, Emily nodded. "True. Well, we better get down to the root cellar."

"Are you sure we have to?"

"I have no great love of root cellars, either, but it is the safest place for us. I do not think they can get through the MacEnroys and their wall but we should do all that is necessary to ensure our safety. There are a lot of bullets flying about." The sound of a window breaking added a lot of weight to her warning.

"You are right. Come along," Mrs. O'Neal said to her children.

Emily grabbed Neddy by the hand and followed the others down into the root cellar. Over the last few days they had done all they could to make it comfortable, putting wood and carpet on the dirt floor and a few chairs. They had also added a cache of food and drink. It had been done just in case they were attacked but no one had really anticipated this. She felt Neddy start to tremble and understood. It all brought back some frightful, painful memories for her, too. Just the smell of the earth had memories rushing to the fore but she fought them off so that she could comfort the child shaking in her arms.

"It is all right, Neddy," she said as she sat in a rocker and held him on her lap.

"Bad men. Where Iain? The bad men will get him."

"He is keeping those bad men away from us. He and all his brothers."

Neddy nodded but stuck his thumb in his mouth. Emily rocked slightly, hoping to calm him but her mind was not so easy to settle. She recalled the pain of her wounds, the damp smell of dirt as she had crawled out of the root cellar. It was the race for the shelter that played out the clearest in her mind, the need to stop the bleeding of her wounds even while doing all she could to keep Neddy safe. Time had never crept by so slowly nor terror been so persistent and chilling. She did not think she could do it again.

"The lad has gone to sleep, dear," said Mrs. O'Neal.

Glancing down at Neddy, Emily relaxed a little. Better he slept than stayed awake and terrified. She rather wished she could find that peace.

Her thoughts went to the MacEnroy brothers. They were out there fighting to keep her and Neddy alive. Guilt was a heavy stone in her belly. She should never have dragged them into her troubles. She could go for days forgetting her troubles in the warmth and friendship of living in Iain's house and then something like this happened and she was ashamed of herself for her thoughtlessness. The MacEnroys had already suffered too much from the greed of her class. She closed her eyes and began to pray that not one of the MacEnroys paid too dearly for what they had to do to keep her and Neddy safe.

She found herself thinking of her sister again. Emily could not understand how Annabel could have broken their one firm rule, the one they had made when they had realized their parents had been murdered. Emily had worked unceasingly to uncover that dark truth and the one that had told them who was behind it but Annabel had been so slow to believe it, passionately arguing with every one of Emily's facts. She had always disliked Albert but Annabel had considered the man the perfect English gentleman. After the first attempt on their lives that had failed, Annabel had appeared to accept the truth and understand what it meant. The mere hint that David or her child could be killed had appeared to make her accept the rules made. It was now obvious that she had not fully accepted the dark truth and the longer they had gone without a threat the less Annabel had worried.

"I should have known better," she muttered.

"Pardon, dear?" asked Mrs. O'Neal.

"My sister. I should have known she did not fully understand the danger she was in. It was not really in her nature to be able to do so. Perhaps she did not understand that it was a threat that would stand for a long time. Not even the possibility of her husband's death, or her son's, could make her fully believe Albert meant to kill us or how it could be dangerous to contact anyone in the family. She always thought he was the perfect gentleman."

"It can be hard for some to accept when it is their own blood causing their troubles."

"I fear that in our class, it is most often someone of our own blood." Emily sighed over that hard truth. "She agreed, swore she understood. I know David did."

"He was not one of your class though, was he."

"No, he was not and I am not sure Annabel always fully understood how *not* like our class he was. She was a sweet woman but not always the most thoughtful of people."

"I am sorry, dear. Sorry you had to discover that about your sister when you can't talk it out with her, maybe finally get her to see. Sorry that it was such a silly mistake that cost you so dearly."

"It cost her more," Emily said quietly. "And, one reason it troubles me so is I cannot help but feel sad for David more than her. That shames me some. But, the man did not deserve what happened to him just because of who he chose to love."

"No, he didn't. But that part is over and done, dear, and you have to push it aside. They left a beautiful lad in your care and that is what matters now. That is what those men are fighting for out there."

"I know. I . . ." Emily frowned and sniffed the air. "Do you smell smoke?" She was not sure if her memories of the last time she was stuck in a root cellar were causing her to just think she smelled it.

Mrs. O'Neal sniffed the air and then cursed. "I do. The bastards have set a fire."

Emily handed Neddy to Mrs. O'Neal. The boy whimpered once then snuggled up against the woman and quieted. She still felt bad about the MacEnroys fighting what she considered her battle but she was damned if she would let their home be damaged or destroyed because of it.

"What are you going to do?" asked Mrs. O'Neal as she stroked Neddy's back.

"Find the fire and put it out."

"But the bullets . . ."

"If the MacEnroys can face them so can I. It is my enemy after all. Do not let Neddy get away from you," she added as she headed up the stairs.

The heat of the fire was the first thing Emily noticed as she cautiously stepped out of the stairwell. She hurried to look into the kitchen, saw the fire was not burning there although a window was broken, and grabbed a bucket. Once she had filled it with water she moved down the hall. It too was not on fire but it was filled with smoke. Then she looked into the dining room and cursed. After all the work she had done, it seemed a cruel twist of fate that this was the room they had chosen to set alight.

After tossing her bucket of water on the fire she ran back in the kitchen. It was going to be hard work to quell the flames since she was the only one working with a bucket. She wrapped a damp cloth around her nose and mouth as the bucket filled with water.

Finding a second one, she stuck that under the pump as well.

Going back to the dining room, she threw the water on the flames, making sure she got some on every part of the line of fire forming in front of the windows. It was diminishing and she prayed that wetting the area where it burned would keep it from flaring up in the time it took her to gather more water.

As she ran back and forth with her buckets of water, she heartily cursed men who could only fight by burning down everything around them. She was just pouring water on the flames again when a bullet smashed through one of the windows in the room. Emily wondered if they could see her efforts and tried to stop her.

Dragging the buckets behind her she did a strange crouched scramble back into the kitchen. If she had to fight the fire under a rain of bullets that would make it difficult. Yet, if she did not continue to fight the fire it could spread and take a section of the fine house Iain and his brothers had made. Emily refused to allow that to happen.

She moved as fast as she could to gather water and ignored the growing sting in her palms. Emily was determined to save as much from the fire as she could. After what seemed a very long time the fire was just smoldering and she sank against the doorframe and fought to catch her breath. When that proved a troublesome exercise due to the lingering smoke she stumbled back into the kitchen and filled her bucket, leaving the second one she had been filling behind. She went back to the doorway and leaned against it again as she watched the spot where the fire had blazed. If it showed even the tiniest spark of life she would be ready.

Ian sighed as he watched the men scattered over the land in front of him. They appeared to be giving up but he did not dare believe in that. Some were belly crawling back toward their horses but he was not sure how far they would get. The Powell brothers were proving to be lethal shots.

"We give up," yelled one of the men, and it took Iain a moment to find him amongst the dead.

"And why should that matter to me?" he called back.

"Just let us get to our horses and we will be gone."

"So ye can come back another time?"

"We ain't that stupid."

Iain was not sure of that but he was tired and there were a lot dead to deal with. He was not looking forward to all the digging. He did not think he wished to know just how many they had killed, either.

"Take your dead with ye," he said. "And leave your guns. I dinnae see ye drop them to the ground and I will drop ye."

"All right. All right." The man stood up, revealing that he was wounded, and tossed his rifle and pistol to the ground.

"And dinnae forget to tell the man who hired ye that he failed. Again."

One by one a few more did the same. They each grabbed one of the dead but by the time they were gone there were still a sizeable number on the ground. Iain continued to wait until he saw one of the Powell brothers signal him and there was no more sound of horses.

"They didnae take that many with them," said Matthew.

"Suspect they took the ones they knew."

"Which means we have a lot of digging to do."

"We'll see if we can use the plow for some of it." He looked toward the house. "If a fire was started it seems to have gone out."

"Bastards. Always trying to burn things."

"They wanted us to run to the house because they kenned there were women and children inside." Iain continued to watch the land in front of him and then shook his head. "Suspicion they are gone. We best go see how Nigel and Duncan are."

Matthew signaled the others that the fight was over and then followed Iain. "Was one of them hurt?"

"Nigel had his arm burned by a bullet but nay more than that."

When he saw his two younger brothers sitting and leaning up against the wall looking as exhausted as he felt, Iain breathed a sigh of relief. He had been worried about them and had felt guilty about ignoring that worry as the fight had continued. So far they had been lucky in this fight but he was not sure how long that would last, especially if the man was going to keep sending an army against them.

"You lads get any more hurts?" he asked.

"Nay, we are fine," said Duncan in a subdued voice, and knew the young man was already feeling a sickness over what he had had to do.

Looking over the wall, he saw the dead and sighed. He patted Duncan on the shoulder but had no words to give him. They had all killed today and must each sort that out in their own way. Then he realized there was at least one thing he could say that might help.

"They were here to kill a bairn, lad. Dinnae waste any grief on them."

Duncan looked a little stronger and nodded. "That fire they tried to start didnae happen?"

"Dinnae think so but havenae gone inside yet." He sighed. "Better get that done and then we have some burying to do." He could almost smile as his brothers all groaned. "Come on, lad"—he helped Duncan stand—"we best get that wound seen to properly."

He was just about to head down to the ground when he saw a man move. The man sprinted for the back door and Iain cursed as he got down from the wall as fast as he could. Obviously this man did not realize the others were dead or had quit. He moved quietly around the house and watched the man kick at the door. He knew his gun was emptied so Iain pulled the sword free of the scabbard and went after the man. He reached the back door just as the man broke it open and went inside.

His heart pounding with a fear he refused to recognize, he stepped quietly up behind the man. The man was heading right for Emily. He watched her hurl a bucket at the man and stayed back to avoid getting hit. It did not stop him for long and he started after her again.

The man staggered a little and Iain used that uncertain movement to hide the sound of his boots on the hard floor. He could see Emily trying to find something to use against the man and Iain stopped closer, readying his sword. Then he thrust the blade into the man so hard and deep his hand bumped up against the man's back. He felt a twinge of horror when the man just hung there on the point of his sword and tried to pull it back. When it did not come out as easily as it had gone in, he placed a foot on the man's backside and shoved his body forward.

When the dead man fell to the floor he saw Emily's face and almost swore. He was not sure his saving her life was going to make her accept what he had just done. One thing his father had never told him was how gruesome a death one could cause with a sword.

Chapter Twelve

Emily coughed as she threw a bucket of water on the fire just to make certain it was out. That produced even more smoke and she stumbled back to the sink. Clutching the side of the large sink, she coughed until her ribs hurt and quickly used a damp cloth to clean her face. She then filled the bucket up again and cursed Albert and the men he had hired. Why did they always have to burn things down? And why did it have to be in the dining room? She had only recently scrubbed the whole room. She could not get over how much that annoyed her, petty though that it was.

Looking at the damage already caused by the fire, smoke, and water almost made her cry. The MacEnroys had worked so hard to build themselves a home and yet again some English gentry were trying to destroy it. Iain had come to this country to get away from her kind. It was so wrong, so unfair, and she wished Albert were there himself so that someone could shoot him.

That bloodthirsty thought was oddly satisfying and Emily hurried to douse the last of the fire one final time. She was setting the empty bucket on the kitchen table when she heard something at the back door. Emily tensed when she realized she had not barred it after she had let Mrs. O'Neal in. Distracted by the woman and her children she had simply locked it.

Just as she decided she might have a chance to go into the root cellar without the man kicking at the door seeing her, it was too late. The door crashed open and the man started toward her. Emily hurled the bucket at him, hearing the man curse as it clipped him on the shoulder. He staggered a little then started for her again. Emily was backing up and frantically looking for something to defend herself with when the point of a sword appeared out of his chest. Emily met the man's horrified gaze, certain her own was the same. Blood began to pour from his mouth and she felt her stomach churn. He sagged and then was propelled forward to lie on the floor.

Tearing her gaze from the man's body, she looked up and there stood Iain, his expression fierce and a bloodied sword in his hand. She started to shake and forced herself to stop. She did not wish to make Iain think he had caused her fear. Emily also did not want him to think she was too horrified by what he had done although she feared he could read it in her face. She had to let him know it was the death that upset her, not the fact that he caused it. The man was planning to kill her and she was more than grateful that he had been stopped. Cautiously she moved around the table. As soon as she had a clear path, she ran into his arms, hearing the sword hit the ground as he wrapped his arms around her. She could smell sweat, blood, and smoke on him but nothing had ever made her feel so safe before.

"Are ye okay, lass?" he asked, rubbing one hand up and down her back.

"I am fine." Emily stepped back and he was slow to release her. "Best pick up your weapon in case others come."

"No others left to come." He bent, wiped the sword clean on the dead man's coat, and then stood up. "We killed a lot of them and as the men began to fall, others changed their mind about it all and fled. We accepted the surrender of others. We will keep a watch in case some eluded the Powell brothers."

"The Powells?"

"Aye. They came running and ended up on the backside of this lot. Hid themselves well and, I cannae say how many, but I dinnae think many of the ones who ran away got very far. I am hoping we'll find one alive."

"So many dead," she whispered in shock.

"They intended to kill ye and the boy. Dinnae waste a moment of grief on them."

"No grief. Just shock. I begin to think Albert is more than greedy. He must be mad." She looked around. "Oh, Iain, your lovely home. They have ruined it." She felt tears sting her eyes.

"It will be fixed, love," he said quietly.

"Smoke, fire, ash, and blood are not easily banished."

"Dinnae fret. We will do it. There is no damage to the main structure. Where is Mrs. O'Neal?"

"Still in the root cellar. Is anyone hurt?"

"Nay. A few nicks and bruises is all. How about ye go and fetch her, but take it slow so I have time to get this body out of here. Dinnae want the children seeing it."

"Yes, I can do that." She took a deep breath and reached for calm. "I am glad none of you were badly hurt and I am so sorry for all of this."

"Ye have nothing to apologize for. This wasnae your doing, never think so. It was all the fault of that greedy bastard Albert. I would sorely like to find him. He is a man who badly needs killing. Just keep that thought in your head. This is all Albert's doing."

"I am so sorry you were forced to do that," she said, and nodded toward the dead man.

Iain pulled her into his arms and kissed her, all the fear he had felt that he would not stop the man in time adding a fierceness to the kiss. "There was a choice before me. Ye or him. That was a simple choice to make." He let her go and nudged her toward the door leading to the cellar. "Go and let the others out."

She nodded and headed to the root cellar, trying hard to ignore the sound of a body being dragged out the door. It was Albert's doing. A faint smile touched her mouth. She still felt to blame for bringing this trouble to Iain's door but he was right, the dead were all on Albert's head. All she and the MacEnroys had done was fight to stay alive.

"Em! Fire!" Neddy ran up and wrapped himself around her legs. "We go. We run."

Crouching down she framed Neddy's face with her hands. "I put the fire out, Neddy."

"No fire? I smell it."

"That is just the smoke and I am afraid we will be smelling that for quite a while. But there is no fire. I threw water on it all and I am sure Iain will do a thorough check to be certain."

"He will indeed," said Mrs. O'Neal as she stepped

up and stroked Neddy's hair where he was tucked in the folds of their skirts, then she looked at Emily. "Any injuries?"

"Iain said just a few nicks and bruises."

Mrs. O'Neal snorted. "Men. Let us get up there then."

Deciding she had allowed Iain enough time, Emily nodded. "Just keep the children behind you in case Iain was slower to clean up something than he thought he would be."

"Might be something left that we need to clean up too," Mrs. O'Neal murmured.

"Quite possible," she answered, relieved the woman understood what she meant.

With all the children kept behind them, or their faces pressed into the folds of their skirts, they went up to the kitchen. Emily was surprised but relieved to see Iain mopping up the floor. A quick glance told her the water in the bucket had already been changed so there was little sign of blood. She did wonder what had been done with the body.

"Are the others coming in soon to have their nicks and bruises tended to?" asked Mrs. O'Neal.

Iain smiled faintly at her dry tone of voice. "They will be in as soon as things are tidied up a wee bit."

"Fair enough. Anything done to my cabin?"

"Nay. It wasnae touched and Matthew had a look about to make sure it was also empty."

"Good. Okay, kids, you are to go home and take our little Neddy with you. Emily and I have work to do."

Emily watched as everyone but her and Mrs. O'Neal left the kitchen. It was over, she thought as Mrs. O'Neal watched the children go before searching out the things she would need to put together a hearty meal. No one had been hurt except the ones who had tried to hurt them. She tried not to think much on what the men had to "tidy up" outside. Emily knew she should feel relieved, perhaps even a little triumphant that they had prevailed, but she just felt cold.

The odd mood stayed with her all through the preparation of the meal. She barely spoke during the meal although she carefully studied each one of the brothers to assure herself they were whole. Iain kept giving her long looks filled with curiosity and concern but she ignored them. Emily knew she needed to be alone to shake off the strange mood. For now, she did only what she had to and spoke only when spoken to directly.

"What troubles you, dearie?" asked Mrs. O'Neal after the others left the table and she started to clean up.

"I brought killers to your home, to Iain's home," Emily said.

"Nonsense. They brought themselves, the bastards. Whoever wants you and that boy dead will chase you wherever you go. Better you get to a place with high walls and a lot of strong men than out on the trail or in some boardinghouse," she said as she washed the dishes and Emily wiped them dry.

"This is not Iain's battle."

"Ha! It is the battle of any man with a backbone and a solid sense of what is right. This cousin of yours wants to slaughter a woman and a small child, an infant, a babe with no ability to protect himself, and all for gain. It should turn any decent man's stomach. It is just sad that there are so many men willing to take the money to do his dirty work for him."

"The MacEnroys saved our lives, mine and Neddy's.

It is a poor repayment for that to drag them into this mess."

Mrs. O'Neal shook her head. "When you start thinking like that, do one thing for me."

"What?" Emily asked suspiciously.

"Think of that boy. Think of those big brown eyes going cloudy with death. That is what your lofty principles will gain you if you hang on to them past all good sense. He can stay with us tonight if he wishes." Mrs. O'Neal walked out leaving Emily with the last of the dishes.

Chastised, Emily finished the dishes. She poured herself a tankard of cider and went to sit on the porch swing. She could hear the faint sounds of the men clearing away all signs of the battle and the death it brought. Emily knew the men who had died were ones who had not quailed at the thought of killing a woman and child but she feared for how causing such death affected the MacEnroys. She could not believe it was an easy thing to kill a man, even one who deserved killing.

She tried to make herself think as Mrs. O'Neal did. Albert and any men he hired were willing to kill a woman and a child so they could enrich themselves. It was the lowest of motives for murder although it was all too common. Any man with honor would feel it was right and just to kill to stop such men. None of the MacEnroys had looked as if they were suffering from what had been done.

She looked over at the O'Neal cottage and sighed. They had fought for that woman and her children, too. If the men had overpowered the MacEnroys they would have killed them all. She had no doubt about that. Emily told herself she should be pleased that she had found men who had the honor and the stomach to do what was right and just. She just wished she could have taken care of it all herself.

A small choked laugh escaped her. She had not been able to take of Albert and the men he hired even back in England. The family members who had stood with her were dead. The others simply thought her an hysterical female. It was the height of irony that Scots torn from their home by her kind were the ones who worked so hard to keep her and Neddy alive.

"Emily?"

She looked up and saw Iain move toward her, taking a seat by her side. He did not look as if he carried any weight for what he had done to keep her and Neddy safe. No ghosts appeared to haunt his expression. Emily wondered if there was something in the male mind and heart that made them able to accept deaths caused by their hands if those deaths could be justified.

"It has been a long, miserable day," she said.

"That it has." He put his arm around her shoulders and tugged her closer as he sipped his cider. "But we beat them. That is something to celebrate."

"They tried to burn your house down."

"Actually, we were not sure how the fire started at first. Duncan feared it might have been him because one of his shots went in the house. Could have knocked something over. But I saw the man in the tree shoot a fire arrow at it."

"There was nothing that had a spark. Not in the dining room where the fire began."

"I know. And we calculated that his shot would have gone in the kitchen. Window busted there. So that man got close enough and had the time to shoot in the fire. I will tell Duncan though as he was unsettled by the possibility."

"It is ruined in there."

"Nay, Matthew says the table just needs to be sanded down a bit and redone and it will be good as new. Carpet is a loss but Robbie says he can weave another. Shame though as ye had just scrubbed the whole place down."

Emily gave a watery laugh. "I know and I am ashamed to admit I was so cross and cursing as I put out the fire. Muttering away about all the work I had done and it was a silly thing to fret over when you and your brothers were facing an army."

"Nay. It is sometimes the small things that can really get to a person in such times. When I was keeping the boys safe during the attack that took my parents all I could think on was that they were trying to burn our stuff and what would I do for clothes. Knew it was a stupid fool thing to fret over but I think that happens because ye dinnae really want to think on the real cause of the anger and fear ye feel."

"Yes. That is probably true. After all, the real cause will be waiting for you to face it when you step out."

"What I saw was that my parents had died in each other's arms."

"That is both sad and lovely."

He laughed but it was not a happy sound. "I ken it. Do ye think he will quit now?" Iain hoped she would say no because he did not want to have to explain why he thought this would go on until the man was dead.

"No. It will never stop until Albert is dead in the ground."

He tightened his arm around her shoulders. "Good that ye see that. I ken ye have said something similar before but was worried ye had talked yourself into changing your mind."

Emily sat up and stared at him. "No. I feel a bit sick

when I say it, as it is such a horrible thing to want, but I know this will only end when Albert is dead. He will never give up."

Iain finished his cider, then stood up, pulling her to her feet as well. Wrapping an arm around her shoulders he took her inside and placed their cups on the kitchen counter. He held her hand and peered out into the hallway. He could hear his brothers all gathered in the parlor so he went quickly to the stairs and dragged Emily up them. She hesitated a moment when he led her to his door.

"I saw Neddy going with Mrs. O'Neal's children. Did he come back?" he asked in a whisper.

"No, but all your brothers are right downstairs," she replied in a voice as soft as his.

"And willnae come in my room. Nay without warning."

He opened his door, tugged her inside, and with a last peek down the hallway, shut the door and latched it. Emily stood looking at him. She looked nervous and he smiled gently as he walked up to her and tugged her into his arms.

"Alone at last," he murmured, and was pleased to hear her laugh softly. "I have a craving to prove we both survived. Understand?"

"Yes. I have a craving to forget it all for a time. Is that wrong?"

"Nay, love. It is not so different from what I seek."

He kissed her. Emily curled her arms around his neck and held on tight. She had the fleeting thought that he could not understand what he did to her with his kiss and she did not want him to. Then all the power would be in his hands and that did not seem fair. Then he slid his hand down her back and pressed her even closer to him. She felt his hardness and decided the power was in her hands as well. Emboldened by that realization she began to undo his shirt.

She smoothed her hands over his chest once she had opened his shirt, reveling in the strength and heat beneath her fingers. When he released her mouth to kiss her neck, she tilted her head to give him better access and trembled slightly from the strength of the feelings he stirred within her. Emily became so lost to the way he made her feel she did not even twitch as he undid her gown. She even tugged her own arms free of the sleeves as he tugged the gown down.

Iain tried not to tear anything as he carefully undressed her. Her touch on his skin was making him desperate, however. When he got her stripped down to her shift he pushed her toward the bed until she sat down on the edge. He quickly shed his boots and then knelt to deal with her shoes. Unable to stop himself he ran his hands over her slender legs every chance he got only to discover, to his delight, that Emily was extremely sensitive to such a touch. As he undid her garters and tugged off her stockings, he kissed each newly bared patch of skin. The soft sounds of pleasure escaping her were music to his ears.

Once he had her stripped to only her shift, he stood up and began to shed his own clothes. The way Emily watched him, her eyes wide yet still warmed with passion, made him hesitate a moment before taking off his drawers. Emily was still new to this intimacy and he did not wish to shock her out of her state of desire. Then Iain shrugged and removed them, tossing them to the side. The way she stared at his groin made him a little uneasy until she reached out and stroked him.

He yanked off her shift and gently pushed her down onto the bed. "Nay, love, ye cannae do that. Nay now. I am a desperate man."

"Oh? That makes you desperate?" she asked as she wrapped her arms around his neck.

"Ye make me desperate."

He kissed her and Emily murmured her pleasure. The way his naked body was pressed all along the length of hers would be impossible for her to describe. Every brush of his warm, taut skin and crisp hair made her pulse dance madly and her desire for him grow until she ached.

Then his mouth left hers and he kissed his way down to her breasts. He kissed her there and then suckled her like a babe. The ache she suffered from centered itself low in her belly, and Emily was shocked when she realized she had been rubbing herself against him. She was just discovering that that motion felt very good when he slid his hand down over her stomach and between her legs. She cried out softly when he slid a finger inside of her.

"Ah, love, ye heat up for me so quickly, thank heaven," he said against the swell of her breast.

Emily could not think of what to respond to that and then forgot about even speaking when he replaced his finger with that part she had no name for. With a quiet cry of pleasure she wrapped her legs around him.

Iain moved slowly at first, holding on to just enough control to keep his thrusts slow and deep. Emily's breathing grew faster and uneven and then her body tightened around him. He caught her cry of release in his mouth then continued to kiss her as he thrust harder, faster, and found his own pleasure. Pressing his forehead against hers he managed to keep most of his weight off her as he rode it out, then he pulled away and rolled to the side. It was an effort but he wrapped his arms around her and tugged her hard up against his side, pleased to feel that she was as wrung out as he was.

For several minutes they just sprawled there, their breathing growing more steady.

Emily began to come to her senses and then wondered if she should say anything.

Unfortunately, she could think of nothing to say. Although her knowledge of such matters was not enough to fill a thimble, she had once heard a woman speak of pillow talk. The woman had been quickly hushed, however. So what did one say after such an event, she wondered.

Iain rolled onto his side, saw the faint line between her brows, and said, "Oh, I forgot to clean us off. Be just a moment."

Already blushing, Emily watched as he walked over to the washbowl, poured some water in, and wet a rag. The man was completely comfortable walking around naked. She wished she could have such confidence but she had already tugged the sheet up until it covered her. He washed, rinsed the rag, then marched back and cleaned her off. Emily thought her face would burst into flames, her blushes felt so hot. After he rinsed and set aside the rag, he crawled back into bed and pulled her into his arms. It took a moment but then she realized he was stroking her back much the way he stroked a nervous horse.

"What are you doing?" she asked, putting her hands on his chest and pushing herself up enough to see his face.

"Weel, ye were looking a wee bit discomforted," he said.

She looked down at his chest and idly petted flat the hair sprinkled there. "I am unaccustomed to doing this and know none of the rules."

"There are rules, are there?"

"I am certain there must be."

He cupped his hand under her chin, tilted her face up to his, and brushed a kiss over her mouth. "The only rule is to be sure ye give each other pleasure."

She sighed and rested her cheek against his chest. "That seems impossibly simple."

"Not everything can have a set of rules to it, love. There are rules all round this, and we've broken most of them, but none for the act itself except to give pleasure and not hurt each other."

Emily thought about all the rules they had broken and she ought to be deeply ashamed. Yet, she was not, not in the slightest. All she felt was some unease because she did not know how this man she had given herself to felt about her. He so easily called her "love" but she doubted he meant it as she would like him to. The fact that she loved him made his lack of love words, and the promises that came with them, all the harder to bear.

She sat up, clutching the sheet to her chest and ignoring how the action bared so much of his tall, muscular body. "I best slip off to my own room now."

Iain sat up and pulled her into his arms. "Why? Neddy is staying at the O'Neals, aye? There is no one to ken ye are missing from your own bed."

"But we have already done that," she protested

weakly as he tugged the sheet away and began to kiss her breasts.

"Are ye sore?"

"No."

"Then I think we should take advantage of our time alone as it is so rare."

Emily slowly opened her eyes and was disoriented for a moment. Then she recalled where she was and turned her head to see Iain sleeping soundly. Glancing toward the window she saw the dim light of dawn starting to color the sky. She slid out of bed and yanked on her shift. Gathering up the rest of her clothes, she crept out of the room and dashed across the hall to hers. Once inside, she tossed aside her clothes and climbed into her own bed.

She could not believe she had stayed the night with Iain. That was risky and probably foolish. Now she was painfully aware of how alone she was in her own bed. She craved his warm body next to hers, the way he idly curled an arm around her waist and tugged her close. It was a mistake to have stayed the night with him because now she would be plagued by all she did not have.

Like his love, she thought, then cursed. She could not be sure what he felt for her aside from lust and she had overheard enough talk to know a man could feel lustful toward many ladies. Emily wondered if there was a way to prompt him to declare himself but quickly shook aside that thought. He might tell her he did no more than lust after her and she could not bear to hear that.

Closing her eyes, she tried to clear her mind. It

would be a while before she needed to rise and she intended to spend that time catching up on all the sleep she lost last night in Iain's bed. She set her mind on planning how, and what, to clean up after the fire and soon felt sleep creep over her.

Chapter Thirteen

Glancing up, Iain found all of his brothers gathered around him and frowning at him. "Dinnae ye lot have some work to do?" He had a bad feeling about what they felt compelled to talk to him about.

"A lot of it, but we decided we needed to talk to ye first," said Matthew.

"And just why do ye need to do that now when we are together most every day, all day long?"

"Because Matthew just decided it," muttered Robbie, and Matthew slapped him on the back of the head. "Weel, ye did."

"Before ye two knock each other senseless, why dinnae ye just ask me what ye want to." He noticed they all looked somewhat uncomfortable and decided it would not be bad.

"Iain, what game are ye playing with Miss Emily?" Nigel asked, and ignored Matthew's glare.

"Miss Emily? I believe it is Lady Emily."

"Ye said that without even the hint of a sneer."

"Why would I sneer?" He almost laughed at the narrow-eyed look each brother gave him. "Ah, because she is a lady, one of the gentry?"

"She is not like that bitch who sat calmly on her horse watching as ye and Geordie nearly burnt to death and our parents fought vainly to get to ye. Hell, Emily was just a child when all that happened. Ye cannae be holding all that against her," said Nigel.

"Nay. Not now. It just bites a wee bit every now and again," Iain said.

"Toughen your skin then," snapped Matthew. "Even if Emily was of an age to have been a part of all that, she would not have been. She wouldnae have the stomach for it."

"Nay, she doesnae. Never has." He smiled faintly recalling the day he had caught her playing like a wild child with the kittens in the stables, then getting so upset when one of them nearly got stomped on by a horse. "I admit it took me a while but I did conclude that she wasnae one's usual example of English gentry." He tossed a shovelful of stable muck into the cart, causing Matthew to leap aside and swear at him.

"Damnation, Iain! If we have to stand and listen to Mrs. O'Neal lecture us, ye can bloody weel listen to us," Matthew yelled as he carefully checked to make sure none of what Iain was shoveling had gotten on his clothes.

"Mrs. O'Neal had a word with you?" He stood the shovel up and rested his arm on the handle as he looked at each one of his brothers. "Burned your ears with a lecture about me, did she?"

"Aye," Robbie muttered, then glanced at Iain and blushed. "She is concerned about Emily. She said Emily has been through so much, lost too much, to be played with by you."

"She thinks I am playing?"

Matthew shrugged. "I think Mrs. O'Neal sometimes has a harsh opinion of men."

Iain chuckled and shook his head. "She thinks of us as all just boys, but, aye, she does have some odd, and stinging, opinions of men. Obviously, her Tommy was the only exception. I am nay playing with Emily."

"Then what are ye doing?"

"Damned if I ken." Iain shoveled up some more muck and nearly laughed at the way his brothers hastily stepped back. "The lass is educated. I am not. The lass is gentry born and bred. I am not. The lass has, and always has had, money and I do not have much of that at all. I could go on but I think ye see what I speak of."

All his brothers frowned at him and Iain sighed. "She and I are as different as night and day. I can think on her and me and see it working out weel and other times I can see it being the worst of disasters."

"So what the hell are you going to do?" Robbie asked.

"I thought I would woo her and see how that works."

"Woo her?" Matthew shook his head and stared up at the stable loft. "Ye are doing this all backwards. Ye should woo her then bed her, nay bed her and then woo her, ye daft fool."

Iain shrugged. "I suspicion more do it the other than ye ken."

His younger brothers looked thoughtful before nodding. Their silent agreement swiftly ended when the three older ones scowled at them. Iain decided it was a good thing Emily did not know how many were discussing their intimate secrets or they would all pay dearly. He knew it was undoubtedly wrong for him to care so little for Emily's need for secrecy and discretion, but Iain knew that he only catered to that need because he wanted to. He had no concern himself about who knew she was his lover.

Once he pushed aside the pinch of guilt that crept over him, he thought of all that had passed between him and Emily. Emily had been willing, her passion running as hot and urgent as his. There had been no denial of his attentions and little hesitation. Since thinking of Emily's passion immediately caused his body to harden, Iain forced himself to clear his mind of all thought, all hint of desire, until his body relaxed.

"So how do you mean to woo her?" asked Nigel.

"Why do ye need to ken the how of it?" Iain asked.

"One of us could, weel, lend a hand now and then."

"Tell tales of your great bravery or extraordinary resourcefulness," drawled Matthew.

Robbie choked on a laugh then struggled to look innocent when Iain looked at him. "I think we could come up with a few things," he murmured.

"Please, and I mean this most sincerely, dinnae try to help me."

Iain laughed at their expressions, an odd mix of annoyed and crestfallen, and rolled the small cart out of the stable. He walked out of the compound to dump the contents of the cart onto the growing pile already there. Then he forked a heavy cover of hay over the whole lot. Not one of the more pleasant duties on a farm but they all took their turn.

Something else he and Emily did not share, the knowledge of hard work. She might not be a lady of the sort of Lady Vera, but he doubted she had ever done any true hard labor. There was a good chance that, until she had come to this country, she had rarely been around the ones who worked hard for their living. He briefly thought of how she had been scrubbing their house and decided that, although it was undoubtedly hard work, it was not really the same thing. For one thing, she would never have worried about smelling like manure or reek of sheep.

After he put the cart and shovel away he headed into the house. He needed a change of clothes and a wash. Mrs. O'Neal was just stepping out of the front parlor and she scowled at him. Iain just smiled and, before she could begin talking to him, hurried up the stairs. He had already heard her lecture from his brothers and was not about to let her corner him for one.

Once clean of the smell of the stables, Iain headed out to check on the flock. The Powell brothers were excellent shepherds but he did not want to become one of those who only cared for the money his stock brought him. He wanted to be involved in it all, from the lambing to the shearing. He had plans to improve the quality of his sheep and the wool they produced for him. Iain dismounted near to Owen, who was watching the sheep.

"How is the wooing going, boyo?" asked Owen, and he grinned when Iain scowled at him. "That well, eh?"

"I havenae begun yet."

"Why not?"

"Needed to do some planning. Never wooed a lass before. Want to do it right." He rubbed the back of one of the sheep. "This lass is getting a bit old, aye."

"She will not be lambing again, I think. Good girl though. She keeps the others calm when it is needed."

Owen rubbed the ewe's head. "If you are looking for mutton though . . ."

"In no rush for it. Hate picking one out for slaughter. Always have even though I have no trouble filling my belly with the meat."

"I will let you know when we have one."

"Fair enough." He checked over one of the lambs and then stood up. "Still pondering a fence. Ken it willnae solve the problem but think it might make it more difficult for the wolves."

"Well"—Owen rubbed his chin—"cannot say that would be a bad thing. Been so long since we had anything to do with wolves I have little knowledge or experience with them." Owen looked at Iain and slowly smiled. "Just why are you out here? I don't think you really have anything important to discuss about the flock."

"Only one thing I feel ye need to ken. If I decide to build the fence in what could be a vain attempt to keep the wolves away, I will have to get a loan. I will put the flock up as collateral."

"Your flock."

"I was trying to find out how ye feel about that."

"As I said, it is your flock. And what else would you put up? Your house? Your land? No, that would not do. And there is also the small fact that I know you will do everything you are able to do to pay it off in time so the flock will not be in any real danger. Trouble can come though, no doubt of that. Warning you though, you may lose the flock but me and David ain't leaving our cabin." He grinned.

Iain laughed and slapped the man on the back. "Fair enough."

"So go and start your wooing."

"Shut up, Owen," Iain said as he walked over to his

horse and swung himself up in the saddle, then rode off to the sound of Owen laughing.

Emily watched Neddy running around with Mrs. O'Neal's boys and smiled. He had never really had anyone to play with before. Rory and Donald were older than him but never pushed him away or ignored him. The friendship was slowly helping Neddy with his speech, too. She wished she knew some women with a child closer to his age though. It was always good if a child had children of an age with him to play with.

"Here," Mrs. O'Neal said, holding a glass of cold tea out for her. "Best to have a drink now and then when you sit in the sun."

"Thank you," Emily said, and smiled at Mrs. O'Neal when she sat down beside her on the bench. "I was just thinking of moving into the shade so this is very welcome."

"A bit of sun is good for a person."

"Not allowed for a lady. Why, you might get some color on your delicately pale, pale skin." She grinned when Mrs. O'Neal laughed. "I was forever being told that."

Mrs. O'Neal suddenly looked over her shoulder and frowned. "What is he doing back home? I don't think this was his day off. It's Duncan's."

"Day off?" Emily asked but Mrs. O'Neal was already standing and heading toward the gates Iain had just ridden through.

Iain looked at Mrs. O'Neal as she frowned up at him. He dismounted and grabbed the reins so he could walk his horse to the stable. It took him a moment of thought before he realized he had frightened her with his early return to the house.

"Nothing is wrong," he reassured her. "I am simply done with what I wanted to do."

"Oh. Gave me a bit of a fright for a moment. Things being as they are and all."

"Fine. No trouble. I just thought I ought to tell Owen what I was thinking about doing and what I would put up as collateral for a loan. He didnae have a problem with it. Did tell me that if I did lose the flock he and David would not be leaving that cabin." He grinned when Mrs. O'Neal laughed.

As he headed to the stable he noticed Emily was sitting outside watching the children play. He put his horse away and took out the small bouquet of wildflowers he had tucked carefully into his saddlebags. Frowning at them he thought they looked a little rough but he shrugged and walked back outside.

Emily was sitting alone watching the children play with the ball. Not the best setting for his first attempt at wooing her but he decided to go ahead. They could at least speak with no one listening, he decided. Sitting down beside her, he smiled at her when she looked at him.

"I brought ye these," he said, and held out the flowers, inwardly wincing over how awkward that was and wishing he had practiced the action a few times.

Emily took the flowers and studied them. They were not what she was accustomed to and then she decided there were really no places around that sold fancier flowers. She suspected he had picked them from some field when he was out with the sheep. The poor things also looked as if they had been roughly handled. The image of Iain out in a field picking flowers for her touched her deeply and she smiled at him.

"Thank you. Are they wildflowers?"

"Aye. Got them out in the fields." He looked at the children and found all three boys staring at him. "Why are they staring at us?" he asked quietly.

"I have no idea. I also think I do not wish to ask them."

"Probably a good idea. One can never be sure of what a child will answer. Can ye leave while they are out here or must ye stay and watch them?"

"Well, unless Mrs. O'Neal wanders back out here, I think I have to stay. Not for her children but because Neddy is out here. He does rather need an eye kept on him."

"Especially when he is with the older boys."

"They are good boys but they play harder and some things they get up to can be too difficult for Neddy or he ends up tripping or falling."

Iain decided he needed to pick a better time. He took her hand in his and lifted it to his lips to brush a kiss over her knuckles. The faint blush she tried to hide by ducking her head just enough to make her hair fall forward and hide her cheeks made him smile.

"Then I shall see you later."

Emily watched him walk away and frowned. For the first time since she had met him he had acted a bit awkward. The flowers were nice but the way he gave them to her was a bit odd, abrupt, and with no flattering words accompanying them. It was a lovely gift but left her unsure of what he was doing.

What she wanted to do was put her flowers into water but she was stuck unless Neddy decided he wanted to go inside. Then Neddy ran over to her and wanted her to take him inside because he needed to relieve himself. Emily went inside with the boy and as Neddy took care of his personal business, she filled a little vase with water and put her flowers in it. Once in water and loosened from the snug bunch they were in, the flowers looked quite lovely.

"Pretty," said Mrs. O'Neal as she entered the kitchen. "Iain brought you flowers, did he?"

"Yes. I believe they are wildflowers."

"Oh, they are indeed. A fine selection." Mrs. O'Neal looked at them more closely. "Think he didn't handle them very carefully."

"They are fine."

Mrs. O'Neal just glanced up at the ceiling and sighed. "The man is trying to court you."

"Oh, no, of course not. He just found a few flowers he thought I would like is all."

"Of course, all the men are forever pausing in their work to pick some flowers," she drawled, and ignored Emily's frown at her sarcasm. "Well, we will see. Now here comes the little man and I think he is very tired." Mrs. O'Neal knelt in front of Neddy. "Are you tired, my boy?"

"No." Neddy yawned and seeing Emily sitting at the table walked over and patted her on her lap. "Sit, Em?"

Emily picked him up and put him on her lap. "You have had yourself a busy, busy day today, love."

"I have. Playeded ball with Rory."

"I watched you but, do you think, a nap, a short rest, might be something you would like to have? Just a little one so your eyes can stay open again."

Neddy nodded and she picked him up. He rested his head on her shoulder as she carried him upstairs. By the time she reached the room where his cot was the boy was already asleep. Emily smiled as she put him down on the bed. She took off his shoes, kissed him on the forehead, and then quietly left the room only to bump into Iain.

"I thought you left," she said as she pulled the bedroom door shut.

"Nay, I just had a good look over the walls. I do it every once in a while, to make sure they are still sturdy. They are. Gates are sturdy, too." He took her by the hand and tugged her toward his room.

"Where are you taking me?"

"Where I can kiss ye senseless without interruption."

Emily almost laughed. She had not expected him to answer so honestly. She did not fight as he pulled her into his room and shut the door although the way he latched it made her a little nervous. Emily was not sure just how far she would allow him to go or how far he might try to go and if she was fully prepared for the consequences of that. She was no longer pure but there was no sense in becoming simply a mistress to a man out in the wilds of a new country.

She should say no. She should walk away but, as he pulled her into his arms, she lost all urge to do so. Everyone thought he was courting her. It would be foolish to walk away now when he might just be working his way to what she ached for, a permanent relationship.

His kiss made her senses reel and her heart pound. Emily wrapped her arms around his neck and held on tightly. She craved his kisses and knew that was her greatest weakness. How could any woman keep her senses when a man kissed like he did?

Iain desperately wanted to toss her onto the bed and make love to her but too many people were around. He eased away from her, ending the kiss slowly as he did so. He was trying to woo her and making love to her again, in secret, sneaking around so she was not shamed, was not the way to court a woman.

"There. I have been thinking about that all day." He brushed a kiss over her forehead.

"You have?"

"Aye." He gave her a quick kiss on the mouth and then opened the door.

After a look down the hall, he led her out and started down the stairs. Iain led her by holding on to her hand. Her silence told him she was puzzled by his actions but was too polite to say so. Iain was puzzled by them too. He was wanting her all the time yet he knew he should not give in to that want. That, he reminded himself with a twisted smile, was not the way to woo a woman and that was what he was supposed to be doing.

"Is there anything ye would like to do?"

"I cannot think of anything. Not here. I do not wish to go back into town for a while as I think it will make me nervous or afraid. I do not really know what people do around here, either. In England it is a lot easier even if all one does is wait for invites. There are also walks in the park, plays, musicales, and so on."

"True. There is little here like that. Well, I shall have to put some thought to it. We should get away from the house now and then, just us."

"That would be nice. It can be something simple. Like a picnic or a walk or a ride."

He nodded. Then, when they reached the bottom of the stairs, he stole a quick kiss and went out the door. Emily stood there wondering what was wrong with the man. Then she shook her head and headed for the kitchen. It might be time to help Mrs. O'Neal with a meal. It would be good for her to do something ordinary and occasionally boring.

When it was time for supper, Iain felt he had himself straightened out. It was a good thing too, he thought, or Emily would be wondering about his sanity. He was not all that sure of it himself. What he was sure of was that he had set his course and he needed to stick with it. No more trying to get her alone so he could satisfy his baser needs. That was the act of a cad, and he was trying to show her he was a beau, a serious man courting her.

He glanced at her cutting up some meat for little Neddy. She looked perfectly calm as she talked to the boy. That made him feel better. He had not scared her with too much attention—strange behavior from him, strange to her at least. It would have been difficult to explain what he had been doing if he had. The real problem was that he had never dealt with a young, untried woman before. His experience, little as it was, was with the whores at the tavern who required nothing of him except payment. One could have a good time with them and not worry about offending them.

He would go back to simple courting. Stay with flowers and candy and maybe another small gift or two. He was not sure he would be good at it but he might even try playing the beau. And, he thought, he needed to consider a better way of handing her his offerings. Today he had been no better than one of Mrs. O'Neal's sons. Although he had a feeling even they would be more gracious and more like a true beau than he had been. That thought almost made him laugh and he took a quick look around the table to be sure no one had noticed his strange behavior.

"I think it might be good to have our reading and writing lessons soon." Emily took note of the complete lack of interest and sighed. "Well, when you decide you would like to read and write just let me know." She was a little disappointed as she had hoped she could give back something for all the care they had given her and Neddy.

"I think I want to," said Rory, glancing at his mother, who quickly nodded with approval.

Several of the MacEnroys nodded and Robbie just smiled. Emily smiled back at him, knowing she had at least one very willing pupil. She would start work on figuring out when and how and create a few things to make lessons easier. She had to begin to teach Neddy so whoever wanted to join in when she did that they would be welcome. She recalled what Robbie had said about wanting to read a book so she felt rather certain he would join in.

When she finally found her way to bed that night, Emily was ready for sleep but her mind was not. She worried about what Albert would try next. The man was quite possibly mad as a hatter, she thought. No one could think killing off so many in one family would never raise any suspicions. And, by now, she would think a sane man would have given up. A sane man certainly would not resort to increasingly large groups of men openly attacking them. There was no subtlety to that and secrecy had seemed to be what Albert wanted. Now he was just lashing out.

Then there was Iain to wonder about. What was she to do about him? She could say she would not be his lover anymore but she knew there was little chance of her holding to that. Could she coax him into saying what he felt and what he wanted? Emily was not sure she could do that. She was not sure he was the sort of man one could coax. What she needed from him was a return of the love she felt for him but she had no idea of how to get that or ask for it.

She also worried over whether she should take Neddy and get back to England, try to reach her grandfather. He would keep them safe. He could even afford to hire people to hunt down Albert. All she had to do was get him to believe that Albert wanted her and Neddy dead. The dead had continued to pile up though so he might be ready to listen to her. That had not gone well the last time she had tried it so she was reluctant to try again but she did not see that she had much choice. She was very reluctant to risk Neddy's and her life to do so, however.

Reaching up she rubbed at her forehead, feeling the strong hint of an aching head forming. First she would sleep, she told herself firmly, for she badly needed to. Then she would think over things and come to a few decisions. It was past time to stop just letting the MacEnroys take care of her and get a better control over her own life. She was now a woman alone, one with the full responsibility of her sister's child, and it was past time she acted like it.

Chapter Fourteen

Emily rolled out the pie crusts for Mrs. O'Neal's pies, her mind awhirl with thoughts of Iain and what game he played now. Instead of his usual hot and cold moods, he was a perfect gentleman. Since part of that included not making love to her any chance he got she was a little concerned. For a week now he had brought her small gifts from candy to flowers. Instead of stealing kisses when they sat on the back porch he wanted to talk, about her, about him, about what they both wanted in life.

Talking was nice, she told herself firmly. It was good for them to get to know each other as well as possible before they continued the affair they had stumbled into. Emily knew that was right and proper. Her body, however, was not the least bit happy with right and proper. It wanted passion, heat, and excitement. Her body wanted kisses and caresses, not talk.

She sighed. Emily had not realized she could be so shameless. What she wanted broke every rule she had ever been taught. Family and society both heartily condemned such things. Emily wondered why that did not trouble her more.

"You are being unusually quiet," Mrs. O'Neal said as she set down the fruit for the pies.

"Just thinking." Emily glanced at the bowl. "What did you put in with the apples?"

"Some of the berries you and the children collected. Took out what I needed for the jam and had a few left. Thought they would add a nice touch to the pie."

"I suspect they will."

"So what are you thinking on?" Mrs. O'Neal nudged her with her elbow. "Iain?"

"And why would I spend time thinking on him?" Emily asked in her haughtiest voice as she began to place the crust in the pans Mrs. O'Neal had set down.

"Humph. You had a dreamy look in your eye."

"I did *not* have a dreamy look in my eye."

"Oh, yes, there certainly was." Mrs. O'Neal did a dramatic imitation of such a look and Emily had to laugh. "I also noted that the man is courting you."

"Is that what he is doing?" Emily decided that was not a bad thing although she wondered why he even bothered when she had already given him what her mother and other older women had said men always wanted.

"Flowers, even candy. Which was very good, by the way. He has even started painting a picture for you."

"What?" Emily stared at Mrs. O'Neal in shock. "What painting?"

"One of the little gorge up the trail. But I shouldn't have said anything. Must be a surprise for you so best remember to act surprised when he gives it to you."

Emily watched Mrs. O'Neal put fruit in the pies and then put some of her crust on top. Iain was painting her a picture of a spot she had idly mentioned to him. It was going to be a struggle not to try to find which room he was painting in and go have a peek. She inwardly shook her head. There was always the chance Mrs. O'Neal was wrong and Iain was painting it for himself.

There was the echo of a knock on the door and Emily frowned as she wiped her hands to go and see who was there. Her eyes widened when she opened the door to find the Bannisters. She had managed to make the trip into town a few times to have tea with Charlotte but had not felt it safe to ask the woman out to the MacEnroys yet. There did not need to be anyone else pulled into the dangerous mess that her life had become.

"Charlotte, how wonderful to see you." She opened the door wider and smiled at little William. "And you William. Where is George?" she asked Charlotte.

"He is speaking with the MacEnroy brothers. Is it all right that I wheedled a ride with him?"

"Yes, of course it is all right. Come in." She smiled at William. "Shall I find Neddy?"

"That would be lovely," said Charlotte, "although I do not know how long we are to stay."

"I suspect until Mr. Bannister and Iain are done with their business." She brought Charlotte and little William into the parlor and Emily then excused herself to fetch some tea.

Mrs. O'Neal was already putting a tea tray together for her. "I think this is the first time we have had a visitor here. Well, except for the occasional fellow who comes to speak to Iain about business. Do you want me to send Neddy in?" Mrs. O'Neal grabbed some small cakes she had made and kept in the pantry for the children.

"Oh, yes, please. She has brought her boy with her.

I was hoping the two boys would become friends. I can carry the tray in if you could find Neddy for me."

Emily carried the tray into the parlor. It felt odd to be so pleased to offer Charlotte tea and cakes. She only briefly mourned the lack of the fine bone china they had drunk from in the manor house back in England. Such things broke too easily for the life she led now. When Neddy was brought in she and Charlotte talked quietly while the two boys got to know each other. As soon as the awkward first moments had passed and the two boys began to happily play, Emily smiled at Charlotte.

"Success," Emily said, and shared a toast of tea with Charlotte then settled in for a pleasant talk.

Iain shook George's hand when the man came into the stables. "You already have news?"

"Not the news you sent out the letters for. Not yet. Did think you would be interested in why the fool at the bank tried to cheat you."

"Aye. I have had a few people asking me to sell them all or a piece of my land but couldn't figure out who would try to cheat me out of it all or who would use the bank to do it for them."

"Morrison. Harold Morrison."

"Ah. That does explain why the banker did what he did. Morrison would be a nice catch as a customer. He and the old man hated each other which is why the man travels a fair distance to deal with a bank in another town. Man would impress his da if he caught Morrison as a customer."

"Well, his father was convinced his firstborn would soon ruin all he had built so he took him out and gave the seat to his younger son. That fellow is painfully honest and truly understands the job."

Iain laughed and shook his head. "I willnae ask how the fool's da found out the truth." He stroked the nose of the horse he had been grooming and went on to the next in line. "Did you find out anything about those people I asked about?"

"Not much. One thing, a close friend of mine, a classmate from Harvard, told me that the Duke of Collins Wood is an important man, a power within the gentry."

"Ye had a classmate that kenned such things?"

George nodded. "He was English, called himself minor gentry, but claimed to know most of the gentry. He said most of them know one another, or, at least, about one another. Said they were an incestuous bunch. I decided he had something he was bitter about."

Iain grinned. "It certainly sounds that way."

"Well, the duke is not as old as one would think with him being a grandfather and all. He must have wed young and had his son married off young. Stanton is the family name. The man rarely does anything of notice but, according to my friend, he is constantly there at every important event or decision. He suspected the man was a quiet power but one to be reckoned with."

"Did he happen to tell ye how to reach the man?"

"Send a courier, secretly. Address it as being for him and him only."

"Then do so."

"Done. Anything else?"

"I am certain there are a dozen but I have trouble deciding which direction to take in all of this. The priority is to keep Neddy and Emily alive. We cannae keep fighting off the men he hires. At some point one of them will get through and do the job he was hired to."

George shook his head. "I still find it difficult to believe a man would kill a child or that he can find so many men willing to do so for him. It is chilling to think there are men out there willing to do so for a title or fancy properties or money but they do kill for such things all too often."

Iain nodded. "And this man doesnae see Neddy as just a child; he sees him as an obstacle to what he wants therefore he must be removed. And we have to do more than stand against the men he sends hunting us. I am tired of burying the dead," he added in a soft voice.

"I can only imagine." George smiled faintly. "I have not even fired a gun."

"Do ye nay ken how to use a weapon?"

"No. Never had the need that I know of and did not join any of the sporting or shooting clubs at Harvard. So, I do not even own one although I have been informed, numerous times, that I should get a gun and learn how to shoot it."

"If ye decide to do so, we can teach ye."

"I will keep that in mind. So what should I have this courier say to His Grace?"

"His Grace." Iain laughed and shook his head. "Never thought I would ever have one damned thing to do with a person who sat that high at the table. It doesnae surprise me that the duke has a greedy relation, however.

"As for what to say, just that. Albert has killed Annabel and David and now tries verra hard to kill Neddy and Emily. Feel free to tell him about any or all of the attempts. Tell him who she and the boy are with and where. Annabel already let Albert know by writing to the wrong cousin so that willnae matter."

"It is a shame we do not have a photograph of the boy. Maybe seeing what is at risk would move the man. But, I will do what you ask. Let us hope the danger finally gets through to the man."

"Aye, because Emily needs to ken that what is left of her family is on her side."

George nodded and put away the small book he made all his notes in. "I will get right on it. I hope it brings a response but I have to warn you, these things can take months."

"I ken it but we really only have to get through the fall and then most everything comes to a halt. I dinnae think even Albert will do much then and he or whatever men he sends against us will be a lot easier to spot."

Iain just grinned when George laughed. He then shook hands with the man and walked to the house with him so he could collect his wife and child. Iain grinned briefly when he saw Emily in the parlor with Charlotte. The two small boys were arguing genially about whose little wooden train car was better and the women were talking quietly as they sat together on the settee.

"Oh, it is time to go," said Charlotte as she rose and brushed down her skirts. "William, we have to go home now."

William got up with clear reluctance and came over to Charlotte with an obvious dragging of his feet. Emily put a hand over her mouth to hide her smile. It had been a pleasant visit and felt very nice to have a chat with a woman her age. It was also very good for

Neddy to play with a child his age. She followed them to the door and said how Charlotte had to come again soon. She meant it but hoped George would understand that care had to be taken. Neddy ran up, took her hand, and said a very polite farewell.

"Eat now?" asked Neddy the moment the Bannisters were gone.

"Neddy, you just had two of Mrs. O'Neal's little cakes," Emily said as she ruffled his curls. "You cannot be that hungry."

"Aye, I can."

She had to bite back a smile at the way he used the word *aye* just like the MacEnroys. "We will have dinner soon, I am sure, so why not go see what Riley is doing outside."

"Fine."

Although his tone was that of a disgruntled child, he ran off to find Riley. Emily turned to look at Iain, who just lifted his eyebrows in a silent question. She debated whether she should even ask about his business but Emily only hesitated for a moment.

"Did you finish your business with George?" she asked.

He wrapped an arm around her shoulders. "I did. The bank has a new head. The older brother was the one I dealt with and he was quickly replaced by the younger one who actually enjoys bank business. No answer to the letters I sent out a little while ago but George did get news about your family. And he is going to write a note and send it by courier to your uncle, the duke."

"I hope that works. I hope he finally listens."

"All we can do is send him word but ye would think the dead family piling up would have already told him what is happening. And what other information

we have tells me nothing that makes me think the
man will ignore so many dead, shrug it off as silly
coincidence."

"All I want is for him to believe me and I think I
will be satisfied. It is very hard to be in danger and the
head of the family thinks it is nothing but frivolous
talk."

"He will listen this time. I feel it in my bones."

Emily poured the bucket of hot water into the tub
and then tested the temperature of the bathwater.
Most everyone was asleep and Neddy had wanted to
go sleep with Rory so she actually had time to enjoy
her bath. It did not need to be a hasty one as in the
room off the kitchen with the constant sound of
people talking right outside the door. She smiled as
she sprinkled some bath salts she had bought in the
Trading Post over the water for she realized she was
spoiled when it came to her baths.

She stripped off her clothes, checked to make certain her clean garments were laid out on the bed so
she could dress quickly, and then slowly lowered her
body into the water. It was not the nice tub she was accustomed to but it served. She put some soap on the
washrag and began to bathe. When she finished scrubbing herself clean she washed her hair, grabbed the
toweling she had put near the tub, and wrapped it
around her head. Then, because the water was still
nice and warm, she sank down into the tub and just
soaked in it.

Despite her efforts to clear her mind and just
relax, Emily began to think on Albert and how to get
him out of the way. She had already sent one letter to
her grandfather but it had been just before Annabel

and David had been killed. He was the only one she had considered it was safe to write to. Her grandfather might not believe her story about Albert killing her parents but he would not reveal anything to anyone else. She had told Annabel the duke was the only one she could write to but her sister had never warmed up to the man and did not want to. Emily might think her grandfather was a bit pigheaded but he was also wise enough to not let any information get into Albert's hands. He might not fully believe in her suspicions but he would never give any information to one she feared and hated.

Since she had never heard back from her grandfather she had to assume that he still did not believe her. That was sad because he was a man with the power and wealth needed to get rid of Albert. In England he would have to merely have a word with a magistrate and Albert would have been dragged to gaol. Over here, his title would not mean much out in Arkansas but he still had the money and the skill to get others to deal with things for him. He had power and skill and used both ruthlessly when he needed to.

The sound of a door opening pulled her from her thoughts and she frowned, wondering who had come back into the house. Then she shivered and opened her eyes for she felt as if she was being watched. Glancing up she squeaked in shock and crossed her arms over her breasts. Iain was standing right next to the tub.

"Ye dinnae like the room off the kitchen?" He crouched by the side of the tub and dragged his fingers through the water.

"There are a lot of people who go in and out of the kitchen and there is always someone talking in there so, even with the door closed, one can feel exposed."

"Ah, so ye like a lot of privacy for your bath."

"Yes, or the illusion of it. So perhaps you could leave so I can go back to illusion of privacy. So, shoo." She took one arm out so she could make a shooing motion with her hand but, to her annoyance, all that got was a wide grin and Iain making himself more comfortable.

"Iain, you should not be in here. What if someone comes up?"

"They won't. Mrs. O'Neal is tucked up with the boys and my brothers have gone to the Trading Post but don't intend to visit Mabel's side." He laughed when she frowned and then her eyes widened slightly. "Yes, love, they are going to visit the ladies."

"Oh. You did not go?" It hurt to even ask him as she was terrified he would say he was.

Iain gave her a disgusted look instead of answering that foolish question. "Nay, I had no inclination to go. Water is getting cool, love, and your skin will get wrinkly." He stood up, grabbed the other towel she had brought in, and held it up for her.

"You expect me to just stand up?"

"I believe I do."

Before she could tell him he would be frozen in place before she did that, he grabbed her under the arms and pulled her up to her feet. She grabbed at her towel but he was already wrapping it around her. Then he kissed her and she forgot all about the games he was playing with her.

He carried her to her bed and put her down. Then he shed his clothes. The man had no modesty, she thought, but realized she did not care. He was tall, lean, his muscles firm, his skin taut, and he was a pleasure to look at. Emily watched him tug off his pants and then his drawers. There he was in all his glory and she was annoyed that she still had no name for that part of him that jutted out and gave her pleasure when he put it to use. She was just about to ask him what it was called when he gently sprawled on top of her.

"Iain, my hair is all wet and will ruin my pillow," she said, trying to think of practical matters before the feel of the man's body against hers scattered all her wits.

He yanked the pillow out from under her head and tossed it on the floor. "There. Fixed the problem." He gently undid the towel he had wrapped around her and bent his head to kiss her breasts.

Emily wrapped her arms around his neck and held on as he drove her wild with his kisses and caresses, even the occasional little nip soothed by a stroke of his tongue. She then ran her hands over his back and slowly down until she caressed his backside. When she lightly dragged her fingernails over the taut skin there he moved against her and made her desire rise to a fever pitch.

She shuddered as he kissed his way down to her stomach. It moved his body out of her reach and she ached to touch him. A shock went through her when he kissed her thighs and his soft hair brushed against her. Then she froze, torn between shock and piercing pleasure when his kisses moved to the place between her legs. Emily tried to pull away but his hold on her legs kept her still until she lost all urge to flee his kiss.

He teased her until she felt as if she would come apart then leave her there, on the edge of something, and return to her breast or her legs. Emily thought it pure torment even as it brought her great pleasure. Then he slid a finger inside her even as he tortured her with kisses and she knew this time she would break.

It came over her in a wave, a blinding surge of pleasure, and she cried out, arching off the bed. Even as she still rode that powerful wave, he joined their bodies and she wrapped her legs around his waist. Clinging to him like a person afraid of drowning, Emily felt him pound into her, not minding the ferocity of his movements, and then he clutched at her and held her still as he groaned and shook. When he slipped away from her, he pulled her close and held her tight as they both struggled to catch their breath.

Once they were both calmer she reached down and took hold of the part she was determined to get a name for. "What do you call this?"

"Right now? Happy. If you would just move your hand up and—"

"I am serious. It must have a name. I know the doctors have given everything names."

"It is called Lancelot."

Emily just stared at him and then she started to giggle. "No, it is not. I am serious. What is it called?"

He lifted his head and frowned at her. "Ye really dinnae ken?"

"No, I really dinnae ken. Who would tell me? I was just about marriageable age and being prepared for my season during which I would hopefully find a husband. There were very few girls my age about and the adults did not teach us anything. So no, I do not know what this part is called or what my part is called."

"Your sister told you nothing? She was married and the two of ye shared a house."

"I asked her and she, well, got hysterical. Also gave me a scold on how I should never ask such things even of a married woman." Emily shrugged. "So no. I am totally ignorant of these things."

Iain bit back a groan as she moved her hand over him. "Doctors call it a penis."

"That's it?"

"Yes, sorry it isn't more grand. The various euphemisms are much grander."

"I was just thinking it was such a sorry word for something most men consider very important." She smiled when he laughed. "I ought to at least know what parts I am, well, dealing with."

"I have the penis and ye have the vagina."

"A what? Honestly, that is better than the name they give your part but still not what one would think it should be. Suppose that has to do with all the Latin the doctors love." She frowned a little. "What do they call what we just did?"

"Fornicating. All the other words I know are really not for your use."

"That is so like physicians. Take something special and slap a boring name on it." She frowned when he started laughing. "'Tis true. Well, now I know, but I doubt I will ever use any of those."

"Ye thought it would be something exciting or poetic?" he asked, and grinned.

"And why not? It is responsible for the whole human race. If we did not use the parts, there would not be any of us."

Iain laughed and Emily decided he had a nice laugh, infectious. He pulled her over as he rolled onto his back and let her body sprawl on top of his. His penis was nicely nestled between her legs and she could feel it slowly grow harder and bigger. She lay there petting his chest and began to think about what he had done to her and wondered if she could do the same to him.

She began to slowly kiss her way down his body. As she teased his stomach with kisses, licks, and little nips then soothed by her mouth or tongue, he began to make some low, rough noises which let her know he was pleased with it all. Then she slid down a little farther and ran her tongue up the length of him. His whole body jerked and grew tense and she feared she had just found one of those things men could do but women could not. Iain slid his hands in her hair and held her in place, however, and she decided she must be doing something right.

Iain watched her as she loved him with her mouth. Her blond hair was drying and was in a wild tangle around her face. It brushed against his legs and drove him crazy. Then she took him into her mouth and he lost all ability to think straight. For someone with no skill or experience she was doing very well. It was not long before he knew he was teetering on the edge of release so he caught her under the arms and pulled her up his body. As he kissed her, tasting himself on her mouth and adding to his growing frenzy, he joined their bodies and moved her as he wanted her to move until she caught on. To his delight she rode him to the end and they both cried out softly as they found their release.

Iain slowly woke up and looked for Emily, who had fallen asleep in his arms. She sat on the edge of the bed brushing her hair and dressed in her shift and stockings. Glancing out the window he cursed softly, drawing her attention. He sat up and looked for a clock.

"It is two in the morning. I think I heard some of your brothers stagger home."

"Damn. Falling asleep was not in the plans."

She smiled as he moved to drag on his drawers. "You make plans for these, um, evenings, do you?"

"With so many people in this house one rather has to. Oh, damn, I was going to help you empty the tub."

"Not to worry. Plan to use the watering can and pour it out the window into the garden." She smiled as he walked around to her side of the bed and kissed her.

"And that might be a mistake. Too many of those and I willnae leave." He buttoned up his shirt and brushed a kiss over her lips. "Try to get some more sleep. Night, love."

She watched him leave and sighed. He kept calling her *love* but she did not dare take it to mean anything more than an easy word to use for an affectionate pet name. And she had let another night together slide right by without pressing him to tell her anything about how he felt about her. Emily braided her hair, tied it off, and slid into bed. One good thing—at least she was too tired, and satisfied, to stay awake long fretting over things she could not change.

Chapter Fifteen

Emily kept a close watch out as she and Mrs. O'Neal drove the buggy into town. Neither of them actually had a dire need for anything but the MacEnroys had taken all the children fishing and Mrs. O'Neal had been eager to go to the shop, to look over the goods in the store at her leisure. Emily had not had the heart to say no, so even though she did not really like being outside the walls of the MacEnroy home, she had come shopping with the woman.

She stiffened her spine and told herself to cease being a frightened little mouse. Now that she thought on it she did not even go riding anymore unless one of the men went with her. Iain insisted on it but she had not complained either. Emily knew it was because she was glad of the extra protection. It was time she ceased cowering behind the men. This was her trouble and she would face it. Like a man, she thought, and grinned.

Mrs. O'Neal called out a greeting to a Mrs. Potter who was outside her home beating her carpets. She then pulled up by the fence, introduced Emily, and began to talk with the woman about a lot of people

Emily did not know. Emily was uncomfortably aware of the fact that she now had a big secret the women who loved their gossip would just love to sink their teeth into.

It was not until they were back on their way to the store that Emily realized something. "Your name is Mary?" she asked Mrs. O'Neal.

Mrs. O'Neal briefly frowned at her. "Yes. Didn't you know that?"

"No. No one told me. They all call you Mrs. O'Neal and that was how you were introduced to me."

"Well, of course the boys call me that. Need to. I have to hold on to some kind of proper place in that household. But you can call me Mary if you must. Don't much like the name myself. Rather boring name, truth be told."

"Mary is a good name. A lot of people use it."

"Especially amongst the Irish, but, be truthful, it is a boring name. There is no lilt to it, no hint of liveliness or beauty. It just sits there."

It was not easy but Emily quelled the urge to laugh. "Well, it goes well with O'Neal."

"I know that but I am not Irish, am I? It is one thing about me Tommy's folks liked." Mrs. O'Neal frowned at the mention of her late husband's parents. "It is the one real fault I had in their eyes. If I had been Mary Callahan or Mary O'Leary and had a crucifix round my neck I would have been completely welcome. Instead I was just plain, Mary Smith, that Protestant."

"It was Mary Smith?" Emily thought she deserved a prize for not falling down laughing.

"It was. As plain a name as anyone could think of. Still think they just got weary of trying to find something clever or original. My siblings all had much better names. Instead I was just Mary Smith, the Protestant girl their son would go to hell for. Do you know they have never come to see his sons, never even written to ask after them?"

"That is sad. Your husband was their only son, you said?"

"He was and my Rory is the spitting image of him."

"They may not know how to get here or cannot afford to. Were the children all baptized Catholic?" Emily could already see the answer to that question in Mary's cross expression.

"No. I had them baptized into the Protestant church."

Emily winced. "I suspect that did not help."

"No. Tommy took great delight in telling them though." Mrs. O'Neal smiled.

"Have you sent them a letter or two?"

"I can't write, can I. Tommy got someone to send them a note with each child born. And, yes, I know you can teach me and you're teaching all the others, but I have twenty years or more on most of them. Too damned old to be doing schooling. Once you get the children taught they can read anything I need read to me. Tommy's folks can't read, either, though I know they find someone to read to them if they have a want to know. Probably one of Tommy's siblings."

"I will write a letter for you. Maybe there is someone in this place who takes photographs and we can send one of them as well. That is, if you wish."

Mrs. O'Neal frowned in thought for a few moments then nodded. "We'll do that. If I get no answer I will be certain the split between my Tommy and his family was final."

Emily just nodded and looked around carefully as they entered the small collection of buildings they called a town. Photography had gained popularity and she hoped that, even in this area, some person had what was needed to offer such a service. Either that or a traveling one would pass through at some time. When they halted in front of the Trading Post she noticed that Mrs. O'Neal was careful not to park anywhere near the door to the tavern.

Once inside the store Mabel and Mrs. O'Neal fell into a friendly argument over the prices of her material. Emily went to the front window and studied the area. She had seen such places in her travels to the cabin she had shared with her sister. There was nothing more than what was absolutely needed and she suspected it would never truly become a real town. It would disappear as soon as people were able to safely go to a town that actually warranted a name. Even the bank was no more than a small house that had bars on the windows and a room for a large safe. It was more a place to stop briefly in one's journey than an actual town.

Then she caught sight of several men walking toward the bank. One of them was very well dressed and tall, with hair as blond as hers and she froze. A heartbeat later she ducked behind one of the curtains that framed the window. She peered out again and her heart raced with alarm. What was Albert doing here, so close to her and Neddy and so soon after his last failure?

"Mrs. O'Neal," she called softly.

Turning to look at her, Mrs. O'Neal frowned. "What are you doing? Why are you hiding?"

"Yes," she hissed, "I am hiding. Can you see the men about to go into the bank?"

"I see them. Five of them. One of them's a tall fellow in fancy clothes. Why?"

"That is Albert."

Mrs. O'Neal hurried closer to the window. "That Albert who is causing us such trouble?"

"Yes. No, don't pay attention to me. Act like you are studying the items in the window." Mrs. O'Neal started studying a tea set that Emily suspected had come from someone in need of money, either someone passing through or even someone in the area trading for goods. "I need to get out of here without being seen."

"What is going on?" asked Mabel as she walked up.

"Some fellow that's working hard to kill our Emily and her nephew is over at the bank so she's trying to hide. Don't want him seeing us leave." Mrs. O'Neal put her hands on her hips and scowled. "Man shouldn't look so good. Ought to look like the evil snake he is."

"Want me to shoot him?" Mabel stared at the man. "Could hit him easy from here but you'd have to pay for a new window."

Emily stared at the woman in shock. "You can't just shoot him down in the streets of town."

"Why not? Want him shot somewhere else?"

"No! I just want to get away from him without him seeing me."

"Shooting the bastard would solve that," said Mrs. O'Neal and then she frowned at Mabel and said, "even if it does cost us the price of a window. A cracked window, too," she grumbled, pointing to the crack that ran down one side.

"Cracked not broken. I shoot that fellow and it'll be broke then, won't it." Mabel frowned out at the men in front of the bank. "Bit of a shame to shoot him 'cause he sure is a pretty fellow."

Emily stared at the two women and then shook her head. "You cannot just shoot him. He is doing nothing to us at the moment. What explanation would you give for shooting him?"

"That he planned on doing something illegal," said Mabel. "You said he was after killing you and the boy. Reason enough for me."

"But he is not after us right this moment, not shooting us, not even looking at us. You would simply be killing him on the street. No, just show us how to get out of here without being seen. I do not know how the laws work here but where I come from you cannot just shoot a person even if you know he is rotten to the core."

Mabel shrugged her wide shoulders. "Seems fair to me. But I can get you out of here without him seeing though it looks like he will be going into the bank soon."

"The bank has big windows," said Mrs. O'Neal. "With our luck he will be looking out of one just as we try to slip away."

"Go out the back. I will bring the buggy around and you can ride out of here without him seeing." Mabel took one last look at Albert and shook her head. "Man that fine-looking shouldn't be so dirty on the inside." She looked at Emily. "Get going out the back. Only take me a few minutes to pull around with that buggy. Waste of a day so far," she muttered as she started toward the door. "You bought nothing and I didn't get to shoot that man."

Emily shook her head and looked at Mrs. O'Neal. "Mabel is a bit of an odd stick."

"I know." Mrs. O'Neal started for the back of the store. "Wanting us to pay for the window just 'cause she'd break it doing a kindness for us. Just trying to get someone to pay for the window that is already cracked, if you ask me."

It was not just Mabel who was odd, Emily thought as she hurried after Mrs. O'Neal. They stepped out the back of the store onto a narrow landing and waited for Mabel. The woman drove the buggy around a moment later and stopped it right by the stairs leading down from the landing.

They climbed into the buggy and Mrs. O'Neal thanked Mabel, promising to get back to shop as soon as she was able, then snapped the reins and set off for home. Emily kept a close watch behind them until they were a good distance from the little town but no one followed. Although she did not feel particularly safe, she relaxed a little.

"No one chasing us?"

"No," Emily answered. "It appears we got away without him seeing us." She frowned as she thought on what she would tell Iain. "I suspect the MacEnroys will think I should have let Mabel shoot him."

"Yup. She would have killed him too. Woman can shoot really well."

"But it would have caused her trouble. He was just standing there and I suspect no one really knows what he has been up to. It would have looked as if she just picked some random fellow on the street and killed him."

"Might have. Might not have. Never can tell with Mabel. She knows a lot of people and they'd listen to her. Don't think anyone in the area would be willing to see her hang for shooting a man none of them know and who doesn't live here. And the boys would've gone in and told everyone why he needed killing."

Emily was beginning to think she should have let the woman kill Albert. It would have solved a lot of their troubles. It certainly would have ended the trouble she had brought to the MacEnroy house. She began to suspect she was about to get an earful from the MacEnroys when the story was told.

"Why the devil didnae ye let her shoot the fool?" demanded Iain as he filled his plate with food.

Emily sighed. They had waited until the evening meal to tell the brothers what had happened in town. She was surprised at how they had all stared at her as if she was mad or witless. Yet, she could not really say she would have acted differently.

"I rather thought that she could go to jail for it."

"Nay." Robbie shook his head. "We would have spoken up for her."

Thinking of all seven brothers swearing to what a threat Albert was made her think that there had been little threat to Mabel. It all would have been cleared up quickly. She was not even certain there was any sheriff or constable in the town.

"Then I apologize. It appears I made an error in judgment."

Iain almost winced. She was speaking in her very proper, very English tone, which meant she was upset. The more upset Emily got the more precise her accent, the more like gentry she sounded. He suddenly realized that the accent did not bother him as it once had, just the realization that she was upset.

"Weel, since ye saw him in town, it might be a good idea if we go and see what we can see. Might even find him"—he smiled coldly—"and have ourselves a little chat."

"I can see how that might be a good idea but I can also see how it could get someone hurt or killed. Yes,

I want the man gone, but I don't want anyone hurt in the doing of it."

"Weel, the fairies willnae come and whisk him away," said Robbie, who then muttered a curse when Matthew smacked him on the back of the head. "Just pointing out that no matter how one would like it all to be so gentlemanly and no one hurt and all, there will have to be some fire and lightning. Always will be when dealing with a man like that."

"I know," Emily said, and sighed. "But one cannot help but wish for something better now and then."

Mrs. O'Neal nodded but said, "You get a few more years on you, dearie, and you will see the better and nicer is one of those miracles that only comes once in a blue moon."

"We will think on what needs doing and try to get ye one of those blue moon miracles but dinnae put too much hope on one," said Iain.

"I will not." She looked at Mrs. O'Neal and said, "I am sorry your day of shopping was ruined. I hope we can arrange so you have another day free to do it."

"We will take them fishing again when ye decide ye want to go and it is safe," said Iain. "Nay many days left for fishing unless ye wish to dress up like a bear to hold off the cold."

"I will tell you when I am of a mood to go. Thank you," said Mrs. O'Neal.

"So he is in the town. I have to wonder if he has been there all along or only just arrived because the men he hires keep failing." Emily frowned. "I wonder how he knows that?"

"Could be he has someone telling him or could be a survivor goes back to him." Iain shook his head. "Would not be a bright one because anyone with a brain would ken that Albert is the bigger threat. That is a man who would shoot the messenger."

"Oh, most certainly. Especially ones like those men. Albert is very aware of his own consequence. Everyone else is an underling and can be easily disposed of. There were rumors that some of his servants were killed for things like dropping a napkin but no one could prove anything."

"A man who goes about killing his own kin will do just about anything," said Mrs. O'Neal.

Emily glanced at the children who sat at a shorter table in the far end of the kitchen. They did not appear to be listening but she was sure they would find out later. It was probably not the best of talk to have around the children but there were few other times when they all sat together and could talk things out.

"Is there no law around here?"

"About a day's ride away," replied Iain. "They are never too interested in dealing with anything that requires they leave their town, which is near to a city compared to our little hole in the wall. No use going to them, trust me on that."

That news depressed Emily's spirits so much she just wanted to get away somewhere and sit, possibly by the water. No law, no just shooting the man, and no way to turn an army of armed men toward him. Everything worked against them. She wondered if that was fate at work or something far worse.

"I forgot to say but I got something that was being sent to ye. Picked it up when I went to get my horse shod." Nigel patted all his pockets and pulled out a letter before handing it to Emily. "It looks to have been moving about for quite a while. Dinnae ken how it got here from your sister's place. Someone out there told them to send it to you here."

Emily's hands shook faintly as she took the letter. "That would have been Maggie. She and her family lived only a short walk from us. Well, what would be considered short by those who live here. I wrote to her once I knew Albert already knew where Neddy and I were. I believe this is from her actually. Which means it may take me a while to decipher it."

"She cannae write?"

"She can write quite well but she is from England, too. Yorkshire. They have so many different ways of saying things and then her family came here and landed in Boston, so you have a New England way of talking mixed with the Yorkshire." She shook her head. "And then she married and moved here. You really cannot understand half of what she says when she talks and when she gets excited or emotional it is truly like a foreign tongue. But we shall see. She may have had someone else help her if she felt she had something of great import to say. I think I should wait until after dinner to read it."

"Can ye actually do that?" Iain teased as he watched how she kept looking at the letter as if she could read some of it through the covering.

"You can read it when we put out dessert in a bit, Emily. Dessert is not so distracting," said Mrs. O'Neal.

Emily nodded and was finally able to set the letter aside. She hoped there had been no trouble at any of the other houses or any of the other people got hurt. One could never be sure about rough men willing and able to slaughter one family and burn their house. In their disappointment over failing to get what they went for they could easily have wreaked destruction on others.

* * *

Emily sat in the parlor on the settee and found herself flanked by Iain and Robbie. She carefully opened the packet that held Maggie's letter and was amazed by the lengthy note the woman had written. Even better she had sent three of her drawings of David and Annabel. The woman had not liked Annabel all that much but Emily had always suspected the woman had been sweet on David.

One drawing of Annabel was of her sister sitting on one of the high rocks and staring toward England. Another was of David, who sat on another rock and stared at his wife. The last was of David and Neddy and, by the look of Neddy, it was from shortly before they had been killed. She handed the drawings to Iain and opened the letter.

As Emily had feared Maggie had written the way she talked, which would mean a slow read for her. She read through the condolences quickly and she could tell Maggie was brokenhearted about the death of David and explained why she had been so deeply fond of him. He had looked and acted like her eldest brother, who had been killed in a fight on the ship over. Now to know David was murdered brought it all back to her.

The bad news hit Emily hard. Someone had dug up the grave marked Neddy. She suspected the men had gone back the next day or sooner and in poking around found the grave marked for little Edward. Then found out it was empty. That was all Albert had needed to get himself out here to lead. She sighed and then looked up at Neddy.

"Neddy?" she called, and the boy looked at her. "Remember Maggie from home?"

"Yes. She is Abbie and Nicky's mom. Is she hurt?"

"No, darling, she has just written me a letter. And she says right here that Abbie and Nicky say hello."

"Can we go see them?"

"Not right now but I will think on it." She shook her head when he lost interest and hurried out of the room.

By the time she finished the letter she missed Maggie like a limb. The woman had been claimed by Annabel, who had then swiftly forgotten all about her. The teas shared were almost always, Maggie, Emily, and David. Even though they were at their cabin and Annabel always called Maggie a friend, she had rarely had tea with them. Emily had guessed that Annabel had detected Maggie's love for David and totally misinterpreted it.

"Well, Maggie says that someone came back to the cabin and checked it all over. In the process they found Neddy's grave and dug it up so they know he was never in there." She looked up to find everyone looking at her in shock. "What?"

"Ye had a grave marked for Neddy?" asked Iain.

"Did you not see it?"

All of the MacEnroys shook their heads.

Emily struggled to explain. "David decided we needed some insurance for our Neddy. If any of us got grabbed we could just say the child is dead, there's the grave. And all that. I thought it a brilliant idea. My sister not so much. Since the boy was who was hunted, we took him out of the running. That was one reason I was so stunned that they killed David and Annabel. With the child supposedly dead and buried there was nothing to gain."

"Except, perhaps, your sister getting pregnant and birthing yet another son. As a, if ye will excuse the language, breeder, she was always a threat." Matthew shook his head. "Where was this grave because we never saw it and we looked all around."

"It was on the other side of the garden. David made it flat so it would not stick up. No mounding. Even made the headstone flat but it had Neddy's full name on it, some religious picture, a weeping angel or something, dates and country. Perhaps because the garden was so full this year it had hidden it, covered the top. I really can't say because, living there for three years or so I was so accustomed to it I never really saw it from day to day. I also tried not to think of it often because it gave me the chills.

"Nothing much else of interest. Some gossip about the McDonald wife being very friendly with Jacob Potsdam and a few tales like that. Maggie always blames the hills. She claims it gives folk the idea that they can act like animals, too. And she is carrying her tenth child and plans to do a specific operation on her husband soon as she can find the right knife."

"Tenth child?" said Mrs. O'Neal.

Emily nodded and grinned. "You would never know to look at her. She says she is part rabbit. But she does not look any older than she did when I met her, not in figure or face, and not even graying hair. To be fair there are two sets of twins in that number."

"But ten children." Robbie shook his head. "How on earth does one family care for so many?"

"And how does a woman find the time to draw such good pictures with ten kids running around?" said Iain, still studying the pictures Emily had handed him.

"Our enemy is a tricky bastard but more than that he is completely insane."

"I think so."

"So what does one do with a madman?" asked Duncan.

"Same thing ye do with a rabid dog," said Iain.

"But how does one find him?"

"He will be lurking around here. There are a number of us who can watch for him," said Matthew.

"So you will all take time from your work, your living, to hunt for this maniac? Does that not seem just a bit unreasonable?" Emily asked quietly. "Give him the opening he seeks to destroy what you have? I think he is after more than ridding himself of heirs now; I think he wants to be rid of the people who have blocked him at every turn. You have to think that every small thing you neglect, every bit of income you lose, and so on, means he wins."

"Do ye really believe that?" Iain asked.

"I do. From what I know of dear Cousin Albert, every time he is stopped from getting what he wants he gets angry and he plans to make the one who blocked him pay. I fear we are not simply enemies any longer, we are impediments and dear Albert gets particularly rabid about those."

Chapter Sixteen

Trying desperately not to wring her hands as she paced, Emily wondered how long it would take to find Albert. She wished Iain had listened to her. Albert was clever and dangerous. The man had no qualms about sending people out to kill people he felt were in his way but he was also more than willing to do the killing himself. Emily had the feeling Iain saw Albert only as English gentry, a breed of people who did little with their lives save spend their fortunes, money earned off the backs of others, and who would never actually fight hard for their lives. They would beg or bargain.

"Sit down, Emily. He will be fine." Mrs. O'Neal nudged Emily into a seat.

"Iain doesn't understand what he is dealing with."

"He has gone after a killer. Think the boy knows that well enough."

Emily shook her head. "Yes, Albert is a killer but, in Iain's mind, he is also just gentry, I think. He does not have a high opinion of that group or any true respect."

"But Iain has fought the man already, several times."

"No, he has fought the men Albert hired to do his killing for him. That actually just proves Iain's opinion. He hired rough men who undoubtedly thought hunting down a woman and a child would be easy work. Even if told of Iain and his brothers they would have just shrugged. Fight a group of shepherds? Ha-ha. The men Albert hired probably thought him an idiot and a coward for not doing such an easy killing himself."

"More fool them," said Mrs. O'Neal as she poured boiling water into a teapot and set it on the table to steep. "Those MacEnroy boys are not fools or idiots. I wager they have things figured out and will know how to end that man. I can't think that he will be able to gather any more fools to fight for him. It often astonishes me how quickly word spreads around here about things that happen or who to watch out for."

An ache started behind her eyes and Emily used both hands to rub at her forehead. It was terrible of her but she dearly wished Albert would just go away, permanently. She really should have let Mabel just shoot the man down like a dog when they were all at the store. It would have been justice at last for her parents and Annabel and David. Emily was horrified by that thought and yet also disgusted that she had not seized the chance and worried about the consequences later. Iain was an honest man, however, and that put him at a severe disadvantage when facing a snake like Albert.

"If he cannot gather any more men because word is out about his offer then why are you so worried?" asked Mrs. O'Neal as she poured them each some tea.

"As I said, Albert is quite capable of doing his own killing. I suspect he has some of his own chosen men with him as well. The others he hired were tossed at us to judge our strength." Emily was certain of that now that she had thought on it all night.

"Oh." Mrs. O'Neal slowly stirred some sugar into her tea. "You sound very sure of that."

"I am. What Albert is doing has preyed on my mind and that is the possibility which kept churning up through all the fear and confusion. I know Iain and his brothers think I am making Albert some sort of grand, heroic figure of evil and just shrug aside all I say. Yet, it is the only thing that makes sense. I think the first attack was because they saw us and thought they could avoid attacking this place if they caught me on the road."

"But they wouldn't have gotten the boy and, from what you have said, the boy is the one who is most important."

"Yes, it is important that he get rid of Neddy." She lightly rubbed her chest over her heart. "My, it hurts even to say it."

"That it does. Sweet little boy even when he gets bossy or stubborn."

Emily smiled. "I know. Anyway, it is vital that he remove the heir. I am just a pest. I think the man may want me dead because I tried to cause trouble for him. I know His Grace listened to me. I have no idea if that cost Albert or not because Annabel and I were already on the run."

"Do you think the authorities are after him in England?"

"That would be lovely but we cannot know for sure. Albert could be thinking that, as a close relation to the boy, he could use whatever authorities he found here to help him get hold of the boy after he got rid of me. Once in control of Neddy he would then have the time to make certain the child's death looks like an accident or an illness. There are too many ways that could be done."

"There certainly are, true enough. Let us hope Iain gets the bastard."

Iain secured his mount to the hitching post outside the tavern. A fancy name, he thought, for a place that was just like every other saloon he had ever been in. His brothers dismounted and did the same. They were not certain they would find Albert in the saloon but it was decided it was the best place to start looking. What he would do when he found the man was something he was still not sure of. It would be good to just shoot him, as Mabel had wanted to, but that would require a lot of explaining. There might not be any real law in the area but there were a few people called on regularly to settle such things and he was not on the best terms with any of them. He had never thought being a landowner could be such a contentious job.

As they walked in the girls in the saloon all perked up. Iain suspected a couple of his brothers would slip away now and then to enjoy their favors if there was no sign of Albert. He just hoped they did not all decide to entertain themselves at the same time. Instinct told him he should not allow any of them to be alone until Albert was no longer a threat.

He went to the bar, ordered a whiskey, and then turned around to survey the men gathered in the place. As he sipped his drink his gaze caught on one particular man. He was tall, well-dressed, and had blond hair. At the table sat four other men, all well-dressed, and hard-eyed. He suspected they were

Albert's handpicked guard, the one Emily had spoken of, and would bear close watching.

Now that he was here, within reach of the man, Iain had no real idea of how to go about ending the threat he was to Emily and Neddy. He had a little more understanding of how she had felt when Mabel had offered to shoot him for her. When no immediate threat was there it became too much like cold-blooded murder. He wondered if there was any way to get the man to draw on him and if he was fast enough to beat that draw.

"Wish he was facing our way," said Matthew. "Cannae be shooting a man in the back, even a bastard like him."

"I was just thinking the same," replied Iain. "Got a better understanding of why Emily said no to Mabel's kind offer." He sipped some more whiskey as Matthew laughed.

"Maybe you could draw him into a game of cards."

Iain looked at Duncan, who stood on his left and slowly nodded. "Could try that. Lot of men get heated over a game of cards." He frowned. "I just dinnae think I have the gaming skills though. Never much took to gambling. Didnae have the money to test myself."

"And we have no idea how skilled he is," said Matthew.

"I have heard it said that the English gentry are all hardened gamblers." Iain frowned. "Never heard whether many are good at it or not. Mostly ye just hear about the ones who gamble away all the money, put the manor house into hock, and so forth. But some must be good, aye, and with our luck, he would be one of them."

"And a skilled duelist. Probably should have found out more about the man from Emily."

"I think one of his men has recognized us," whispered Nigel as he leaned across Matthew.

"Good." Iain smiled coldly when the man turned to look at him. "Let him ken that we are onto him."

Matthew shifted in place and set his empty glass on the bar. "I have a bad feeling about this."

Iain stared at his brother. Matthew's bad feelings too often proved a good warning. He wondered if Albert could be ready for them yet could not figure out how the man could be. Iain stared at the man, at the four men with him, and then at the table they sat around. He idly wondered why Albert had a bell on the table. Glancing around the saloon he saw other men tense and watch Albert, as if waiting for a signal. They were all hard-looking men, not locals. He looked back at Albert, who looked far too relaxed.

"I think we should leave," said Iain, and he started toward the door.

He heard the sound of guns being drawn and flung himself to the floor. He watched as his brothers either did the same or dove over the bar to hide behind it. Iain drew his gun and looked for Albert as the shooting started. The man had moved to the other side of the table so he could watch the chaos he had undoubtedly arranged. He held a pistol in his hand but was not shooting at anyone. The locals had all ducked behind their tables and drawn their guns and the men working for Albert were shooting back.

Iain waved Nigel to slip behind him and then get behind the bar. As soon as his brother disappeared behind the bar, he waved at Robbie to follow. Once his brothers were safe, Iain started to edge back himself. He could see Albert had shielded himself with his table and was exchanging shots with some red-bearded man Iain had often seen around the boardinghouse. Then the man looked at him. Iain edged back some more as he watched the man aim at him but then Albert suddenly cried out and clutched his side.

Iain took the moment to stand up and start to move around to get behind the bar. Then something slammed into his head. He fell back against the bar, the pain making his head spin. Then the blackness started to roll over him and he grabbed the bar as he began to sink to his knees. He felt hands grab his arms and pull him. It took too long for him to understand that he was being yanked over the bar by his brothers.

Someone called his name and he realized he was now seated in someone's arms. He looked up but all he saw was blood. Lifting up a shaking hand he wiped it away from his eyes and knew it was his own blood.

"Iain! Did the bullet go in? Are ye able to speak?" said Matthew, but Iain winced for it was as if his brother was yelling in his ear.

"Head hurts," Iain muttered, then slumped, able to hear, but unable to respond.

"Oh, hell, he went out," said Matthew.

"But he is alive," said Robbie, and he placed a hand on Iain's chest. "I can feel his heartbeat."

"Duncan, shoot that bastard," ordered Matthew.

There was so much pain in his head Iain knew he could soon disgrace himself by weeping. All he could do was keep his eyes closed against the insult of any light and not move. He wished he had the strength and sense to speak to his brothers but that proved to be beyond him. He could not even see who held him because the blood was still running into his eyes.

The shooting stopped and he almost wept with relief when the sharp sound of bullets ended. Then the person holding him stood up, dragging Iain up with him. Iain groaned as his stomach churned and his head throbbed. He tried to ask to be set down but all he heard was a garbled mutter. An arm went around his waist and he was forced to take a step. It was too much and Iain gave in to the blackness that had been waiting for him.

"Well, we will be hearing what happened now," said Mrs. O'Neal.

Emily frowned. "We will?"

"The men are back." Mrs. O'Neal frowned as she stood up. "They are riding hard."

That did not sound good, Emily thought. "They have come back?"

Mrs. O'Neal stood up and started toward the front door. "They have run back."

Emily hurried after Mrs. O'Neal. Why would they run back to the house if everything had gone well? She was suddenly terrified of the answer to that puzzle. She stood behind Mrs. O'Neal as the woman opened the door. Matthew was pulling a limp Iain off the back of his horse and she gasped. When she swayed Mrs. O'Neal's hand grabbed her arm and held her steady. Emily took several deep breaths and felt herself steady.

"Get some hot water and rags, child," Mrs. O'Neal ordered, and Emily ran to the kitchen.

Once in the kitchen she grasped the edge of the sink and fought to gain some control, lecturing herself about her weakness. He was still alive, she told herself. He needed help and it was no time to give in to foolish nerves. Head wounds also bled badly. She had learned that as a child. His brothers had looked worried but not grieved.

Feeling more prepared, she got the bucket of hot water and some of the rags Mrs. O'Neal kept in the cupboard. Hefting the full bucket, she started up the stairs. Matthew came down and took the bucket from her.

"Bullet didnae go into his head. Just scraped his head. Got himself a new part in his hair. Head wounds just bleed bad."

"I know," she said as he handed Mrs. O'Neal the bucket and she put the rags on the bedside table where she could reach them.

As she watched Mrs. O'Neal work and handed the woman whatever she asked for, Emily finally got a glimpse of Iain's wound. It was bad but not life-threatening, although she was no doctor so her assurances to herself did little to ease the icy knot of fear in her stomach. It looked to be much similar to the wound she got on her arm. She could only hope Iain's wound healed as well as hers had.

The bandage that Mrs. O'Neal wrapped around his head would have made her laugh if she was not so worried. Emily knew the woman was trying to put the other men at ease when she tied it off with a bow. There were actually a few smiles. Then she shooed his brothers out and turned to Emily.

"The bullet just skidded across his skull but it is a deep cut. I could see the bone in places but it wasn't cracked or anything. But if all goes well he will wake and just have one hell of a headache. If you need a rest from sitting with him, I would ask one of the brothers. I will take care of Neddy for now."

Emily blinked and frowned at her. "*I* am going to sit with him?"

"Yup. Man needs to be watched. Don't want him up and trying to walk for a while or anything like that." She grabbed a chair from the corner of his room and set it by the bed. "There are books to read I can get or I can sit here and you can look for something."

"Why are there books? None of them can read."

"I have no idea. Think they got them clearing out some cabin that got burned or they were left behind by the people who lived there and decided moving here was a mistake and left. They collect up whatever was left when they find one of those, a deserted or burned cabin. Now I will go get you some food but it may be a while before I can bring any up." She started for the door. "If he has to use the chamber pot or something like that just call one of the lads."

"All right. I will be fine."

"I am certain you will be. Do not fret. Head wounds are treacherous but this doesn't look like a really bad one. I truly saw no crack in the bone and there was no movement when you touched it." She laughed at the face Emily made. "I know, I know, disgusting but if you are going to learn how to fix people up you have to be ready for things to be rather disgusting. And in these parts there can be a lot of fixing up of people needed. There's a bell here by the door"—she tapped it—"and a yank will sound the bell in the kitchen if you need something."

Emily sighed and sat on the chair. It was a well-made chair but it was hard and Emily expected she would notice that very painfully soon enough. She sat up straight, as the chair inspired her to, and watched

Iain. She thought he was sleeping restfully. At least she hoped it was sleep and not unconsciousness.

It was not long before Emily knew it was going to be a difficult time ahead for her. Sitting and staring at someone who was sleeping was no fun, was not even vaguely interesting. She began to think of all the things she might be able to do to pass the time. She had a journal she could write in but that rarely took very long. However, she would ask if she could get it. Mrs. O'Neal had asked her if she could knit so there must be the materials needed to do so. Another thing she could do as she sat there.

"Well, Iain, it looks as if you are stuck with me for a while. The fact that you do not appear to hear me talking is somewhat alarming but, then, it might be good since you are stuck with me until you decide to wake up."

She leaned forward and took his hand in hers. It was still warm and that eased her mind. "I should have warned you better about him. Told you more about him. At the time it just did not seem important, that it was all just my opinion. And there were seven of you." She shook her head. "Matthew said you hit him so we may be lucky and he'll die. Poisoning of the wound from the bullet or blood loss or something. You will want to be awake for that."

"How is he?"

Startled by the voice when she had not heard anyone come in, Emily clasped a hand over her heart and looked at Matthew. The man stood on the opposite side of the bed and his expression was so rigid she knew he was deeply worried and fighting to hide it. Emily wished she knew more so that she could give him some uplifting news.

"Mrs. O'Neal says . . ."

"I ken what she says," Matthew said, his tone almost snappish. "What do ye think?"

"I think what she does. I know nothing about wounds. I grew up in pastoral Hertfordshire, Matthew. I know little to nothing about doctoring. He is not feverish and I know that to be a good thing but, sadly, it is still early. His head is whole, no bones cracked or broken, and he is strong. Head wounds are a mystery to even the best of physicians."

His shoulders slumped. "Fool stayed on the wrong side of the bar for too long, making sure the rest of us got behind it. Same damn thing he always does, puts himself out there while shielding us."

Emily smiled. "He is the oldest. It is his place and he is very aware of that."

"He has carried us for too long. Didnae even do so when the bairns were of an age to scream a lot. Hungry? Scream. Wet? Scream. Too much noise? Scream." He shook his head. "He was even doing most of the watching of us when my parents were still alive. It was Iain who went after Geordie when he ran into our burning house. I always wondered why it wasnae our mither or da. I guess some people are just made that way."

She nodded. "And that is what made him go after Albert, I suspect. That need to protect."

"Weel, Albert was becoming a problem. I was getting fair sick of digging holes for all the fools he sent after us."

"Oh." She had never given a thought to what happened to the bodies left behind. "Rather gruesome thought."

Matthew laughed at the face she made. "Had to be done. Draw the scavengers if ye dinnae."

"Oh, Matthew." She pressed a hand to her stomach

as he laughed again and became aware of the fact that she still held Iain's hand. "Maybe we can speak of other things?"

"I went and found the locals who helped defend us and thanked them. That is something I think old Albert didnae consider, that the others in the saloon would give us a hand."

"No, he would not. I just wish I knew how he figured out where to set a trap for you. I have thought and thought and I do not believe he saw me that day I was in town."

"I had a look around, looking at the line of sight from bank to store and then store to bank. I noticed something. If one looks in the bank windows at the right time of day, just about the time of day ye were in the shop, they just reflect all that is around them. He could have seen you in the short time you stood in the window or he recognized Mrs. O'Neal. Everyone kens who she is and who she works for."

"I see. But if he saw me why did he not come after me?"

"Ye didnae have the boy with you."

"Of course. And knowing I went to town, saw him, he would assume I would tell Iain."

For a moment Matthew stared at Iain and said nothing. Emily felt uncomfortable, certain the brothers had to blame her, in some small way, for what had happened. Albert was her enemy. Without her and Neddy here the man would not pay any attention to the MacEnroys as, to Albert, they were just poor farmers. She would take that threat away if she could but she had to think of Neddy. If she and the child were on their own, she was certain they would soon be dead.

"I best get back to work. Ye will let us ken when he does wake, aye?"

"Yes, of course I will. I suspect I will also have to call on you for help now and then."

"Call away. We will be near at hand and there is always at least one of us lurking close to the house."

"Did you discover where Albert went to after the attack in the saloon?"

"Nay. He and his men all rode out and disappeared into the hills. We have been looking around the hills but have found nothing. Maybe he has fled home."

"One can only hope."

Matthew left and she sighed, idly patting Iain's limp hand. What Matthew had told her about Iain came as no real surprise. It did worry her a bit, however, because Iain's protective tendencies could keep putting him in Albert's path and that could prove deadly next time. There was no changing a man's nature, though. Iain would stand between danger and the weaker for as long as he could. She had guessed that about him and Matthew's stories had confirmed her opinion.

"Brave fool," she muttered. "This is not your fight and we shall have to have a good talk about that when you recover your senses."

She could not have him getting himself killed for her sake. She would never survive that sacrifice. There had to be something she could do to get him to stop taking chances. There should be something she could do to get help in ridding her of Albert's threat. Letters had gone out to Iain's acquaintances so perhaps she should send a few out to hers. If she could get word to the duke perhaps he would finally accept that Albert was a threat and responsible for every family death in the last few years. He had not really believed her when she had claimed that Albert had killed her parents. It was true that her proof was thin and she mostly used her own feelings about the man but her grandfather had to have been considering the possibility that she was right.

The duke was a reasonable man so she was sure he must have been thinking on what she had said. It had not been quick enough for her but it might be useful now. The dead were piling up and she knew Albert would not stop until he added her and Neddy to that sad pile. What she had to do was compose a letter detailing all her suspicions, rational points needed to be made, and then he might consider the possibility.

She had to get past the fact that he had been Albert's guardian for many years before the man had reached his adulthood. Emily did not think there was any great affection there but the man felt as if he had a duty to Albert. What she needed to do was make him remember that he had a larger duty to his other family as well. It was shrinking every day through Albert's need to be rid of anyone who stood in his way or worked to make his goal more difficult to reach. Perhaps she should even mention how, once he was rid of all the other obstacles to his goal, he would start eyeing the duke himself. Her grandfather was not so very old and could live a number of years yet. That would shortly begin to annoy Albert.

As she composed the letter in her mind she had to smile. The words she thought of had a bite to them but it was past time for such a snappish tone. Now Albert was showing a willingness to kill off anyone who offered help.

Emily nodded and went and rang the bell. Mrs. O'Neal came up a few moments later carrying a tray with some cider and food. One look at the food was enough to remind Emily that she was hungry.

"Thank you kindly," she said as the tray was set on the table. "I had not asked for food but now find I need some."

"I thought you might. What did you want then?"

"Paper and a pen. I need to write a letter to my grandfather. I hope to finally get him to act on this. It is far past time he accepted that the boy he cared for for years is a killer."

"You said he didn't heed you before. Why would he now?"

"Because I am going to put aside all thought of his position and speak to him as a man whose pigheadedness is costing too many people their lives."

Mrs. O'Neal smiled. "Be right back with that paper and pen."

Chapter Seventeen

Wincing, Emily shifted in her seat so that she could rub away the painful twinge in her back. Sitting in a hard chair for three days was beginning to cost her but she knew she would not relinquish her place at Iain's bedside. Her hatred for Albert, the anger she felt, was a poison that churned inside her but she could do nothing about it. The man still lived and that only added to her anger. It was just wrong that a man like him continued to have such good luck.

How had Albert known the MacEnroys were coming for him? Matthew's explanation was the only one that still held. It was hard to accept that mere chance and bad luck had been what had brought Iain to this bed, unconscious for three long days. Emily supposed she would have to accept that unknowingly she had been the one to cause Albert to set that trap. Somehow he had seen her and known that she had seen him and acted on that alone to prepare for Iain's arrival in town.

Iain gave a soft groan and she tensed, watching him closely. There was movement behind his eyelids and she felt her hopes rise. His wound had not festered, was not considered serious despite how it had bled as if an artery had been opened, but it was a head wound. There was no ignoring the fact that no one really knew what damage could be done. Emily had not needed to hear all the horrific stories Mrs. O'Neal had told her to know that head wounds were dangerous. She clasped her hands together and watched his face, silently praying that this time that groan meant he was waking up.

Iain struggled to open his eyes. His head ached, a dull throb much like the one that lingered after a fierce headache. As the fog of a too deep sleep cleared from his mind, he began to remember. Albert had been expecting them to ride into town. If not for the well-armed locals in the saloon leaping to their defense he and his brothers might have died. He then realized he had absolutely no memory of his brothers getting out of the saloon safely.

He opened his eyes then groaned as the light seared them. He caught a movement to his left and then saw Emily run to the window and yank the curtains shut. Iain took several deep breaths and let them out slowly as he fought to soften the pain something as simple and welcome as sunlight had caused. Then he realized he was thirsty, his throat as dry as a desert.

"Water?" he asked, startled by the croak of sound he produced. Just how long had he been asleep?

Emily hurried to get him a glass of water then slipped her arm beneath his head to lift it just enough for him to drink. He nearly finished the whole glass before the strength needed for that simple chore fled and he slumped. She eased his head back down on the pillows and set the glass on the table.

"My brothers?" he asked, pleased to hear that though his voice was weak, it sounded almost normal now.

"They are all fine. A few bruises from leaping over the bar and then dragging your carcass around. You were the one most badly injured. They feared that you had been shot in the head but it appears you narrowly escaped that fate. The bullet just skimmed across your skull. According to Mrs. O'Neal, your very thick skull."

"The woman adores me."

"Of course she does. It is quite evident."

He wanted to laugh but feared it would hurt. "Knocked me out."

"And that probably saved your life. According to Matthew, everyone was aiming at you. You dropped like a stone soon after that bullet grazed you so they all thought they had hit you and finished you."

"How did my brothers escape unharmed?"

"Well, it appears the locals do not care much for Albert and his friends, old and new. I did not realize so many people went about armed to the teeth in this country." She shook her head. "Anyhow, they all shot back at Albert and his men and that allowed your brothers to grab you and run. Several of Albert's men were killed or injured before he got himself out of there. Matthew believes Albert was hit, too, but the man still ran out."

"I cannae understand how he knew we were coming in."

"Despite how much I dislike the man I have to admit that he is clever. Always has been. I suspect he heard about me being in town. Actually, Matthew thinks he might have seen me looking out of Mabel's, caught a reflection in the bank window. But once he was sure I had been in town and figured I must have seen him, too, it was highly possible you and your brothers would come looking for him. So he planned for it. Very carefully. Matthew found out all the men round here spent a lot of time in the saloon so he had obviously decided that was the best place to lay a trap for you."

"Damn. Wily bastard."

"Oh, yes, most certainly. Wily, sly, conniving, and all other such ills you can think of."

"Should have just shot him but he had his back to me. Suspicion that was planned as well."

"Quite possibly. He would have taken the time to find out everything he could about you and yours." She sighed. "I even wonder at times if our coming out here played right into his hands. Big, wild country. Perfect place to kill a few people and then sail on home. All he had to do is find us and my sister helped him with that. I am so sorry," she said quietly, taking his hand in hers. "I should have let Mabel shoot him."

"I understand why ye didnae. As I said, I thought about shooting him myself but could not bring myself to shoot a man in the back. Any of the locals get hurt?"

"Not badly. Albert was not interested in any of them and, as soon as he realized his grand plans had taken a wrong turn, he fled with his men, leaving the ones he had hired on to fight it out. Unfortunately, Albert got in one telling shot before he left. The one that skimmed across your skull. But even though he thought he had taken you down, six more men were shooting at him. So he ran. Matthew is certain he hit him once but he did not take him down, does not even know where or how bad the wound was."

"But that could make him easier to track."

Emily sighed. "Could do but, depending on how badly he was hurt, his men might take him to an actual town or city to find a skilled doctor. If he is too badly wounded, they may even consider taking him back home to England thinking that is where he is sure to want to be buried. I can imagine him leaving such orders with his closest men, the ones who came here with him. It would be nice if that is what is happening now." She shook her head. "And just listen to me, wishing for a man's death. My parents would be appalled."

"He murdered them, took your sister and her husband from you, killed three other relatives I think you mentioned, and was doing his best to add ye and Neddy to that tally. Maybe then your grandfather. More than reason enough to wish for such a thing."

"I suppose so but I do resent him for causing me to do so, as much as I detest him for what he has done. But you seem quite wide awake for a man out cold for three days. I suspect you would like a meal."

"Aye. Have ye taken care of me all that time." He smiled when she blushed.

"Matthew or one of the others came in to see to your, er, personal needs. I got some watery broth down you from time to time. Oh, and I cleaned your wound, which is healing very nicely. And I, well, I cleaned your teeth yesterday."

He grinned despite the ache in his head. "Ye cleaned my teeth. Was my breath so foul then?"

"No. I have been ill a few times and slept for long periods and the one thing I hated the most about it all was the feeling in my mouth when I finally woke up." She made a face and shuddered at the memory. "So I was just sitting here watching you breathe and decided I would rescue you from that particular horror." She grinned. "You may thank me now."

"Thank you. What has put ye in such a gay mood?" He frowned when her expression changed abruptly and a hint of fear revealed itself briefly on her face.

"I am just pleased that you finally decided to wake up." She stood up and smoothed down her skirts, hoping he did not understand how true that statement was. "I will just go and see what we can put together for you and send Matthew up with a tray."

Before Iain could say another word she was up and out the door. Once outside, she leaned back against the door and let the tears fall. It was foolish because he was obviously going to survive but she could not stop the tears; they were washing away the fears she had lived with for three days. When she was finally able to control them, she wiped her face with her skirts, straightened her posture, and went down the stairs.

Iain frowned at the door. The change of her mood was so quick it left his head spinning. She had seemed to be happy and joking and then sad. He was sure he had seen tears in her eyes. Emily had no true skill at hiding her emotions. He thought over what he had said and could see nothing that would have caused it.

Sighing, he closed his eyes. He was too weary and his head ached too much to try to figure out a woman's moods. He smiled slightly. It was rather nice to even be faced with that small trouble.

Matthew strode in and stood next to his bed to stare at him. Iain looked up at his brother and frowned.

After a moment of looking at each other, Iain began to get irritated.

"Are ye going to say anything or are ye just going to gawk?"

Matthew grinned. "So ye finally decided to wake from your wee nap, did ye?"

"Aye. And since ye are here, maybe ye can give me a hand to get to the damned chamber pot."

Chuckling, Matthew helped him out of bed. Iain found that he was not yet ready to do much walking as Matthew steadied him. He hated this part of being an invalid, no matter how short the time one was stuck abed. Once done, Matthew led him back to bed and Iain nearly fell into it. Only Matthew's strong hold made his settling in less abrupt.

"Jesu, I am as weak as a newly whelped lamb."

"Weel, I think even one of them can walk about better than ye can right now."

"Thank ye kindly. My head is aching badly and right now I cannae see too weel because of it. So ye are safe from my fists."

"That will pass," said Matthew with a grin.

"When did ye become a doctor?" grumbled Iain.

"Recall last year when I fell out of that tree?"

"Ah, aye, verra graceful. Ye landed on your head. Ye were out for a while, too. So how long did your head ache?"

"About a day or so after I woke. An annoying deep throb and real pain when I tried to lift my head on my own. And, even though I had been sleeping for a couple of days, I still felt tired."

"I have too much to do to lay about for even longer than I have."

"Ye either lay about or ye land on your face when ye try to go somewhere."

Iain sighed. "Then I guess I will adopt a slothful attitude until the aching eases. Do ye think Mrs. O'Neal has anything to ease the ache?"

"I can ask but I dinnae recall her giving me anything," said Matthew.

"She might have just felt like torturing you as I recall her being verra angry that ye were even up in the tree. But, aye, do that. I am also starting to feel hungry."

"There will be a tray brought up soon. Mrs. O'Neal will bring it up. Seems ye upset Emily." Matthew frowned at him. "Ken ye feel miserable but . . ."

"I said nothing to upset her. One moment she was smiling and making a joke then she went all quiet and sad and left."

"Ah. Then it must just be because ye didnae die."

"I only had a bullet burn on my head. That doesnae usually kill a man."

Matthew shrugged. "She was a wee bit teary-eyed when she came down the stairs and then she hurried out to fetch the boy. So, Mrs. O'Neal figured ye had snapped her head off about something."

"Naturally." Iain frowned. "Why would she get all teary-eyed because I wasnae dead?"

"Because ye can be a right bastard and she was sorely disappointed that we wouldnae be playing the pipes over your grave?"

Iain wished he had enough strength to at least slap the grin off Matthew's face. "Verra funny. Her change of mood just didnae make any sense."

"Nay? Ever hear of weeping for joy?" Matthew shook his head and looked at Iain sadly when his brother just looked confused. "The lass has sat with ye for three whole days just watching ye sleep. Then, ye wake up and she realizes ye are truly no longer in danger and she cries. That was what it was."

"Oh." Iain thought about that and smiled. "So happy tears, as our mither used to call them."

"That was what I figured it was. Must have been hard on the lass sitting here for so long just checking that ye kept breathing. Ye aren't the most interesting thing to look at."

After one sharp rap on the door, Matthew hurried over to let in Mrs. O'Neal. The woman carried in a full tray of food. Matthew helped Iain sit up against the pillows and she put the tray on his lap. Iain noticed that, although there was plenty and it was hearty, filling food, it was also the kind of food that sat very easy on a stomach. Since Iain's stomach was definitely uneasy, he appreciated the woman's efforts.

"Eat what ye can, son, and pleased ye came back," said Mrs. O'Neal. "We will have you up and about real soon." She pointed at a glass with some milky-looking liquid. "This might help your aching head. Always keep some on hand for when I get a bad head. Ain't tasty so be ready for it," she warned as she left, assured that he could manage the simple meal on his own, and busy arguing with Matthew about why she had not given that cure to him when his head had ached.

Iain gave into the demands of his growling stomach. He ate slowly and took drinks of Mrs. O'Neal's potion in between. When he realized he was full and there was still food left on the tray, he was surprised. It embarrassed him that he had not finished the food

the woman had made for him. He had, however,
finished her headache potion.

Matthew returned and helped him to the chamber
pot. Iain was feeling too sick and weak for that to
bother him but he knew it would as he healed and re-
gained his strength. He was back in bed and falling
asleep when Mrs. O'Neal came up to collect the tray.
She left some water on the table next to him and he
mumbled a thank-you, falling into a deep sleep even
as she shut the door behind her.

Emily crept back into the room and sighed when
she found Iain asleep. She had wanted to talk to him
more to reassure herself that he was healing. Unfortunately, she had had to flee the room as soon as
possible before making a fool of herself by crying like
a child. Scolding herself for weeping when the man
had actually woken up, an event she had been waiting
for for three long days, had not helped.

She sighed as she thought on her weak moment. It
had to have been because she had been so worried
and afraid. The fact that he had revealed he was re-
covering had just been too much for her after the
long wait. The funny thing was she had been so happy,
so completely pleased to see his eyes open. It was as if
some dam had broken inside her.

Emily picked up the lap desk Matthew had made
for her and set out her writing tools. It was time to
write to her grandfather if only to tell him the truth
about the boy he had raised. Now that Albert was
gone she felt free to write to anyone and had already
sent out two letters to some cousins she had been
close to, including her closest friend. She hoped they
would read them. After not hearing a word from her

in almost four years she really would not blame them if they just tossed the unopened letter in the fireplace, but she prayed they were more forgiving than that.

It took her a long time to even start the letter to her grandfather. There had to be some way to gently lead in to speaking of Albert's possible death and his crimes, to let him know what happened to David and Annabel, but the words were not coming for her. She finally gave up on thinking of something profound yet comforting and just began to write. He had once told her he liked her chatty letters because he could hear her talking, that it was almost as if she had come to visit. He had said his wife had written letters in the same way and she had been so flattered. Emily was not sure she believed that but decided he had said it so that was what he would get again. She just hoped the news about Albert did not break his heart.

"Who are ye writing to?"

Iain's voice suddenly sounding in her ears startled her and she left a blot on the letter. "Wait just a moment. I have blotted the paper and want to write a little apology for that." Once she was done, she looked at Iain and smiled. "I am writing to my grand-father."

"Telling him about Albert?"

"Yes. I can only hope that in these last few years he has come to learn more about Albert and so will not be too heartbroken, that he knows the man is a killer. It is still hard news to tell him because he raised him. He took him in when his parents were mur-dered and they seemed to get along together just fine."

"Which is a little hard to believe."

She chuckled. "I know. That makes it even harder to sound all appropriately sympathetic. I am offering him condolences about a man's death when I feel no regret at all."

"Is this the kind of thing ye are teaching us to do?"

"Yes. Writing a letter with your own hand has several advantages. You can say what you want without having to tell some other person what that is and you are certain the words you wanted are the right ones written down."

"Good point."

"I am sorry if you are finding it tedious."

"Oh, nay. Weel, sometimes. But I have begun to see the advantages of kenning such things. I think it is just my age. Learning something new once ye are older than a schoolchild is hard, for many different reasons."

Emily nodded. "It is easier for me to teach someone older, though, if only because you have the maturity to understand what I am trying to get across to you. Like the sounds of the letters."

He started to nod, found that hurt too much, and just grunted his agreement. "For all our whining, I think my brothers and I are catching on faster than we thought we would."

"You do not whine. You grumble." She grinned when he gave her a fierce frown then reached out to pat his arm. "Just wait until you have enough skill to sit and read a book or even the newspaper, if they have one round here. Then you will find it much more enjoyable."

"Robbie is the one who seems the most anxious to be able to sit and read a book."

She nodded, recalling when the young man had once stated his wish to read a book. "I can still recall the first time I was able to just curl up in a chair and read, all by myself. It was a simple book for children but I was so pleased with myself."

"Weel, teacher, we will soon prove your success, I am sure of it."

"I am sure you will."

She moved to help him have a drink of water. It was obvious he had already strengthened since the first time he had opened his eyes. She expected he would be up on his feet soon. That would be when they would have trouble holding him back from doing too much too soon. Recalling her own time of convalescence, she vowed to hold her patience with him. She would just remind herself of how she had suffered the same frustrations.

Emily stared at the man struggling to get his boots on and sighed. Repeating that reminder of her own troubles after being shot was wearing thin. She was sure she had not been as annoying as Iain was. He was pushing hard at the limits of her patience. Even though she was giving him private lessons on his writing and reading, she wished he was further ahead in the learning than he was. Having either skill would have at least given him something to do as he rested.

"Must you?" she asked on a sigh. He sat up straight and she saw how he had to steady himself.

"Aye. I am going mad just lying there with nothing to do," he replied. "Worse, my mind keeps showing me all that needs doing before winter slips in."

"I know. It is just that you are only a week away from being shot in the head."

"At the head. Nay in. Aye, I ken it was a bad wound and could have been far worse than it was, but I am nay so weak I need to remain lying on my back and I have slept enough I could probably stay awake for days."

"Please do not try."

He laughed. "I ken I am nay healed. But I truly cannae just lie in this room any longer. Having all my brothers take turns to come in and keep me entertained is nay helping." He had to smile when she blushed.

"They did not mind."

"I ken it and it was good to hear what had been done. But I need to be moving around if only to tire me out. Last night I lay there for what felt hours before I could even keep my eyes closed. The mere thought of lying awake all night horrifies me, especially kenning my days are spent the same way."

"I know." She sighed. "I hated it as well. Just promise me you will sit still here for a few moments. You made yourself light-headed when you pulled on your boots and do not try to deny it."

"I willnae," he said, although he had been thinking to do so.

"Good. I will go down and start cooking something for you. Just sit quietly for a few moments and you can come down to sit in the kitchen and eat it. Would you pull the bell before you leave the room? It might be good for me to come and go down the stairs at your side."

"Nay. There is a rail I can cling to. I cling to ye and we could end up doing more on the stairs than just walking down." He laughed when she blushed bright red.

"Men," she muttered, and went out the door.

"Definitely has spent too much time with Mrs. O'Neal," he said to the empty room and lay back against his pillows.

It would be a few more days before he could return to his plan to court her. He hated to admit it but his body was not quite up to doing much. Iain promised himself he would be careful, would baby himself no matter how much he would hate it. Then he would get right back to courting Emily and he would not be needing her help to see him down the stairs.

Chapter Eighteen

Iain waited as Mrs. O'Neal packed a basket for him. He intended to take Emily on a picnic. It was a sunny, warm day, and he wanted to take advantage of what could be the last of such days. It was also one of the things he had written on his list of things he could do to woo her and he felt he now had the strength to do that. His brothers had their moment of hilarity over his list for which he had thrashed them soundly. He also knew that they thoroughly approved of him courting Emily.

"How long should one court a woman?" he asked Mrs. O'Neal, and pretended not to notice how she rolled her eyes.

"Until ye have won her," she answered, and set the basket on the table with enough force to make him jump. "And I don't mean just into your bed."

"Ah. I ken your opinion on all that. All my brothers told me." He stood up and picked up the basket. "It is why I am working hard to woo her."

"Ye have done this backwards."

"Been told that, too," he said, and walked out.

He found Emily in the stable saddling the mare he

had gotten for her. She had named it Fancy and it made him smile. Iain set the basket near the doors and walked over to her, bending to kiss her neck then dodging out of the way when she jumped and her head went back. Seeing her pleasure over both mare and saddle had brought him a lot of pleasure, and the blushing gratitude she had offered had been very hard not to soothe with a lot of kisses.

"Careful, lass," he said, laughing softly. "Nearly broke my nose there."

Emily blushed. "I am sorry. You startled me."

"I ken it. Bad thing to do to a lass who has been hunted. I am here to take ye on a picnic." He pointed toward the basket. "Mrs. O'Neal packed us a basket."

"That was very nice of her. You are going to take me on a picnic?" She went to the basket and peeked in. "Good heavens, the woman packed enough for a small army."

Iain laughed and picked up the basket. "I thought we could ride out to that place on the trail ye like." He set the basket down again as he saddled his horse and then hung the basket from his saddle. "Are ye willing to come with me?" He walked over to her and held out his hand.

Emily laughed and placed her hand in his. "Lead on, sir."

He set her in her saddle then swung up into his own. For a while they rode side by side, saying nothing, simply enjoying the day. It was probably one of the last warm, sunny days they would be able to enjoy, Emily thought, as there were too many signs of the coming fall to ignore. She lifted her face to the sun and savored its warmth.

"Fall is coming," said Iain.

"I was just thinking the same. The only thing I do

not like about that is that fall is followed by winter."
Emily smiled at him. "I suspect that does not trouble
you hardy Scots as it does me."

"Nay too fond of the cold, actually. That is why we
put in so many fireplaces."

"I did not think there were that many."

"Nay, ye probably grew up with one in every room.
It is a lot for a shepherd's house." He smiled when
she laughed. "Took a large bite of the money we had
brought with us plus three beds made by Matthew
and two rugs woven by Robbie. Mabel has one of
those fancy iron stoves in her shop and we have been
working on a trade for it with her. A little trade and a
little money."

"That must be fun." Emily laughed. "I bet she drives
a hard bargain."

"Ye have no idea, but we are close."

When they reached the spot on the trail, Iain
secured their horses and helped her down a short
path to a flat grassy area at the side of the gorge. The
sound of the water was soothing and the water glis-
tened in the sun. He spread out a blanket and set the
basket down before he sat. Then he patted the spot
on the blanket right by his side. Emily grinned, shook
her head over his antics and sat down.

"I did not see this spot when I rode by," she said. "I
thought there was nothing but rocky cliff."

"Hard to see unless ye go right up to the edge and
even then ye can be distracted by the water. So, let us
see what Mrs. O'Neal put together for us."

They spent a pleasant hour eating Mrs. O'Neal's
fried chicken, a crunchy salad, and fresh bread and
butter. There was some apple pie and she had even put
in a jar of fresh cream to top it with. Emily groaned

when she finished her pie and fell back on the blanket, her hands covering her stomach.

"I ate too much. You will have to haul me home in a cart," she said.

Iain smiled a little as he put the things back into the basket. He wondered if she even realized she had called his house home. It had been said so easily, so unconsciously, he knew she felt it and that suited him just fine. Finished with packing the basket he set it aside and lay down beside her, turning on his side so that he could look at her.

"Want some wine?" he asked.

"You have wine?"

"We arenae totally uncivilized out here. Actually, Duncan makes it. It isnae the kind ye are probably used to but it serves."

"I did not see any grapes around."

"There are some wild ones he uses now and then but he uses whatever is at hand. I think the bottle he gave me was blackberry."

"Huh. Never had that. My aunt Catherine used to make wine. Some of them were nice. Some, well, not so much. I liked her elderberry wine." She sat up and he handed her a glass then watched as she took a sip. "Different but tasty."

"Aye. A wee bit sweeter than I like but he does it weel." He took a sip. "Hmmm. Not as sweet as last year's batch. Better. Stronger, too, I think. I begin to believe we may be planting some grapes if he keeps up."

Emily laughed. "You are a very gifted family. Furniture, weaving, painting, wine making. There are three brothers left. Do they have a skill as well?"

"Weel, Matthew can talk to horses, calm the most jittery of the beasts. Funny, but I wouldnae have thought horses in this country would respond to the Gaelic, but they do."

"That is odd, but still a gift. Gaelic, really?"

"Aye, Gaelic. Occasionally sings an old song." He grinned when she laughed softly.

"Still leaves two brothers," she said, and smiled at him.

"They havenae found anything yet." He leaned forward and brushed his lips over hers. "I have something for ye. I have been holding it for a while, giving ye time to, weel, grieve."

Emily blinked then quickly drained her glass of wine. She guessed he had something that had been David's or Annabel's. While she felt she was over the worst of her grieving, she did not think she was ready to see some personal item of the people she had lost. She had dealt with her grief mostly by not thinking of their deaths. Then she took a deep breath and let it out slowly, grabbing hold of a thread of calm and sanity. The question to answer was when would she be ready and there was no certain answer. Better to brace herself now and get it over with.

"Emily?" He reached out and ran his hand up and down her arm.

"I just needed a moment." She looked at her empty glass and set it down. "And something to brace myself with. So, what do you have?"

Iain studied Emily for a moment. He could see that she did not want to see what he had, did not want her memories stirred up again, but she would do it. He wished there was some good time, a more appropriate time, to give her the things he had taken from the dead, but doubted there would ever be one. He pulled the small wrapped package from a pocket in his pants and held it for a moment as he studied her.

Unable to decide what her expression meant, he sighed and gave it to her.

Emily's hands trembled faintly as she opened the small package and spread it out on her lap. She reached for Annabel's locket first, opened it, and felt a sharp pain in her heart as she stared at the small pictures. She could recall when Annabel got it, the day they got the pictures, and even when Annabel had put them in the locket. She had spoken of keeping her boys next to her heart as she had tucked it inside the neck of her gown.

Putting the locket down, she picked up the rings. They shone as if freshly cleaned. Inside each one was part of a maudlin saying about united hearts. Annabel had spent far too much of their money for the things when they were in New York getting Neddy's birth certificate verified by every member of the gentry they could find and she had said they needed them to let everyone see they were married. David had been angry at first but too much in love to stay angry. Emily absently brushed aside the tear that rolled down her cheek.

"Why?" she managed to ask, her gaze fixed on the portrait of Annabel holding Neddy and taken at a time when her sister had bubbled up with happiness.

"I thought ye would want something to remember them by. And the rings?" He shrugged. "They seemed like the sort of thing a parent might pass on to his child."

"Thank you."

"I didnae want to make ye cry."

She smiled, leaned toward him, and brushed a kiss over his mouth. "You did not. It was seeing her when she was at her happiest. Then the rings, they reminded me of all she could not forget."

"What do ye mean?"

"They cost far too much, and we did not have all that much anyway. Yet she never thought on that; it never occurred to her. She just took the money for them and was hurt because David was angry about that. I had to sell a few pieces of my jewelry to replace the money she took and that also bothered David. Annabel did not know how to change who she was." She managed a little smile. "But you are right, when the time comes Neddy will appreciate them."

"That is sad." He watched her rewrap the locket and rings and tuck them into a pocket in her skirt. "Do ye think her husband kenned it, saw that she didnae want to change?"

Emily opened her mouth to say that David had loved Annabel. He had but that was not the right answer. A memory came flooding in and she realized he had understood his wife could not change, did not even want to try, and still loved her. She had been weeding the garden and David had been stocking the woodpile. Annabel had been sitting in a chair in the shade, fanning herself. At one point Emily had looked up to find him staring at her, his eyes sad. He had then smiled sadly and said that she was a good girl, that she knew what was important, and had the strength to accept change.

She felt Iain's hand stroke her hair and knew she had just spoken out loud. She had not intended to, did not like to voice any criticisms of her dead sister, but also found she did not really mind when it was Iain. Emily did not resist when he pulled her into his arms. She slid her arms around his waist and laid her cheek against his chest.

"How old was your sister?" he asked.

"Eight and twenty when she died, so four and twenty

when she married David. She was six years older than
me. David had just turned thirty. Too young to die.
They were both far too young to die and definitely
did not deserve being murdered."

Iain was doing some quick subtraction in his head.
"Ye are only two and twenty?"

"Yes." She frowned up at him, wondering why he
interrupted her serious thoughts on her loss with
questions about her age. "What does that matter?
Actually, I will not be two and twenty for a few
months yet. I am only one and twenty until the end
of November."

"I thought ye were older." He grimaced for he suspected that was not what a woman wanted to hear.

She laughed a little. "And how does that matter?"

"It doesnae. It was just a surprise."

"How old are you then?"

"Eight and twenty. My birth date is the first of
November." He told himself to shut up because he
sounded like an idiot worrying over things that did
not matter.

Emily kissed the hollow at the bottom of his throat.
"So old. I might need to rethink this liaison." She
nearly screeched with laughter when he suddenly
pushed her down onto the blanket and tickled her
mercilessly.

Iain's intentions quickly shifted from playful to
amorous and he kissed her. He turned them onto their
sides so he could more easily undo her gown. When
he tugged it down, he had to pull her arms out of the
sleeves and he sensed a growing tension in her body.

Kissing the swells of her breasts over the top of her
shift, he murmured, "It is all right, Emily. No one will
see us."

"They only have to look down," she protested.

"The only ones who use this trail are my kin and the Powell brothers and they all know the horses tied up there means do not look down."

"You have brought another woman here."

The hint of an accusation in her tone made him grin. "Not me. But there are few places around here to be private."

Emily was not sure whether to believe that or not. Then he pulled her shift down and began to kiss her breast, stealing away all thought of a need for privacy and a possibility of other women in his life. Nothing else mattered but how he could make her feel.

He sat up to take off his shirt and she waited tense with anticipation. She loved how it felt when their skin touched. Nakedness was vital to lovemaking, she decided. All that skin touching was almost as stirring as one of his kisses. She welcomed him back into her arms when he returned and met his kiss with an equal ferocity.

When he had to reach beneath her skirts to shed her drawers she had the passing thought that at least they would not be fully naked in the broad daylight. Then his hand slipped between her thighs to torment her and she arched into his touch. Surprise peeked from beneath her passion when he used his clever fingers to bring her to release.

The force of that release was just easing when he joined their bodies. Emily clung to him and he moved lazily almost to bring her passion back to a peak. Muttering his name she tightened her grip to urge him on to a greater ferocity when she hit and then went over another peak. She was still gasping from the strength of it when he joined her, groaning her name into her hair as he held her close.

Iain finally rolled over onto his back to fix his pants

and glanced over at Emily. She lay on her back, her clothes in disarray and her arms flung out to the sides. She looked well pleasured, he thought, but suspected she would not appreciate him telling her so. He would love to compliment her on how beautifully responsive she was but also thought that might not be a thing a lady would consider a compliment. She did look tempting lying there with her breasts bared to the sun, but he smothered his growing interest, bent closer, and brushed a kiss over each breast.

"Ye do look fine basking in the sun like that," he said quietly, and almost laughed at the speed with which she opened her eyes, glanced down at herself, and then began to yank her clothing back up.

"Rather like a fresh-caught fish . . ." he began, then laughed out loud at the outraged look she gave him and held her back when she would have clapped a hand over his mouth.

"Such a funny man," she muttered even though his laugh urged her strongly to join in.

"Back to real life."

"I know. Not that real life around here is such a travail." Using her fingers as a comb she put her hair back in order.

"There are days it can seem so."

"Even on those days, it is not so bad. Of course, I have nothing to do with the raising of the pigs. I gladly leave all that to Mrs. O'Neal and her children. I am not fond of pigs."

"Ye dinnae see any of us mucking about with them, either, though they do provide us with a fine meal now and then."

She grinned. "I know. I just wish Mrs. O'Neal would not tell us the name of the pig the meal came from."

"Aye," he agreed, and chuckled. "I just cannae

figure out if she does it because she is pleased about what the poor pig produced for us or if she is trying to put us off eating any because she doesnae like to kill them."

"I did ask her once, commenting on how she names them all and appears fond of them. She said she is but she is also raising them to feed people, that that is their purpose in life, and that the life she gives them is a 'demmed good one' so she doesnae feel badly when she ends it."

"Very practical, our Mrs. O'Neal." He stood up and then pulled her to her feet. Emily held firmly to his hand as he went back up to their horses. It was a pleasant place and she had enjoyed herself, in ways she would never tell anyone, but she was not sure she would like to picnic on what was no more than a cliff too often.

When they reached the house and dismounted, Emily saw Mrs. O'Neal standing with one of her larger pigs. She suspected that was one of her problems with the animals, they could grow so huge. Walking over to Mrs. O'Neal, she put herself on the opposite side of the woman from the pig that was noisily enjoying a bucketful of scraps from the table.

"Has he finished living his good life?" Emily asked.

"Humphrey here is close," said Mrs. O'Neal. "Just trying to decide if he is for a regular meal or should be saved for a holiday. I am thinking he would best serve for one of the winter holidays. Handsome fellow as he is, he deserves to be something special."

Emily looked at the pig and figured only a pig lover could see something beautiful in the animal. "I suspect he won't find it all that special."

Mrs. O'Neal laughed and Emily started toward the house, leaving Iain there to discuss Humphrey's fate.

There were certain aspects of farm life that took some getting used to, she decided. The manor house had had farms but she had only ever seen them in a picturesque setting, the less pleasant side of farming kept out of her view. She was heartily glad she was not the one who had to make the decisions about which animal would grace the table tonight and she fully intended to keep it that way.

Iain finally left Mrs. O'Neal having her last days with Humphrey and went looking for Emily. He was not fond of picking the animals to use for the table but was accustomed to it, but she was not. Although she had not looked sickened or truly upset, he could read the unease on her face.

As he started up the stairs he realized he had completely used up his newly found strength. It had, perhaps, been a little early to use his picnic idea but he did not regret it. Iain knew Emily and Mrs. O'Neal would harangue him about it though. He was about to go into his room when Emily came up beside him and put an arm around his waist. It was only then he realized he was swaying a little.

"Too soon," he said as she helped him to the bed.

"I suspect you will recover quickly though." After settling him on the bed she stood up and grinned at him. "I was just thinking of going to the kitchen and getting myself some cold tea and a nice small piece of pie."

"Ye just had pie."

"A small piece. Adding another will not hurt. Mrs. O'Neal has all the boys off picking berries with her and thought I would enjoy the quiet."

"So will I." He started to sit up and she pushed him back down with one small hand against his chest. "I am not feeling so poorly I cannae go sit in the kitchen to eat pie."

"No, most likely not, but rest for a few more minutes then come on down and if you feel the least bit unsteady on your feet, ring the bell, and I will come up to give you extra support." When he just frowned, she said, "Promise me."

"Fine. If a short rest doesnae cure me, I will ring for your aid."

She kissed him and, laughing, skipped out of the room. Iain shook his head. It was humiliating to find out he was still prone to moments of weakness but he should have realized something like that could bother him for a while. He would give himself a short rest period and then go down to the kitchen for pie and Emily.

Chapter Nineteen

"Albert!"

Emily backed up as the man stepped in through the back door. He looked terrible. He was a sickly shade of pale, his hair was dirty, snarled, and oily, and his clothes were dirty and torn. There was a fierce glint in his eyes that terrified her. And just him standing there in the kitchen was terrifying enough without all that was now wrong with him. It had been two weeks since the confrontation in the saloon. Had he healed from the gunshot? Where were his men?

He stepped closer and she realized he also smelled bad, almost as if something was rotting on him. Albert had always been so fastidious. It was then she realized he had been hit with a bullet and he had not healed from the wound he had gotten. She could not see it but knew it was there. Then she saw the gun in his hand.

"Where's the boy?" he demanded.

"Albert, he is only three years old. A mere babe, for mercy's sake."

"A babe who holds *my* title, *my* lands, and *my* bloody money. Now, where is he?"

"You cannot kill a child."

"Watch me. I suspect I will do a very good job of it. Tell me where he is. There is no point in trying to hide him. How many others do you want to die because of that brat?"

"That *brat* is your blood. So was my sister. So were those three other relations of ours whose only crime was trying to help me and Annabel. And my mother and father. And it was you and only you who killed them. Do not try to shove your sins on others. Did you kill poor Constance, too?"

"That stupid cow? No, no need to. She left your fool sister's letters in one of the prissy keepsake boxes you women fancy. Right on her desk in plain sight. So, I invited her to go for a ride with me in my carriage and, when she ran up the stairs to change, I went through her things. Did not even lock the demmed box so I saw the letters and had a nice read. Your sister did love to blather on. Then I put them all back so she would not even know. All I had to do was listen to her. Less than an hour spent listening to her empty, senseless chatter and I had all I needed. Though there was a time or two when I did consider the joy of putting a bullet in her constantly moving mouth."

Constance was obviously very fortunate that Albert had been in a good mood that day. "You do not need any of it. Not the lands nor the money. You have your own. You just want it. One can sometimes sympathize with ones who commit crimes because of desperation, poverty, or need. Even revenge. What you suffer from is pure unrelenting greed. How can you do this to Grandfather? He took you in, raised you. You were like a son to him."

"Not enough of a son to be named his heir."

"Your parents left your care to a good, generous man."

"Something they had been about to change. Why do you think they were killed? I saw their will, saw who would take me in yet they were going to change that and stick me with a wizened old woman who was as good as destitute. I have been planning all this since university, you know."

"You killed your own parents?" Emily did not think anything could have shocked her more and she waited to hear him forcefully deny it.

"Fools. Both of them. And one like me should not have to deal with fools. They had the Duke of Collins Wood as a friend and never made use of him, never made use of that most advantageous connection." Albert shook his head. "My father was shocked at my suggestions that he do so. Several times I patiently pointed that fact out to him, the fact that he was missing a grand opportunity by not taking advantage of the old man. He just kept saying, 'The duke is a trusted friend; I could never do that.'

"Then a friend of mine at Oxford shot his father. He did not kill him for the years of abuse he had suffered at the man's hands, just shot him in the hand that had so regularly beaten him and fondled him. My father was so shocked. He asked how could a son shoot his own father? I happened to be carrying my pistol so I showed him. Shot him right between the eyes. Then my foolish, foolish mother ran in. Why would any rational person run right toward the sound of gunfire? Stupid cow. She screamed at me. Me! Her own son! Shot her to shut her up."

Emily listened to the man talk with a growing

horror. He was mad. He may well have always been but she thought it had become too much for him to hold back when he had shot his own parents. It was that act that had brought all his illness roaring to the fore. She could not even blame this on the infection he now suffered from. The man should be shackled up in Bedlam or someplace similar.

"You kill people like others flick a piece of lint off their coat sleeve," she said softly, suspecting her look of horror would not calm his murderous urge but unable to hide it.

"That is because the people I kill are no more significant than a piece of lint. They are an annoyance, a blockade. They are foolish, stupid people. I should not be forced to deal with such people."

"Neddy needs to be none of those if you just leave. He will stay in this country."

"You expect me to believe that? Who will make him stay when he is grown and realizes what awaits him back in England? You expect him to actually choose to herd sheep or cattle? Maybe become a farmer? Over here they seem to expect the landowner to do the work himself." He shook his head over what he obviously considered an obscene attitude.

He spoke of those things with such scorn she did not even try to defend the many ways of earning a living. "He would stay because all he loves would be here."

Albert laughed. "Any man with sense would decide he can love whatever he wants, wherever the best living is. I happen to love being very wealthy. I will love getting the title and I will most certainly love having that power. A royal dukedom would be better but I will settle for one gifted by the great Elizabeth."

* * *

Iain stood as still as possible just outside the kitchen door and listened. The man was supposed to be dead or gone, not still plaguing them. He did not know exactly how long Emily had kept the man talking but it was evident there was no talking such a man out of his murderous plans.

There were a lot of reasons to kill Albert, including his current weakened state that would make physically fighting the man impossible. He could kill the man easy though, especially knowing he planned to end the life of a bairn. That that bairn was Neddy, a little boy they had all come to love, would make the killing even more acceptable, he thought with an anger he had never felt before. He would also like killing him for terrifying Emily. He had been able to hear that cold fear in her voice although he doubted Albert had noticed.

Walking back into the parlor as silently as he was able to, Iain took the sword off the mantel there. He had left his gun upstairs and feared he would lose what strength he had if he went back up the steps. The trip he had taken today might have been a pure delight but it had cost him just when he needed his strength. Iain also admitted that it would be good to kill that man with his father's sword. From what he had overheard, Emily was backed up against the kitchen door and Albert was near the back. He went out the front door and walked to the back, slipping up to the kitchen door as silently as he was able.

Through the slight opening in the lace curtains over the window in the door, he could see the man's back. He could also see how tightly the man held on to the chair by the kitchen table. It appeared he may well have been injured and he was not at full strength. The white of his knuckles revealed Albert had a real tight grip on the chair. Iain had to wonder if it was needed to keep Albert upright and steady.

That would work to his advantage, Iain thought. Even the idea of killing a wounded man from behind did not cause him any hesitation. He had also seen the gun in the man's hand. The man's obvious love of hearing himself talk was all that was keeping Emily alive.

Closing his hand around the door handle Iain began to slowly turn it, thankful that he had begun to make sure all door handles were well oiled. That time he had killed one of Albert's hired men in the same way he planned to kill Albert now had made him very cautious about having silent doors. As he began to slowly open the door he almost smiled. He must have been firmer about the chore getting done regularly than he had thought because it was opening without a sound.

Stepping into the kitchen was difficult. Iain wanted to rush as he feared the man was getting to the end of his bragging and would immediately shoot Emily when he was. He held his breath each time he put his foot down, knowing the softest sound of a footstep could alert the man. Iain had no wish to be shot again if only because that would make it difficult to rescue Emily. It felt like hours passed until he was close enough to run the fool through with his sword.

Just before he ran his sword into the man, he whispered, "So very sorry to end your soliloquy."

* * *

Emily caught sight of the kitchen door opening and fought desperately not to fix her gaze on that. She saw Iain creep inside and nearly sagged with relief. She knew things were not safe yet but she felt as though they were.

"Albert, you cannot keep shooting people just because they annoy you or get in the way," she said, using the tone she used on Neddy when she was trying to correct some bad behavior of his.

"You are so cute when you try to talk like a mother or tutor to a small child." His look turned fierce. "I am neither. I am soon to become the Duke of Collins Wood and deserve respect."

"Grandfather is not so aged you can count on him dropping dead the moment you become the heir. Although, shock may do it," she added in a muttered voice that dripped with scorn.

Albert pointed the gun straight at her heart. "How droll. Do you know, he once made a passing comment on how good it would be if women could become the duke and he wished his ancestor had gotten that concession from Elizabeth. Seems the old man is rather fond of you and thinks you would be a perfect duke."

"That is very kind of him."

"That is stupid. Complete and utter stupidity. Now, are you going to tell me where Neddy is or do I have to go through this hovel room by room. Rest assured I will kill anyone in my way. That includes all those brothers you are probably bedding and that woman with her three kids."

Just as she opened her mouth to try to say something she watched a sword point come right out of his stomach. She pressed a hand to her own and she felt something wet splash her face. To her amazement,

Albert only grunted, lightly touched the tip of the sword, and glanced behind him before grinning at her. It was gruesome to look for blood was already starting to pour out of his mouth.

"This is funny, is it not. Killed by a Scot with a broadsword in America. The irony of it all." Then his eyes went blank and his body began to sag.

Iain shoved the body off the sword and watched Emily sink to her knees and close her eyes. There was blood all over her face and he grimaced. After wiping his sword on Albert's frock coat, he moved to the sink to get a wet rag.

"Iain?"

"Right here, love." He crouched down by her side, careful of the blood that was slowly flowing over the floor.

"Please get this off me. I can feel it dripping down my face."

There was a note of extreme tension in her voice and he suspected she was fighting hysteria so he grabbed her and moved her to the table, setting her down on a bench. Then he carefully washed the blood from her hair and face. "Ye will have to wash the gown, I fear, though there isnae much on it. It mostly hit ye in the face with some going in your hair." He felt her shudder and decided he would not say any more about the body and blood.

"You must cease killing people with that sword."

"I left my guns upstairs and decided I should not risk going back up. He was mad as a hatter."

"Most certainly. I think the reins on his madness snapped clean off when he killed his parents."

"His own parents? What did they do?"

"He felt they were stupid. His father for not using his connection to Grandfather and his mother for being so upset that he had killed his father. That became his reason for killing people. They were stupid or they got in his way when he wanted something. It was difficult to listen to him as he, well, he boasted of what he had done. I do not know why he thought I would care to listen to his depravity. What makes me sad is that I know there are many more he has killed but they were not of our class and he must have thought them not worth mentioning. By the way, it looks as if we may be getting Humphrey for our holiday meal."

He smiled. She was obviously trying to calm herself so he let her talk, although she appeared to have forgotten he was there to hear that last little piece of information. "Sounds good." Then he frowned as he noticed she was starting to shake. "Almost clean, love."

"Thank you. For saving my life again and for cleaning my face."

"I caused the mess on your face."

"No, it was actually Albert who did that by bleeding. Did you hear what he said? Even though he was as good as dead, he had to make a comment, had to have the last word."

"I heard it. Not sure if 'irony' was the right word though." The little line between her brows told him she was thinking about that.

"I am not sure. Did you say something to him? It looked like you said something."

"I just told him I was so sorry to end his soliloquy."

"Can I open my eyes now?"

"Aye. Face is clean. Just do not look around the kitchen. Keep your eyes on me."

"I can do that." She opened her eyes and stared at him. "I rather like just looking at you."

When he grinned at her and quickly kissed her, she knew she should be shocked by what she had said but felt nothing. It was as if she was numb all over. Shock, she thought. She was suffering from some kind of shock. Considering all she had just been through she supposed that should not be a surprise but she hoped it ended before she said anything she regretted. Unfortunately, she felt sure it was going to end in a strong bout of tears.

Iain moved to get rid of the body then realized he could not lift it. Advising Emily to close her eyes or find something in the kitchen to stare at aside from Albert, he went out the door and, seeing Mrs. O'Neal, told her that he needed one of his brothers fast and why. Then he went back to sit next to Emily, turning on the seat so he could face her.

"Wish I was stronger, love. I would carry ye upstairs and away from this."

"That is all right although I do like it when you carry me."

He frowned and glanced at Mrs. O'Neal, who had come back in to get ready to mop up the blood. "Poor girl is in shock," Mrs. O'Neal said quietly. "Look at her eyes."

Iain sighed as he noticed the glassy sheen in her eyes. Then his brothers Matthew and Nigel walked in. Even though he never took his gaze away from Emily he explained what had happened.

"Man was mad as a hatter," Iain said as they began to carry the man out, careful to keep out of Emily's line of sight. "He even killed his own parents. Said they were stupid because they did not use the duke to make any gains. Actually, I think he killed his mother because she had the audacity to scream at him, her own son. And I didnae even hear all he said. God alone kens what else he confessed to."

Once his brothers had gotten rid of the body he pulled Emily to her feet and took her out the back door to walk around to the front and get to the stairs. He was pondering Mrs. O'Neal's whispered advice to try to break through Emily's shock but had come up with no idea of how by the time he got her into his bedroom. He suddenly grinned as he wondered why he had taken her there. Aside from the fact that he was ready to get out of the sickroom. He wondered if he was thinking making love to her would pull her out of her shock. Since that could well include her starting to cry he decided against it. He urged her to lie on the bed, propping up the pillows at her back.

"Ye need to have some water, I think, love." He moved to pour her a glass.

Emily sighed. "You always call me love. You really should not. Gives a girl hope, you know, that she might really be your love. I know I am not. I am just the girl you like to, like to, um, shag." She nodded. "That is the word. Shag."

Iain hurried back with the water and made her drink it, fighting to control his laughter, mostly brought on by surprise. "That is not all you are to me, Emily." He hoped she could hear and understand him because he did not like her thinking that. "I have been wooing you. A man doesnae woo a lass when she is just convenient for lovemaking."

"Oh, yes, the wooing."

"Aye. I brought ye flowers and candy."

"Mrs. O'Neal and the children really liked the candy." The numbness was fading and Emily tried to hold on to it; she did not really want to remember what she had seen and heard.

"Ye gave them the candy?"

"Shared it. They were all sitting there with their big begging eyes. I do not know how they knew I had candy but suddenly they were all there. I feel odd, Iain."

"Ye are in shock, love."

"There. You did it again."

"Emily, you are my love and if my wooing didnae make ye see that, I was doing a worse job than I thought I was." He gently stroked her cheek. "Come back to me and we can talk sense and I ken ye will remember what I say then."

"He was so insane, Iain. It was frightening to be in a room with someone so barking mad. He needed to be chained up. He killed his parents and he wanted to kill Neddy. Saw no wrong in it. He even planned to kill my grandfather. He did not kill Constance though, even though he thought she was stupid and talked of how, in the hour he spent with her, he envisioned shooting her in her never-closed mouth even though he was feeling very pleased with himself and kindly toward her at the time. Who thinks like that?"

Her voice rose on the last question and he held her close. "A lunatic. You probably will never know how many he killed. Dinnae fret over it. He is gone now and we dinnae need to worry about his mad plans."

"But he was my relation. Blood relation. What if that sickness is in me?"

"Never. It doesnae run through families like red hair. There would be signs. There is nothing in ye or little Neddy to show it. And sometimes it is just the one. Just some twist that happened. Maybe in the womb. I have seen both. I am nay worried about it.

Maybe it came from the side that is no blood relation to ye."

"You mean it could have come from his mother's side not the duke's."

"Aye." He felt a wetness on his shirt that told him the tears had come. "The man is dead. Ye dinnae need to worry about him anymore."

"You will tell me if you ever see a hint of it?"

"Aye, but I dinnae think I ever will."

"Because I am your love," she whispered.

"Exactly. The wooing was so ye would be of a mind to heed me when I spoke of it."

"So ye want to continue to woo me."

"Do I have to?"

"Not really."

He tilted her face up to his and kissed her, then looked down at her and knew what he was about to say was as true and heartfelt as anything he had ever said in his life. "I do love ye, Lady Emily."

"Oh." She knew she was crying again. "I love you, too. And you do not need to call me 'Lady.' It is my grandfather who is the duke."

"Which meant your father was the marquise. I think that makes ye a lady."

"Is that a problem?"

"Used to be. Nay anymore. If nothing else, ye showed me there are good and bad. Ashamed that I ever compared ye to Lady Vera even once."

"Lady Vera? Lady Vera Compton?"

He tensed. "Do ye ken the woman?"

"Only of her. The duke disowned her. It was quite the scandal. She was only a distant relation but he disclaimed any connection to her and her family. Was she the one who lost you your home?"

"I guess George's friend at Harvard was right. The

gentry is an incestuous bunch. Do ye all ken each other?"

"I do not. Never saw the need. My father had to and complained long and sometimes loudly about it. Refused to take us with them to some house parties. Something about them not being suitable for children. Yet if I mentioned that any of the people my age had been there he would go all stern and say their parents never had any sense. When I was older I decided it was because of drunkenness and maybe something lewd."

"Quite likely. So why did your grandfather disown her and her family?"

"He said they had no feeling, or even the slightest hint of courtesy, for the ones who worked their lands and made them rich. To my grandfather that is one of the worst sins of the gentry. He says our class is wonderful at spending the money but neither thinks nor acts like they know it comes from the work of others. He is called a radical, I fear. Well, I do not care, but it occasionally causes the rest of his relations an uncomfortable confrontation."

"And I suspicion your father was much like him."

"Yes. But he did play the game much better than my grandfather."

Iain laughed. "Older men can get away with being more blunt-speaking. People who dinnae like what they have to say can just tell themselves he is getting crotchety in his old age."

Emily smiled, realizing it was his anger at the gentry that had caused him to go hot and cold in the beginning but that he was well and truly past that. "That is exactly what my grandfather says. He also says he has done enough in the past to please most everyone and earn honors and medals and they just do not have the spine to tell him to shut it."

"I think I could get to like your grandfather." He kissed her. "Do ye wish to go home?"

"It would be nice at some time if only to see my grandfather and some friends. Go to my cottage at the shore. But no, I miss some things and probably always will but I realized the other day, some of the things I can make here. I actually liked the cabin and all that we did to make it a better place to live. I truly felt a part of it whereas the manor is pretty much perfect and has been for over a hundred years. All I would do is move in. And I do not believe you would be happy to leave this place and live over there so what would be there for me?"

"I would go if that is what ye really desired." Even though the words were hard to get out he knew he meant them.

"But why?"

"Weel, a mon should stay with his wife, shouldnae he?" He had to bite back a laugh at how wide her eyes grew. "Lass, I told ye I love ye." Then he grinned. "And if we are wed, I can shag ye whenever I want and not worry about Mrs. O'Neal lecturing my ear off. Dinnae ye wish to wed me?" he asked quietly, suddenly feeling uncertain and hating it.

Emily hugged him, pressing her face against his throat. "Oh, yes, I do. I do. When?"

"Soon as possible. Suspect it will be a few weeks as I cannae see Mrs. O'Neal standing for us just running off to a preacher and getting it done. She will be wanting a proper wedding."

"I think I do, too."

"Good. Need to get to all that shagging."

She slapped his arm. "Why do you keep saying that?"

"Got the word from ye," he said, and watched her blush. "Ye were still stuck in shock and ye told me I only called ye 'love' because I was shagging you." He grinned when she groaned and covered her face with her hands. "I would like to ken where ye heard that word and why ye ken what it means."

"I never said that."

"Sorry, but ye did." He laughed when she swatted his arm again. "Violent woman."

"I think if ye can be calling her a violent woman in that tone she is over her shock and you can get your behind out of there," came Mrs. O'Neal's voice through the door.

Iain sighed. "I guess there will be no celebration of our engagement," he whispered, and stood up.

Walking to the door, Iain opened it and frowned at the woman standing there frowning back at him with her arms crossed over her chest. "We are getting married."

"When did you decide that?"

"Just now. Ye are interrupting our celebration." He started to close the door but was not surprised when she stuck her arm out to stop him; he had seen the glint in her eyes.

"Well then, come on, missy, we have some planning to do."

Emily got up and went to the door. She glanced at Iain and he grinned. Even though she tried to get Mrs. O'Neal out the door as fast as possible she knew it would never be in time.

"Weel, lass, guess the shagging will have to wait until after the wedding," Iain said, then yelled when

Mrs. O'Neal swatted him on the arm. "Damn woman, that hurt."

"Good. Come along, dearie."

Emily fell into step behind the woman and glanced back at Iain still rubbing his arm. She grinned and waved. Her good humor faded when they entered the kitchen. Mrs. O'Neal sat her down at the table and Emily did her best to not look at the spot where Albert had died. Then the woman slapped a piece of paper and writing tools in front of her. It was a rather large sheet of paper and Emily had the feeling Iain was right. It could be a long while before the shagging could be indulged in.

It was time for the meal by the time Emily was done writing and she gazed in amazement at all that Mrs. O'Neal thought needed doing. They were going to be busy if they were going to have a wedding in just a few weeks. She was freed from worry about that when the brothers all arrived and tried to give her kisses of welcome only to start a tussle with Iain until Mrs. O'Neal intervened with her wooden spoon and good aim. Emily laughed and realized she was going to be joining a good strong family. Happy in a way she had not been in a long time, she settled in to enjoy the meal.

Chapter Twenty

Emily could not believe it was her wedding day. Even with Maggie, Mabel, Mrs. O'Neal, and Charlotte all crowded into her room it was hard to believe it. They were now all gathered around her making sure her wedding dress was fitted and hanging on her just right. Mrs. O'Neal and Mabel had made it for her and she had been stunned speechless then cried. Mrs. O'Neal had even lent her her veil, a beautiful work of lace done by her mother for her own wedding.

"Damn, woman, you are looking very good," said Maggie, even as she stood back and rubbed at her rounded belly.

"Thank you. When are you due, anyway?"

"Two months from now."

"And your husband let you come?"

"Came with me, and the kids, didn't he? Man's always afraid if I go somewhere without him someone will snatch me away from him." She grinned and then turned to Mrs. O'Neal. "And thank *you* for letting them in your house. We've been doing our best to keep them quiet."

Emily studied Maggie as the woman talked with Mrs. O'Neal. Her husband might not be as crazy as Maggie could make him sound. Even pregnant with her tenth child the woman was quite stunning. She had a beautiful color of blue for her eyes, nearly purple, and long reddish-blond hair that was so thick and wavy one could not help wondering why it did not weigh her down. Despite all the children and being nearly thirty-five, the woman had a figure that was the type to draw a man's eyes. When she was not pregnant, anyway. Emily had always wondered if it was one reason her husband kept her pregnant, and then she had seen they could still be madly in love with so many children, as well as with each child. They adored each one and she suspected Maggie would happily keep having them until she grew too old or was advised to stop by a doctor.

Emily looked at Charlotte, who listened to the women talk of kids with a soft smile on her face. She was carrying but had not yet announced it to anyone, including her husband. To Emily's amazement she discovered Mabel was married to the man who ran the tavern and had six children of her own. She began to wonder if Iain expected her to perform so well and was not sure if she was pleased with the idea or terrified. Considering she had been ill in the morning for the last three days, if she discovered it was not from nerves, she may be getting an answer to that question fairly soon.

Wanting her sister to be there, Emily pulled the locket out from under the gown and settled it on her chest as Maggie stepped up and slipped her arms through Emily's. "That is pretty."

"It was Annabel's. I thought it would help me, since she cannot be here, to feel her close."

"I am sure it will. She and her beautiful man are watching. I feel it in my bones."

"Oh, I hope so. She used to nag me to find a man."

"Be hard to find a real man over there amongst the gentry."

"There are a few." She smiled when Maggie grimaced.

"Got yourself one now. Are ye going to go back to England?"

"I do not think so. I rather like this place and Iain would never be happy away from all his brothers and stuck with people he cannot fully trust and would probably be disrespectful because he is not one of them. I would not much like that, either."

"Nope. Me and Beech moved here because the place we lived in treated him like trash. His family was dirt-scratching poor."

"May I ask a question?"

"Sure. I don't want to answer and I won't."

"Fair enough. Why do you call your husband Beech?"

"It is his name. Mother named them all after trees she saw through the windows of the house. Some were named after plants too. She couldn't go outside. Her da died of a beesting and she was terrified she might be the same way. So she stayed in all the time. Husband's name is Beech. Just plain old Beech."

"It is actually a nice name." She frowned. "Though thinking on the different trees some would not be so nice to be named after." She smiled when Maggie laughed.

"One reason we left. Once folk learned she named the kids after plants and that she was terrified of the outdoors he was always getting in fights with ones who called his mother crazy. Poor woman was just scared, not crazy."

"No. I have seen crazy."

"He's dead now," said Maggie, knowing exactly who Emily referred to. "Paid in blood for the evil he did, as was right."

Emily took a deep breath and let it out slowly to banish the memories. There was a knock at the door and all the women stared at it. A second knock came but it was a lot lower down on the wood. It was much too low for a grown man.

"I open this door," yelled Mabel, "and I better not see no men or I'll shoot 'em."

The sound of people running back down the stairs made Emily smile. The MacEnroys did not react well to being told "no" and this was their third try to get in.

"They don't stand up to Mabel, do they?" said Maggie.

"I suspect that is because if Mabel says she will shoot you, she will," said Charlotte. "And she never misses." Charlotte looked at Emily. "I assume she only intended to wound."

Emily shrugged. "I would assume that, too. This is a wedding, after all."

Mabel opened the door and looked down. Neddy stood there in his best clothes, clutching the rings and staring wide-eyed at Mabel. Then he looked around, spotted Emily, and ran to her. She put her arm around his shoulders. At least he was not scowling at her as he had been since the day he understood she was to marry Iain. He glared at Iain a lot as well, which just made the man laugh.

"Time to go," Neddy said. "I got your rings." He held out his hand, opened it, and pointed to the largest of the two rings. "His ring." He pointed to the smaller one. "Your ring. See? I 'membered."

"Yes, very good. I am ready to go now." She caught him glancing at Maggie, who had moved to her side.

"What that?" he asked, and pointed at her belly.

"A baby," Maggie replied, and smiled.

"You eated a baby?"

It was hard but Emily swallowed the urge to laugh when she saw his horrified look, and Maggie was not helping by laughing so hard right next to her. Poor Neddy was suffering from a lot of upsetting news lately. No matter what she and Iain said the boy was convinced he was losing her.

"No, honey-pie," Maggie said, her voice still quivering with amusement. "This is where a mommy carries the baby." She took his empty hand and placed it against her belly. "It is growing there and, when it is done growing, it will come out."

Neddy frowned at her stomach. Emily smiled at the fierce look of concentration the boy wore. Then his eyes suddenly grew huge and he yanked his hand back. Emily moved fast to pick him up before he raced out of the room. If he decided to hide, she would need to find another ring bearer.

"It moved. It trying to get out," he said, his soft but hurried words revealing his fears.

"No, sweetheart," Maggie said, getting closer to him but she stepped back when Neddy cringed away from her. "It isn't trying to get out, it's just moving around. Maybe doing a little dance, do you think?"

"Maybe it kicked me. It does not like me."

"Must be a little girl then."

Neddy laughed, then suddenly he started turning back and forth while looking at the floor. "Rings! I droppeded the rings."

All the women started to look but they would not let Emily get down on the floor to help. She was stuck looking where she thought the rings may have fallen from Neddy's hand or where they may have rolled to when they had hit the floor. They finally found them under the bed.

"How did they get all the way over there?" Emily asked as she put them back into Neddy's hand.

"I throwed them when I got scared," he said, closing his hand tightly around the rings.

"It is all right, love," Emily said. "We found them so no harm done." She frowned at the door when a somewhat timid knock sounded and Mrs. O'Neal opened it to reveal a blushing Robbie.

"I think we should go down now," he said. "Iain is getting nervous."

"You are escorting me?"

Robbie nodded. "I won the toss so I get to be the one to hand ye over to him."

Emily laughed and shook her head as she walked over and linked her arm with Robbie's. "Then we had best get moving."

"He really is getting nervous," Robbie whispered.

"Why?" she whispered back. "Does he think I am making an escape through the window?"

"Nay," Robbie said, laughing softly and shaking his head. "I dinnae ken what is wrong with him but he is, um, twitchy."

"Twitchy?"

"Pacing the room, looking up the stairs, watching the clock. All of that. So we need to get down there or my brothers are going to start to thrash him. And the little girls are getting impatient to toss the flower petals. I think Jasmine is hungry, too. She was eating the flower petals in her basket." Maggie burst into laughter at the antics of her youngest daughter. Emily giggled and could hear the other women doing the same.

Iain watched as Emily walked down the stairs, laughing with the other women and Robbie. She looked more beautiful than ever. The gown she wore was a simple one, each white lacy inch revealing the figure he liked to get his hands on as often as possible. Her hair had been left loose, the veil and some fancy silver hairpins all that held it in place.

Mrs. O'Neal pointed a finger at him and he walked across the parlor to stand in front of the preacher. He kept his eyes on Emily as he reached out to slap Matthew on the arm to stop him yanking on his collar. He was not sure why Mrs. O'Neal had insisted he have so many men standing with him as groomsmen. There were more people in the wedding party than in the seats as guests. And just when had he come to know so many people? He glanced at the Powells standing with his brothers and took some comfort in the fact that they looked as uncomfortable in the suits Mrs. O'Neal had found for them as he felt.

He watched as the little girls walked toward him tossing flower petals on the floor, little Jasmine pausing now and then to eat a few. Little Neddy walked very carefully until he reached Iain's side and then he sighed and loosened his fist over the rings he held. The little girls finished throwing petals and scurried over to take their seats with the guests. Then, finally, Emily walked toward him on Robbie's arm, smiling shyly at him.

Once at his side, she leaned closer and whispered, "Are you still sure?"